A NOVEL

THE PROVERBIAL MR.UNIVERSE

MARIA LA SERRA

For more information about the author visit: maria-laserra.com

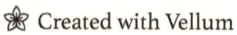 Created with Vellum

For Laura & Sofia, my true universe.

For Mom & Dad, my rock, my lighthouse.

Stranger, if you, passing, meet me and
desire to speak to me,
why should you not speak to me?
And why should I not speak to you?

Walt Whitman

You don't love someone for their looks,
or their clothes, or their fancy car,
but because they sing a song only you can hear.

Unknown

ALSO BY MARIA LA SERRA

LYRICAL LIGHTS

JANUARY

1

GIRL WITH A REALIZATION

OLIVIA HAD FOUND AN ESCAPE ROUTE ON THE FAR LEFT, A RED EXIT sign beckoning salvation but somehow she couldn't find the courage to venture out the door.

"Congratulations!" said an elderly woman, one Olivia didn't recognize.

"You look lovely. Are you having a good time, dear?"

"Thank you ... yes." She would have been, if the circumstances were different. If she weren't an absolute crazy mess.

Loud music and laughter circled around Olivia as she stood in the middle of the crowded room. Who were these people? They were too busy living their lavish lives to notice that hers was coming to an emotional standstill.

"Wow, some shindig you've got going on. I feel like I'm at the ... what's the name of that award show they do in Hollywood?" Paul asked, taking his place next to her.

"Are you talking about the Oscars?" She frowned.

And the Oscar goes to ... Olivia Montiano, for Sham of a Life. Too bad it had taken her five years to realize it.

Paul slightly nudged her arm, handing her a glass. "Are you all right?"

"Yeah, sure ... Why?"

"Well, you look a little pale." Paul playfully rested his hand on her forehead.

"Can you stop?" she laughed, slapping his hand away. "I'm fine."

Her brother Paul had always been handsome, tall and lean, but something was different about him these days. Maybe it was his light hair, freshly cut to a shorter length. Or maybe it was because he'd gotten his act together and now worked for their father.

"Yeah, I guess I'm a little overwhelmed." Olivia glanced down at her glass.

"Shit, do you even know these people?"

"Some," she said, smiling weakly. "It's overdone, right?" Olivia had had no part in any decision-making when it had come to planning her engagement party. Everything from the menu to the tablecloth was the work of Dario and the event planner.

"Well, your fiancé sure knows how to throw a party." Paul brought the glass to his lips but stopped midair. "Hey, isn't that the new mayor?"

Nodding, Olivia took a sip of her drink. "Geez, what is this?" She scrunched her nose.

"Whiskey." He chuckled. "Okay, drink up. It seems like you could use it."

Olivia wasn't much of a drinker—maybe a glass of red wine occasionally. Never in her life had she gotten drunk, because Dario thought it was immature. So Olivia had strived to be responsible ... maybe even a little boring.

Without hesitation she shot back the glass, wiping her mouth with the back of her hand.

"I didn't mean for you to chug it down. You're supposed to sip it." Paul grinned, taking the monogrammed glass, with the initials *D&O*, from her hand.

She cast a glance over her shoulder and whispered. "Paul, do you have your cigarettes on you?"

"You don't smoke." His eyebrows gathered up.

"I'm an adult ... do you have one for me?"

"You're serious? I don't think it's a good idea."

"Come on. I feel like doing something destructive." Who was she kidding? She had never done anything bad in her life.

"I don't know what the big deal is. It's just a cigarette."

Paul peered around him, as if in deep thought. "All right, only this once."

"You're such a hypocrite."

"Do what I say, not what I do," he said, quoting their father.

Olivia rolled her eyes. "Where are you going?"

"I left them at coat check. I'll meet you outside in five."

She watched her brother make his way through the crowd. All night she had kept her composure: smiling, talking to her guests, even laughing at their not-so-funny jokes, never showing a clue about what was going on inside her. *Today is the day*, she told herself. She had reached the point of all she could bear. She needed to escape from this room, filled with people who believed social status and wealth were the only things that gave someone importance. At some point, she had been one of them, too.

Dario approached her from behind. "Olivia, come with me. I want you to meet Mr. Belanger."

"Who?"

"Come on. You know who he is." He cast her a look. "He owns half the commercial buildings downtown."

"Can it wait? I was—"

"Well, no. I don't want to keep him waiting." Catching his reflection in the glass window, he straightened his blue silk tie. He gave her a side glance. "I told you, you should have worn the blue dress. At least we would have matched tonight."

Who were they, Laverne and Shirley?

"I don't believe this shit. I've been trying to close this deal for weeks."

Dario had been irritating her throughout the night. And now, she was less than excited at the prospect of being paraded around the room like she was the show's main attraction. Her fiancé seemed to have missed the point of what should have been a joyous occasion. Instead, he had made it out to be something else entirely. Olivia wondered how she had allowed herself to get lost in someone else's life. Was there any hope of getting her own back?

She nervously spun her ring around, itching to take it off like a cheap wool sweater. This ridiculous, massive diamond ring would have made most women happy.

Not her.

Dario hadn't proposed the way she'd dreamed of; instead he'd brought up the subject of marriage like it was a proposition for a business deal. She knew he wasn't much of a romantic, but still ... When they were ready to take the next step in their relationship, she'd never have thought it would feel like a hostile takeover.

He quickly glanced at her. "God, Olivia, would it hurt you to smile?"

She closed her eyes, held on to her last breath, and walked away.

"Olivia?"

Turning the corner, she opened a door leading to the large terrace. As soon as it closed, there was an instant quiet and serenity. Only the faint sounds of cars and trucks heading east and west came from below. The Place Ville-Marie had the most spectacular panoramic view of the entire metropolis, and this was the reason Dario had wanted to have their engagement at the penthouse. She let her long red dress drag through the snow, walking closer to the end of the gallery.

The beacon light flashed across the sky, forcing her eyes back up, landing on the biggest star. She had a feeling that something was about to happen, something exceptional.

What would she wish for? Happiness? Love? A great career? Didn't she possess those things already? Most of her friends thought so. But Olivia knew the reality: when it came down to the fine print, it was a different story. These days the thread had been unraveling quicker than she could ever have imagined.

For several weeks, Olivia had struggled with the feeling she was not living the life intended for her. Olivia thought about Dario. Even if she had believed in soul mates to begin with, it was clear that Dario wasn't hers. Over time, Olivia had thought she could change him, but it turned out it had been Olivia who had done the changing instead. At first she had told herself that Dario only wanted the best for her.

Lies.

She had thought she could live with the fact Dario was a workaholic, like her father, and it didn't bother her.

More lies.

She had believed Dario was marrying her because he loved her, and not because of her father's wealth or connections.

More. More. Lies.

The truth had been in front of her all along, but she'd refused to see it for many reasons.

"Olivia? What are you doing out here?"

She turned around and found her sister Nina standing there, with the door half open. Her purple dress fit Nina like a glove. Her honey-colored hair, pinned up, gave her the allure of old-Hollywood glamour. Nina was four years older, but everyone said they looked alike. Olivia had never thought they resembled each other much, except that they both had inherited the same big caramel eyes from their mother. Growing up they had been close; all three siblings had their place in the family: Nina was a daddy's girl, and Paul was a mama's boy...and Olivia fell somewhere in between.

"Geez, it's cold." Nina brought her arms up, bracing herself for the winter chill.

"Where's Paul?"

Nina shrugged. "He said you wanted to do something destructive. What's that about?" She paused. "Are you crying?" Nina pulled her dress up, carefully walking closer.

"I can't do this."

"What?" Nina frowned.

"I can't go through with this charade ... I can't marry Dario." She covered her face with her hands.

Nina yanked Olivia into an embrace. "Hey ... Hey, it will be all right. Liv, seriously, stop! You will get mascara all over yourself, and me." Nina pulled back and reached into her purse. "I know what's going on..."

"You do?" Olivia took the tissue out of her sister's hand, wishing Nina could just read her mind.

"It's just cold feet."

Olivia's heart slumped. She knew it was more than that, but how was Nina to know? Olivia had been hiding everything from her family. There was so much they didn't know about her relationship with Dario.

"I had cold feet before I married Peter. It's only normal. It happens to some people."

"I don't believe you. You're just saying that to make me feel better."

"No, it's true. Ask him." Nina's teeth chattered.

"But Peter is good to you."

"Yeah, Liv. All men are brilliant in the beginning. They bring you flowers, sweep you off your feet, and when you marry them it becomes a different story." Nina brought her arms higher around herself, bouncing back and forth. "Suddenly you become this freaking 1950s housewife. Picking up his dirty socks at the end of the bed. Every. Freaking. Morning. Somehow they seem to forget what the laundry basket is for." Nina pulled a face.

"But you love him."

"Sure I do. We've been together for so long, but sometimes I wish we could go back to the beginning." Her smile faded. "Marriage is not a fairy tale, Olivia. Other things come into the picture. Mortgage, bills, kids—life has a way of sucking the romance right out of it. There are days I swear Peter gets on my nerves. I could just choke him ... But when I force myself to stop and think back to the first moment I saw him, and why I love him, it renews my faith in us." Nina's eyes softened.

"I don't know..." Olivia understood that relationships went through all kinds of changes. They evolved into something else, leaving a remnant of their former obsessive, passionate love behind. But if you didn't have the love to sustain the relationship, any snag could cause everything to unravel. She had heard this speech or something like it before, from Aunt Teresa to the sweet Chinese lady next door. It seemed everyone had a piece of advice since she'd gotten engaged.

Her dilemma was simple: what if she was making a terrible mistake by settling down before meeting the person she was supposed to love? Even at the beginning of her relationship with Dario, she couldn't have called it a great love story. Olivia wasn't sure what had sustained their relationship all this time. Perhaps it was love, but lately she had realized it had been her father. He was the one who'd set them up.

There was nothing more motivating than the fear of disappointing a parent.

Nina jumped at the sound of a crackling noise behind them.

"Ma, you scared the shit out of me." Nina placed her hand on her chest.

"Girls, I didn't think you were crazy enough to be out here. Quick, get inside! You're going to catch pneumonia." Their mother's voice came through the open glass door. She looked sophisticated in her shift dress and white pearls, the Jackie O. look. Even though their mother had arrived in Canada as a young girl, she had never managed to lose her Italian accent when she spoke English.

"We're coming, Ma." Nina shook even more. "What the hell are you made out of? Aren't you cold? Please tell me you're ready to go in."

Olivia nodded.

"Are you okay?"

Olivia took in a deep breath. "Yeah ... sure ... I'm just over-whelmed."

She spotted Dario from across the room, standing close to a very attractive blonde.

At what point had she forgotten that there were other choices?

2

MR.UNIVERSE

OLIVIA HAD ALWAYS WONDERED WHY PEOPLE LIKED THE SKEWED version of reality, but now she understood. It was so much easier to live a lie than to face the truth. Ever since the night of her engagement party, she couldn't think about her life without calling everything into question.

"Olivia ... *Hello*, Olivia?"

She turned away from the window and glanced at Dario in the driver's seat. He looked at her with his dark brown eyes. She remembered the first time she'd seen them; her heart used to skip a beat. Now, nothing.

She had almost been nineteen when they first met, at one of her father's charity functions. Olivia had had a weakness for older men—the smartly dressed ones, tall, brown curly hair, and eyes that could melt any woman's heart.

"What's the matter with you?" Dario asked. "You seem distant this morning."

Only this morning?

He had volunteered to drive since her car was at the mechanic. "You're slouching again, sit straight. You have such bad posture," he said.

Now she regretted not taking a taxi instead.

"Geez, Olivia, are you listening to anything I say?"

"Sorry, I have a lot of things on my mind." Her eyes remained steadfast on the window.

Olivia was hoping he would get the drift; she wasn't in the mood for small talk. For the past two weeks, they'd been fighting more and seeing each other less, which she appreciated.

Olivia couldn't understand why she had bothered to reconnect last night by surprising him with dinner. When Dario came home, he told her he had eaten already and went straight into his office, leaving her alone in the kitchen, deflated like a balloon. She had locked herself in the bathroom, crying. Dario was unaware...but would he have cared? She was trying not to pity herself, but then again, she realized that Dario wasn't the first man in her life to disappoint her.

"I'm thinking about the fall campaign ads we'll shoot next week." She looked down at her hands.

"Okay, so what's your point?"

She turned to look at him and wished he could at least pretend to show enthusiasm for once. She had worked so hard on this collection and was proud of the turnout. This was Olivia's opportunity to show her boss what she was capable of.

Olivia frowned. "I'm excited about it."

"Oh, right." His eyes remained on the road. He gave her a side glance, as though he wanted to tell her something, but he took his time, choosing his words carefully. "Listen, I have a lot of work to do at the office—" he cleared his throat—"so I will have to cancel our dinner date tonight."

"Seriously? You're doing this to me again?"

"I have no choice. Everything is on my shoulders since your dad promoted me."

Dario was an architect, and he had worked for her father's company for the past five years. At thirty, with his determination and wit, he had made a good career for himself. Dario was the kind of guy who strategically placed himself where he wanted to be. At the beginning of their relationship, Olivia had found those qualities admirable. Over time ... not so much.

When Olivia didn't answer, he continued. "I'll make it up to you, babe. I promise."

Olivia had pondered those words way too many times, only to be disappointed.

"Next week I'll take you to your favorite restaurant ... ah ... Donna's?"

Lucky guess, but no. It showed how little he knew her. In the five years they'd been together, she'd never eaten there. So who was he having dinner with at Donna's?

She frowned. "Rouge Tomate," she said dryly.

"Right! I'll plan a romantic dinner for next week ... you and me ... I promise," he said, his eyes still on the road. "What's the matter?"

"Nothing."

He glanced quickly. "You're mad?"

"Why wouldn't I be? We're never together anymore." She threw her hands into the air.

"Don't be a hypocrite, Olivia. You, of all people, should understand me. You're always working late."

"Yeah, I work late because who wants to come home to an empty apartment?"

"Oh no, don't put the blame on me. I work hard, I buy you beautiful things, I do everything to make you happy. I do this all for you, all for us."

Dario *had* given her the finest things: jewelry; trips to Europe; beautiful expensive Italian-leather handbags. It all meant nothing. How could it move her in any way when he wasn't capable of giving her the one thing she wanted?

"I am not putting the blame on you. We don't connect anymore..."

"It's not my fault, Olivia,"

"You think it's mine? I make myself available every time you need me."

"Listen, Olivia, working for your father hasn't been easy. I have a lot of stress with this new position, so excuse me if we don't connect lately."

"I understand, I do. I'm stressed at work too. But sometimes I think I'm the only one trying."

He laughed, and that was even more aggravating.

"You can't call what you do at work stressful. Come on, Olivia. You sketch all day." He smirked.

She looked at him in disbelief. "Don't degrade my job. My work is more than that."

"I don't know why you care so much when all you do is complain about it. Anyhow, it's not like you will continue to work once we're married," he said.

"I can't believe you said that!"

"What?"

"I'm supposed to do what at home? What about my dreams and my aspirations?"

He laughed again, which continued to make her temperature rise.

"Exactly! Right here is what I'm talking about. You don't care about me. You don't care about what I like, or—"

"Oh, come on! Stop being such a baby." He paused. "I do care," he said in a not-so-convincing tone.

Her heart was drumming so loudly that it rang up to her ears. She put a hand on her forehead. "Maybe this is all wrong..."

He raised his hand in the air. "What are you saying, Olivia? Are you not happy? Happy with me? Are we back to that again?" He missed the clutch, and his car lurched into first gear.

No, she wasn't. Olivia was sure of her feelings but afraid to say the words out loud, scared of the consequences if she did. "Honestly, I don't know anymore." Her eyes met his cold stare.

Dario shook his head. "I figured something was up last night.

You kept on asking me those questions. You're trying to pick a fight." He looked away. "I think you do this for attention. Your father spoiled you too much. *I* spoiled you too much!"

Whenever they fought, he made her believe she was the cause of it. Her fault they argued, her fault she was unhappy. He never took the blame for anything that went wrong. The car pulled up to the curb, stopping in front of the gray building where Olivia worked.

"Yeah, you're right—" she frantically waved her hands in the air—"I do this all for attention."

"What's the matter with you? Sometimes I think you're unstable..."

"I hate when you say that." His words hurt. They always did.

"Yeah, well, you've been acting fucking crazy lately."

She peered at him without saying another word. What was the point? She had certainly had enough. Olivia opened the car door, slamming it on the way out. She didn't even turn around at the sound of screeching tires. She just stood there motionless, staring at the building. If only she could call in sick, because her heart was about to fall out. Wouldn't that be reason enough?

Instead, she decided to go across the street to pick up a large coffee. Maybe she could caffeinate herself to death—but not before a deep, rumbling voice called out from behind.

"Don't let the shadow follow you around," said a man with a thick accent.

She looked around, and her eyes landed on a homeless man sitting on the snow-covered ground. His face was weathered from the hardship of living on the street. His white hair and beard were growing wildly around him. At first she wasn't sure if he was talking to her, but then she realized that there was no one else.

"What?"

"The fear we are never worthy of anyone better," he replied.

"Sorry?"

"When you subject yourself to pain, repeatedly allowing him to break you with a few words. Says a lot about you," he replied.

She frowned. "What's that?"

"You must not love yourself. I'll tell you, mademoiselle...your life belongs to you. It's a matter of treating your life with respect, and maybe then life would provide you better."

Olivia nodded, not sure what she should have said. She dug into her purse, took out her last five-dollar bill, and handed it to him. Her death by coffee would have to be another time, since the café across the street only took cash.

"Sorry, it's all I got." She smiled and walked toward the entrance of the building.

"Mademoiselle! Wait—I have something for you."

Her inner voice told her to keep walking, but for some reason she stopped and walked back. "For me?" She frowned and waited for him to remove a piece of paper from his pocket, handing it to her.

She unfolded the paper, seeing only a few sentences scribbled there. It was quite a task to read since the penmanship was awful. She looked around once more before reading it to herself.

Dear girl with the red scarf,

Life can be hard at times
but remember it's only
temporary. Be true to
yourself and realize you
deserve someone who will love
you unconditionally. Please
never settle for less.
Trust me, after all,
I am Mr.universe ☺

SHE LOOKED BACK at the man on the street. "Cute. Did you write this?"

He shrugged. "No."

Olivia frowned. "So then who?"

This was addressed to the girl with the red scarf. Coincidently, she wore a red scarf—well, more like red pashmina—draped around her neck.

"Mr. Universe." His smile widened even more.

Looking over her shoulder, she thought maybe this was a joke, like those TV shows where they played tricks on people with a secret camera hidden in the nearby bushes.

"You're playing with me, right?"

"Don't worry. You're lost, but you will find your way. Sometimes it's easy to get lost in the scheme of things. The universe will reveal himself to you when he's ready."

"Right ... okay, thanks for..." She waved the note in the air.

"We are all on stage, my dear. Sometimes we forget our lines, but luckily an offstage helper can whisper our sentences to us, until we get back on track," he continued.

She arched her eyebrow. "An offstage ... helper?" She slowly nodded. This man wasn't making any sense and now she was late for work.

"Metaphorically, of course. Someone to guide you when you've lost your sense of direction."

"Hmm ... right ... of course."

He rose slowly. "Don't stop looking at those stars," he said, walking on by, leaving her to wonder what had just happened.

Olivia looked down at the piece of paper he had given her.

Chills ran up the back of her neck, but it wasn't from the crisp cold air.

Don't stop looking at those stars. It was something her grandfather used to say.

Dear girl with the red scarf,

Sometimes life throws a curve ball,
knocks us to the ground. Trust me,
I've tasted dirt more times than I'd
like to admit. My point is we all have
been there (if you're anything like
me) and most likely be there again.
But you need to get up, dust
yourself off, and move on. Maybe the
best part about this experience is that
you will keep on getting stronger and
wiser. I mean this with every fiber
of my being: I believe in you.
Never give up. Surrender to all the
things your heart desires.

Trust me, after all, ☺
I am Mr.universe

3

WHEN SHE COMES
AROUND

NICK MONTGOMERY'S EYES FIXED ON THE VOID—A BIG WHITE VOID, to be exact—hitched onto the easel right in front of him. He ran his fingers over the coarse fabric of the canvas. It almost depicted his life these days: deserted, uninhabited, vacant. A shell of a life as opposed to what it once had been. Sitting quietly, he waited for it to come—but it never did. When a stream of morning light trickled in from the basement window, Nick got up and walked toward the door, picking up his keys from his desk before exiting his studio.

Later, Nick sat in the café, where he caught sight of a girl. His heart dropped when he realized it wasn't *the* girl—not his girl, per se; not yet anyhow.

Nick had made the fateful decision to walk into that café two months ago, when he'd first moved into the neighborhood, in search of a place to grab a bite. That was the first time he'd seen her, sketching in a notebook. When she'd glanced up, their eyes had met. Nick had never considered himself a sappy romantic.

He had once believed in love, maybe even at first sight, but that had existed ages ago, at a time when Nick thought life was limitless. Now Nick wasn't sure what he believed.

But something had shifted inside him, an instant spark or even magic, because at that moment he had wanted to believe that something extraordinary could happen. The girl with the sad eyes had that kind of effect on him.

And, as after catching a tune on the radio for the first time, she had begun to appear in all the places he went. They crossed paths on multiple occasions, up and down the street of Chabanel, all in the radius of a few blocks in Montreal's garment district. He had become familiar with her daily routine. She would come to the café every morning and take her dark coffee to go. She disliked the color red but wore a red scarf. One morning she announced to her friend with the bright hair that men who wore beanies indoors annoyed her. Was she talking about him?

Good chance.

That morning Nick sat across from her, wearing his beloved gray hat while reading his morning paper, because nobody did that anymore. A few days ago he had considered saying something. But he couldn't even muster enough courage to say one word. Nick sat there quietly at his table with scenarios playing in his head.

SCENARIO ONE HUNDRED AND TWENTY-FIVE:

Him: Are you a designer?

Her: Yes.

Him: I'm an artist myself. You're talented.

Her: Thanks.

Him: Can I buy you a coffee?

Her: Thanks, but I already got one. (Paper cup right beside her)

Crickets...

GOD, why was he so lame?

He worked at a bar; this kind of thing should have come easy. There was another important fact that made him apprehensive. There was somebody else in her life—a good 3.5-karats somebody.

Minor detail.

"Is she here?" his brother Dan asked.

Nick must have missed her this morning, thanks to his brother's need to have his short, golden hair styled and gelled every morning, every single hair positioned in the right place. It drove him insane that Dan thrived on being a perfectionist.

Although there were few physical differences between them, Nick had once been the better-looking of the two. In the last couple of years, Nick had sort of let himself go. Once the notion of mortality came into the equation, small things became insignificant—like personal grooming.

"What?" Nick played with the scrambled eggs on his plate.

"The girl you've been drooling over?" Dan's blue eyes shot up to meet his. "You know, you do this thing with your tongue when she walks through that door."

"I do not!" He laughed at Dan's facial expression, like a dog on a hot day in search of water.

"Stop playing patty-cake and go fuckin' talk to her."

"She's not here, and there's another thing. She's engaged!"

"Whatever." Dan waved a hand in the air. "Amanda was seeing someone when we first met. Look at us now."

Dan had first laid eyes on his beautiful fiancée when Nick was hospitalized the first time. She was visiting her grandmother and had trouble with the vending machine. Luckily for Dan, he was there at the right time.

"Seriously, I don't even know what she sees in you," Nick mused.

"I ask myself the same question." Dan paused. "Let me give you a piece of advice..."

"Dude, you fuckin' give horrible advice."

"When did I ever steer you in the wrong direction?"

"All the time."

"Bullshit. I've given awesome advice."

"All right, the time when you were too lazy to drive me to Christina Jenkins' party. You had this smart-ass idea I should take Mom's car when I didn't have my license."

"Oh, come on, that was a fender bender."

"I totaled Mom's car," Nick said.

"It's not my fault you can't drive in a straight line."

"Oh, here's another good one..." Nick swallowed his bite before continuing. "You thought it was a good idea for Chloe to move in with me."

"Okay, that wasn't my finest. How was I to know she'd turn out to be a closet psycho?"

After a short minute, Nick dragged his eyes back up. "So are you going to tell me?"

"Oh, now you want my advice?"

Nick shrugged.

"For God's sake, ask her out."

"I wouldn't know what to say. Hi, your boyfriend is a jerk, can I take you out sometime?"

On the few rare occasions Nick had seen them together, her fiancé was oblivious to her existence as she gaped at him with those beautiful, elephant eyes, begging for some validation. If she were his girl, Nick would never remove his eyes from her. Never for one minute would he make her feel insignificant. Why did assholes have all the luck?

"I don't get it. You always had girls running in circles."

"Well ... I guess things change. You forgot what the last three years were like." Nick rubbed his scruffy face.

Dan's eyes softened. "No. I was there, remember?"

Nick sucked in the air from his nose. "Who am I kidding? She'll never go for someone like me."

"Why not?"

"She never smiles."

"Hmmm ... not the friendly type."

"I like that about her."

Dan frowned. "Yeah, sure, what's not to like?" Dan leaned in closer. "You know, Amanda has a single friend..."

Nick shut his eyes. "Oh no, please, don't do me any more favors."

"It's been three years since Chloe left. I hate seeing you alone."

Nick pursed his lips. "Hold on. I'm alone, not lonely. There's a difference."

"Yeah, sure, keep telling yourself that."

"I'll have you know there have been other women."

Dan rolled his eyes. "When was the last time you were in a committed relationship?"

Dan had a point. Nick had dated little after his ex-girlfriend walked out. That was because Chloe had poked more than enough holes in his heart, and the remnants of those scars remained. Looking back, he realized the relationship had lasted longer than it should have, but he couldn't walk away. He wasn't like his father.

"Do me a favor. When you see her, ask her on a date. If not, I'm going to do it for you."

"No, don't! I'll do it, alright. Just don't be a dick."

"Please, because I can't take looking at your sorry-ass face anymore." Dan pulled out money from his wallet and Nick pushed the twenty back to him. "Breakfast is on me."

"Sure? Alright, I'm off to the bar. I have a shipment coming in this morning," Dan said, rising from his chair.

"I'll be there a little later. I'm scheduled to close tonight."

"Again? Why don't you let Yannick do the closing?" Dan stared at him. "I don't want you to exhaust yourself."

"I'm a big boy. Don't worry about me." Nick hated when his brother mothered him.

When Dan left, Nick pulled out his sketchbook from his bag and took one last sip of coffee before he began to write.

Dear girl with the red scarf,

Destiny doesn't care about us. We
can't control it or change the
course. Maybe it's just a matter of
surrendering ourselves to it, letting
things happen the way it should. I
know it's difficult to submit to
something with much uncertainty.
Cut the ropes and let yourself fall,
let yourself tumble to a place
where you were meant to be. After
all, destiny is a way for the
universe to guide one thing into
another.
Trust me, after all,
I am Mr.universe ☺

4

DEFINITELY SOMETHING

OLIVIA COULDN'T BELIEVE A WORD OF IT. HIS LIPS WERE MOVING, but at some point she had lost all interest in anything he had left to say. Was this the man she had wanted to spend the rest of her life with? She couldn't even stand to stay another five seconds in the same room with him.

There was nothing unusual or out of the ordinary about finding Dario in his home office, slouching in his chair, his feet up on his desk and a cell phone to his ear when she came home early from work. What had gotten her attention was the form of language he was using, followed by a low, husky whisper.

"Baby, no, I can't ... I told you already. Of course I want to see you tonight."

Those words had stopped Olivia dead in her tracks. And there she stood, behind the half-open door, listening to the rest of their conversation. There was only one thing to justify what she had just heard. Dario was a cheat.

Foolishly, Olivia was holding on to a relationship that was never salvageable. She'd been second-guessing their relationship for months, but Olivia had hoped that, if he'd somehow changed, things would get better between them. Maybe she should have been thanking him. If tonight had gone as planned, they would be at some upscale restaurant where she'd be peering around the room, envying every couple, while he took a business call.

"Where are you going?" Dario followed her into their bedroom. "I don't know what you thought you heard—but I was trying to close a deal."

His expression told her he wasn't sure how much of the conversation she had overheard. He was playing it safe, waiting for her to reveal more before continuing.

"Oh, closing a deal was exactly what you had in mind. I'm not stupid—I was behind the door the entire time,"

As the blood drained from his face, she knew there was more to the story. Like some private prayer, he placed his hands in front of his face.

"Okay ... Can we talk about this?"

"Talk? You're having an affair." She stopped pacing. "I'm calling the engagement off."

"Please, you're making a mistake. You've got this all wrong..."

Olivia observed him for a moment. She should have yelled, called him every name in the book, but nothing came out. Dario was visibly shaken. Was he afraid of losing her? No, more like his job and this lifestyle, and she was the glue holding it together.

"Is it hard for you to be honest for once?" Olivia said.

"Hear me out ... Ann has this thing for me. It's harmless flirting. Trust me when I say nothing has ever happened between us. I swear on my mother's head. Please, believe me."

"God, how pathetic are you? After I caught you telling another woman..." She paused. "Wait ... as in Ann, your assistant — Ann?" How humiliating! Her family couldn't handle another scandal.

"Yes." His eyes veered to the floor.

"The one you took with you on your business trip to New York last week?"

He took a moment before answering. "Yeah ... so what? Nothing happened with that woman, I swear!"

"How long has this been going on?" She searched his face for some answers. "Before the engagement party? Longer?"

His silence confirmed it. She walked past him.

"Where are you going?"

"To get away from you!"

Down the corridor, she locked herself in the bathroom. It was the only way she could get him to stop hovering. She needed to think, to be alone with her thoughts.

"Olivia, I'll do anything to fix this. I'll break it off with Ann, I'll see a therapist ... I promise. It will never happen again. Just... please don't leave me," he pleaded from behind the door. "I'm so sorry, baby."

Olivia leaned against the door. Anyone in her position would be numb with shock, curled up in a ball crying, but at this moment Olivia wasn't capable of mustering even one tear. In the past twenty-five minutes, he had not spoken one word about love; he had begged her to stay, to believe him, but there was no *"I love you,"* no *"I can't live without you."*

She imagined a life without him, and the possibility was exhilarating. Would it be easy to walk away? Then she remembered the handwritten note she had found yesterday, wedged under her windshield wipers, which, until now, had had little meaning. Mr. Universe had written: *A person knows when they're doing the right thing when goodbyes are effortlessly done. There is no lump in your throat, no anguish, no pain in your heart. Then, goodbye is what should be prescribed.*

She opened the door with such force that it made Dario flinch, and he went silent. Maybe he had seen it in her eyes, because she certainly felt it. The glass had finally shattered, and she was now coming through.

"There is nothing left for us to keep on going," she said. "So I think it's best if you leave by tonight."

He nodded in defeat. She eagerly removed her engagement ring and placed it in his black suit pocket.

"Olivia, what are you going to tell your father?" He tried one last attempt, but this time around it wouldn't work. She was finally done—done being manipulated by him.

*

TWENTY MINUTES LATER, Olivia had her friend Jessica pick her up at her apartment, and they went somewhere Dario wouldn't be able to find them.

The place was like every other bar in Montreal on a Friday night, crowded and energetic. It had a modern, chic decor with tables scattered everywhere. A vast canvas on the far wall caught Olivia's eyes on the way in. The subject was a girl walking away from the viewer, her red scarf blowing in the wind. She took another glance before Jessica nudged her.

"There are two seats at the end of the bar," Jessica said over the loud music.

"Why not at the back?" Olivia suggested.

Jessica shook her head, making her red ringlets bounce around her face. "Ah ... no. The bar is where the action is." She nodded her head in the opposite direction. Olivia winced, following Jessica through the crowd.

"Don't be such a downer, woman! I didn't come out with you so you can cry and be miserable about that piece of slime."

Surprisingly, Olivia had done neither—only felt the weight lift off her shoulders. Three bartenders were working behind the bar, and the shortest of the three took their order.

"I wished I had been there to see his face when you told him to move out." Jessica brought the martini glass to her lips.

"I think he still believes we can work things out," Olivia said.

"Just be straight with him. Don't give him any hope. I swear, if you even think about going back to him, I will never speak to you again!"

"No worries there." Olivia knew it was over. It had been for the longest time, but she just hadn't known how to let go.

"I always hated that asshole," Jessica murmured.

Olivia and Jessica had been friends since college, where they'd both pursued a career in fashion. After getting a degree in design, Olivia had worked for a small children's wear company until a position opened at Jessica's company, D.S. Designs. It was Jessica who had encouraged her to apply for the assistant position. Although it wasn't Olivia's dream job, she took it with the hopes of one day being promoted to a designer position with her own label, as promised by her boss.

"You know what I don't understand? How your dad doesn't see right through him," Jessica said. "I mean, he must see him at work. He can't possibly be that good at hiding it."

"My father is rarely at the office, and when he is, Dario is probably on his best behavior." Olivia sighed. "I don't know how I will break it to my parents."

"I'm sure they will be disappointed, but they'll get over it. Whose life is it? Yours or theirs?" She waved her hand in the air. "Speaking about your dad, how are things with him?"

Olivia shrugged. "He doesn't tell me anything. When I ask, all he says is not to worry. I know he's in some trouble, and now, with his diagnosis, I'm not sure what will happen."

Olivia glanced up when she felt a hand on her shoulder. Olivia looked up, and standing there was an attractive man wearing a blue T-shirt two sizes too small.

"Is this seat taken?" he asked.

"Yes, it is. I'm waiting for my boyfriend," Olivia said as the guy gave her an apologetic smile and walked away to better prospects.

Jessica let out a laugh. "My gosh, Olivia! What am I going to do with you?"

"What?"

"What's the matter with you? He was *gorgeous*. You should have let him sit next to you."

"I don't feel like flirting with some random guy. Not tonight."

"You know what they say: the best way to get over someone is to get under—"

"That's so absurd!" Olivia blushed. Dario was the only man she had ever dated, the only person she'd ever known. She hadn't thought about what it would be like to date again, and after what she had gone through with Dario, it was exhausting just to think about it.

"I'm just saying you should meet new people. Figure out what you want."

"I've been single for a little over an hour. What I need now is to be on my own."

Jessica laughed. "Don't be such a nun. I'm not telling you to marry the next guy you run into. I'm telling you to loosen up a little."

Jessica swung her shoulders with the music.

"All right, I give up." Jessica slightly put her hands up in defeat. "You're missing out." Jessica grinned.

"Well then, too bad for me."

"Yup, too bad." Jessica narrowed her eyes. "Especially for that guy down there who's been checking you out since we arrived."

"Jesus, do you have a built-in radar or something?"

"I'm a woman of many talents. What can I say?" Jessica winked.

"So who is it? The guy with the checkered shirt?"

"No, darling, that guy is checking *me* out." Jessica smiled wickedly. "I'm talking about the bartender standing in *front* of the man in the checkered shirt."

Olivia tried to glance back timidly. Her eyes widened with wonder. Something about his face tickled the back of her mind. Where had she seen him before? He appeared to be in his mid-twenties, tall, slim build. His hair was a little longer on top, and some stray strands would trickle in front of his bright eyes every so often. He wore a loose T-shirt with a pair of poorly fitted jeans.

He wasn't hideous; he just wasn't what she wanted in a significant other. Olivia had never thought herself to be shallow, but she liked guys who took their appearance seriously. His eyes met hers, and she shyly glanced away.

"Oh, that guy..."

"Yeah, that guy."

"Jess, none of these guys in this room are my type."

Jessica turned and gave her a surprised expression. "Seriously? Because they are not wearing a Hugo Boss suit? Sometimes I swear you're such a snob, Olivia." Her eyes narrowed in. "Do you even know what your type is? And don't describe your father's—you know how that one worked out."

OLIVIA BIT HER LOWER LIP. She had a point.

"Well, I wish you luck on that one." Jessica brought her glass to her mouth.

"Can you tell me why I came out with you tonight?"

"You came so I can shake sense into you. Make you open your eyes. Have fun, Liv; you've only got one life. Dario is your father's dream, but what's yours?"

Olivia didn't know what she wanted anymore. She'd been trying hard to please her father all her life, and now she was about to disappoint him once again.

Dear girl with the red scarf,

Sometimes people just show up in our lives without
any explanation. But if you should find love
begging at the door of your heart and choose not
to open it, then there is a good chance that you
will deprive yourself of some happiness. I believe
that nobody is terrified of love, only scared of
all the other crappy stuff that love brings along
with it. Stop playing it safe, letting your mind
rule where the heart is the only one who could
understand. Taking chances is what love is all
about.
            Trust me, after all,   ☺
            I am Mr.universe

5

MUSIC AT THE START

"Hello, ladies." The bartender's eyes went from Olivia to Jessica. "See that handsome guy over there, with the green checkered shirt? Well, he sent you this." The unshaven bartender placed a pink alcoholic drink in front of Jessica.

"Well, thank you. My night just got interesting." She gave Olivia a side glance. "Sorry, hon, no offense."

"None taken."

Jessica turned in her seat and waved flirtatiously at the guy down the bar. "Do you mind?" She nodded in the direction of the cute stranger.

"I thought you came out to console me?" Olivia said coyly.

"Yes, and I did."

"All right, go. I'll be fine. I'll just sit here all by myself," Olivia mused.

"You're not alone! You've got this charming, handsome man in front of you." Jessica cross-examined the bartender, who was smiling. "Go easy on her. She's going through a tough time." She whispered, placing her hand on Olivia's shoulder. "She just broke up with her fiancé."

Did a shadow of surprise cross the stranger's face?

"Jessica!" Olivia hated to reveal any part of her life, especially to strangers.

Then Jessica leaned in closer to Olivia's ear, "Try to be nice. You might have fun." She walked away, leaving Olivia alone with the bartender.

"Shit, now your friend left you too ... rough night."

Her head snapped right up. "Oh—I wasn't dumped."

"No, I'm sure you weren't." He frowned. "I didn't mean to assume..."

She stared at him for a moment until her phone buzzed from within her leather handbag. It took several seconds to get to it, buried underneath receipts, gum wrappers, and now several notes from Mr. Universe.

"What?"

He grinned. "Need help?"

"I'm good, thanks." She smirked sarcastically, waving her phone in the air.

Fifteen missed calls from Dario. There was no way she would call him, because there was nothing left to say. Olivia thought about her father and what this would do to him. It would be another blow, and he'd be crushed when he learned that his future son-in-law was a narcissistic cheat.

No, tonight she didn't want to think about it.

God, she needed a drink.

"What's in there?" He attempts to peek inside, but Olivia pulled her bag away.

She dropped her phone back into her purse, losing it inside again. "None of your business."

Olivia noticed a subtle smile linger on his lips. She amused him.

"So, what's your story?" The bartender began to organize things behind the counter.

Olivia sighed. "Believe me, you don't want to know."

"Try me?"

"It's nothing."

"You will have to tell me something better if you want to keep me interested." He smiled gallantly.

"O ... okay..." She glanced up at him. "How about...none of your business!" She flashed him a sweet, innocent smile, twirling a strand of hair that had come undone from her bun.

"Ouch! Aren't you a feisty one?" He chuckled.

"Sorry, I don't want to be rude, but—"

"Too late for that, darling." He frowned.

She glared at him. "Please don't call me that."

"What?"

"I'm not your darling." Olivia knew this stranger had done nothing to deserve her fury; it should be saved for Dario.

Another buzzing sound came from her bag. This time, it was her mother. Olivia cringed, knowing Dario had been calling around looking for her. She placed her phone on the counter and her eyes meet the bartender's amused face.

Yes, that's right, funny guy. My life's a mess.

Olivia had a talent for keeping things together, bottling up her emotions for no one to witness. Now she was losing control, and the thread kept unraveling. Olivia wasn't sure if there would be anything left of her once everything was said and done. Her heart pretended to be unable to imagine how it would end, and now she found herself at the mercy of the stranger's soulful eyes, and Olivia thought she might cry.

"Listen." His eyes softened. "If you need someone to talk to..."

"You can't possibly understand what I am going through."

"Yeah, you're right. What do I know of messy breakups?"

Olivia could tell by the look in his eyes that he had been through something. She recognized the lack of brightness and life in his gaze, because she'd seen it every time she passed a mirror.

"You know what you need? A stranger who doesn't know your backstory. I promise I won't judge."

"Oh my God, you're a walking cliché." A sarcastic laugh escaped her lips. "No, I'm fine, thanks."

"You know, I'm a good listener."

He was relentless.

Olivia glanced around the room. "Oh, I'm sure you're qualified."

His brows came together. "Hey, who's being judgmental? Didn't your mother teach you not to judge a book by its cover?"

"Yes, and she also taught me not to talk to strangers."

He chuckled. "Well, we aren't exactly strangers." His eyes said something more.

Maybe he had recognized her but from where?

"Do we know each other?" Perhaps he was one of the fit models that D.S. Designs occasionally hired to do their fittings, but he didn't look like model material. Most models she worked with were attractive and charming, and he was fashionably challenged like he'd just rolled out of bed.

"Not necessarily, but you've seen me around."

What was he talking about? This was the first time she'd been in this bar, the first time she'd ever seen this man...she thought.

"You don't know a thing about me, so please don't act like you do."

He smirked, as though he could prove her otherwise.

She narrowed her eyes at him. "Oh, what's so funny?"

"Well, I already have a feel for you ... just by your appearance."

Olivia glanced down. She was wearing her blue turtleneck with a gray pencil skirt. She considered her outfit professional enough to wear to the office. "What's wrong with the way I dress?"

"Nothing, you dress lovely." He smiled with a hint of animosity. "But it says a lot about your personality. Just an observation." His eyes swept over the top half of her, which made her uncomfortable.

She leaned further in her chair, placing her arms on her chest. If he was judging her based on what she was wearing, then what he wore said nothing positive about him. He wore a lame, wrinkled T-shirt with bold red letters: DEATH BEFORE SHAVE. Which Olivia regarded as *immature*.

He followed her gaze down to his tee, then snapped his eyes back up to meet hers. His smile widened to one side. "Like what you see?"

Olivia couldn't form any words, and the blood rushed to her cheeks. Why on earth was she blushing? Olivia straightened herself, trying to compose herself. "Okay, Mr. Bartender, so tell me ... what does my appearance say about me?"

He observed her. His eyes trailed the length of her face, pausing briefly on her lips. "Well, the turtleneck and your hair tied at the top like that—says you're incapable of fun. You're uptight, afraid of people finding out the real you." He leaned back on the counter behind him.

"You're wrong. I'm not uptight! I know how to have fun—*fun* is my middle name." As the words rolled out of her mouth, they didn't sound convincing, not even to herself. Olivia gazed at him from the corner of her eye. "Did you get your degree from a Cracker Jack box?"

"Aren't you a smart one." He chuckled, placing his hands on his hips. "No, I got it from the same place you got your attitude from."

Ugh.

Who was this guy, making her flustered and aggravated? Why couldn't she get up and go?

Yes, she should. She grabbed her purse and phone.

"Wait, I was kidding." He cleared his throat. "Well, not really ... But I'm sure you're nice ... at least to someone out there." He chuckled, but halted when Olivia flashed him a look. "Please stay. I promise I'll be on my best behavior."

Olivia glanced down to where her friend sat with the handsome stranger. Jessica was laughing and having a good time. Her stomach tightened. She had been awful to this guy who didn't deserve it. Maybe she could try at least to loosen up just a little? After all, this guy's description of her wasn't far from the truth.

"You know, I like you," he stated matter-of-factly.

Her face burned with heat, a good sign that he had had an effect. "No offense, but I'm not your type," Olivia spat. "I mean, you don't want to deal with someone like me ... uptight and all." Olivia sighed.

He studied her for a moment. "I disagree."

"Really?" Olivia glanced around the room. Sitting at a table farther down were two attractive women. They had been trying to get his attention, but he was oblivious to their efforts. "Those girls over there seem interested in you. You'd have better luck with them than with me tonight."

He followed her gaze until his eyes landed on the pair of enthusiastic, smiley blondes. "Oh, those girls are not my type. Beautiful brunettes with a smart mouth are," He had a twinkle in his eyes. "The sassier the better." He joggled his eyebrows.

Olivia picked up the glass to conceal her smile. She had lost her touch; shutting guys down and crushing their hopes was what she did best. Somehow, she couldn't seem to shake his annoying, relentless, heaven-sent attitude. Gosh, she wanted to hate him.

"I bet your boss wouldn't be pleased you're here flirting with me instead of doing your job."

His smile faded. "You're probably right, but I think you're worth getting fired over."

"You think you're charming?"

"Well, it all depends on how it's working for you."

"Not so good," she said flatly.

He rubbed his jaw. "Okay, so what will it take for you to go out with me?"

Olivia looked at him in disbelief. "Well, for starters I am in no condition to start anything with anyone, sorry." She shrugged.

"Well, that's a shame."

"A shame for whom?" She let out a laugh.

"For you."

"Of course." Olivia rolled down her collar.

"Look, you seem like a nice guy, but I'm still in a relationship."

"Yeah, apparently with someone who's not right for you," he added. "I think we're meant to be more than just two ships passing in the night."

"Hm ... might I remind you, your ship is sinking."

"Really?"

"Pretty much since we began this conversation—*oh*, look at that! Your ship is completely underwater."

He laughed. "That bad?"

She nodded her head slowly. "I'm afraid so."

"But you never know. I might be the one you're looking for." His eyes twinkled with amusement.

She was taken aback. "I ... I'm not looking for anyone. The only reason I'm here tonight is to get *away* from someone."

"Right, and here you are—you found me instead. You can't deny it's serendipity."

"Serendipity?" Olivia frowned.

"Look, I believe you walked into this bar tonight, and not by chance. You and I were meant to be here together." He motioned with his hand.

Olivia giggled. "Oh, come on. Do girls actually fall for this kind of stuff?"

"Maybe some," he said, laughing, hiding his sudden bashfulness. "All right, look, we got off on the wrong foot. Can we call it a truce?" he said honestly.

Olivia bit her lip. She hated to admit it, but she was having fun. Well, maybe just a little. He had gotten her to forget her problems, at least for the moment.

"Nick Montgomery," he said, holding out his hand.

"Olivia ... Montiano." She took it and noticed how warm his skin was.

"Is that your real name?"

"Yeah, why wouldn't it be?" Her brows drew together.

"You're not one of those girls who like to toy with men? Give them a fake name and number?"

"Do I look like the kind of girl who would do such a thing?"

He tightened his eyes.

"Okay." She laughed. "Yes, Olivia is my name. I was named after Olivia Hussey."

"No way!"

She caught his sarcasm and narrowed her eyes at him. "Are you familiar with Olivia Hussey?"

"Yeah, sure. Everyone knows who Olivia Hussey is—okay, not really."

"She's an actress, obviously. One of my mother's favorites."

He shrugged. "Anyhow, it's a lovely name." He tapped his fingers on the counter. "Montiano ... where have I heard that name before? Sounds very familiar."

She shrugged innocently. Her surname had been all over the news for the past year.

"Hey, you know what I realized? We share the same first four letters in our surname. You have to admit it's more than a coincidence," Nick said.

"Wow! A good observation." She smirked, not seeing what the big deal was.

He studied her for a moment, raising his hands in the air in defeat. "All right, Olivia Montiano, I give up. I see you're a woman of many well-kept secrets, and you may keep them if you like." Nick winked.

After a moment of silence, she said, "So, what's your story?" She was trying to be a little friendlier.

"Nope, I will not tell you a single thing."

"All right, I deserve that," Olivia replied.

"Okay, you don't have to twist my arm. I'll let you in, but over dinner."

"You don't give up? No, that won't be possible."

"Are you afraid that you will find me interesting? See, I'm the type of guy who stays on your mind, long after you've met me." His eyes danced.

Oh great, he was one of those. Full of himself. She should introduce him to Dario. "For sure. You're not a guy who is ... forgettable." Olivia giggled.

"Are you making fun of me?"

"You're a strange man, Montgomery."

He took out a blue pen from under the counter. "Give me your hand," he asked.

She hesitated for a moment before allowing him to take her hand in his. "You're not going to write your phone number, are you?"

"Only a fake one." Nick smiled.

His hands were soft to the touch, making her feel out of her element. She watched him as he drew a little heart with jagged edges going down the middle on the inside of her wrist. The surprising thing was that she didn't want him to stop.

"What's this?" Olivia asked.

"The first and most important clue about me." He gently let go of her hand.

"Someone broke your heart?" She frowned, regretting being such a bitch.

"Want to know more?" His eyes softened. "Ah—don't say I didn't warn you."

"So, I'm right?"

"Let me buy you dinner, and I will tell you more about it." He smiled.

"But you didn't say anything." Olivia recognized a ploy when she saw one. "Sorry to break it to you, but your plan is not working, Romeo." She looked at the time. "I should be going." Olivia didn't want to get involved, and if she stayed, she might be tempted to say yes, and that would only lead him on further.

"Stay, this is fun."

"As tempting as that might sound, I can't ... I've had a long day." She turned away to get down from the stool.

"Roshambo," he blurted out.

"What?" she said with a half laugh.

"Roshambo me for it. I win, you let me buy you dinner."

"What's Roshambo?" She giggled.

"You never played Roshambo before?"

"Hmm ... ah—no."

"Rock, Paper, Scissors?"

"Oh yeah, sure. Like when I was six," she spat.

"I was wrong ... You're way beyond uptight." He narrowed his eyes.

"I'm not."

"Prove it. If you win, I won't bother you anymore. Fair enough?"

She took a moment before replying. "All right—fine."

Olivia followed his lead.

"RO. SHAM. BO," they said in unison.

"You lose! Scissors cuts paper. Better luck next time, Montgomery."

Had she said *next time*? Olivia hadn't meant for it to come out the way it did. She beamed brightly while Nick shook his head.

When Olivia realized her friend had gone, and so had the stranger, she called a taxi and placed her phone back on the counter. Olivia asked how much she owed him for the drinks; Nick refused to take any money. He told Olivia it was the least he could do since he had ruined her night. Though she would never have admitted it—not to him, anyhow—Olivia had a good time.

And just when she was about to enter her cab, she heard Nick's voice calling out. She turned to find Nick holding out her scarf and her phone in his hands.

"You forgot these," he said, making his way to where she stood.

"Thank you." She smiled.

He handed her the phone but refused to give back her scarf. Before Olivia could understand what he was trying to do, he lifted her collar, draping the scarf around her neck.

Suddenly it came to her why Nick was so familiar. He wasn't wearing that dreadful hat, and that was why she hadn't recognized him. Their gaze lingered a moment.

"It's you," she said in amazement, but he remained silent. She had thought of all the times they had come face-to-face and never said a single word to each other. Like two perfect strangers, but now they weren't strangers anymore...not exactly. "Thank you," Olivia said again, as she was the one first to break away from his gaze.

"Sure—"

Nick opened the door, but before sliding into the back of the cab, she gave him one more glance.

"I know you won't believe it, but I have this feeling we will see each other again," he told her.

"Are you telling me you're a psychic as well, Nick?" Olivia smiled. "Of course. You're the 'Where's Waldo' in my life. I seem to find you everywhere I go."

His half-smile turned into a whole one. "See you around, Montiano."

"Catch you later, Montgomery." She slid into the back of the cab as he closed the door behind her. She looked through her calling list as the cab drove off. Olivia didn't understand why she was so disappointed when she discovered Nick hadn't programmed his number into her phone. What had she expected?

Olivia placed it back into her purse, slouching further into the seat as it drove into the night, toward what she had hoped would be a very, very lonely apartment.

Dear girl with the red scarf,

You learn a lot about love when you lose it.
You learn a lot about life when you have
your heart broken. We blame ourselves for
everything that went wrong in the
relationship or we think we're just not
loveable. That can't be further from the
truth. See we all crave for someone to
make us feel like magic. We want to see
ourselves in someone else's eye, but here's
the kicker: this will never be unless you
believe you are magic yourself.
Trust me, after all,
I am Mr.universe
☺

6

A MAN WALKS INTO A BAR

NICK ARRIVED AT THE BAR WITH A STOOL TUCKED IN ONE ARM AND A canvas in another. His brother Dan was behind the counter, taking inventory and stocking up for the evening. Nick hadn't realized what he was getting himself into when he'd agreed to work for his brother over a year ago, but he needed the money, and it had freed up his days to create art. That was something he had desperately wanted to start again. Dan handled the administration while Nick ran the bar when his brother wasn't around.

"Sorry, we're closed ... Oh, it's you."

"I see someone's in a good mood." Nick smiled coyly.

"Yeah, well..." Dan flipped through the papers laying on the counter.

"You had another argument with Amanda?"

"Something like that."

Nick slid the barstool under the counter and gave his brother a sideways glance. "Hey, were you ever planning on telling me about the blind date?"

"Yeah, about that..." Dan smirked.

"Why didn't you tell me this morning when I saw you?"

"I tried. Besides, don't look at me. It was Amanda's idea."

Nick blinked. "So you guys planned the whole thing behind my back? Didn't you think maybe you should have run it by me first?"

"It wasn't behind your back. You weren't there when we discussed it." Dan grinned.

Nick shook his head in disbelief. He wasn't upset, because he knew his brother's intentions were always good. Nick had just thought that, based on the last disaster with Amanda's cousin and her issues with his medical history, they had given up hope of setting him up with anyone again. "I appreciate what you guys are trying to do, but honestly, I don't think I'm up for it," Nick said.

"Wait, hear me out. Amanda's friend Lucy, she's smart and cute. I know you guys would hit it off."

Nick was skeptical when people tried to set him up. It always started the same way: the girl was beautiful and brilliant, and they'd have so much in common that she was destined to be his soul mate. Guaranteed.

But Nick had already given it enough shots to know it always fell short of something. He didn't choose to be single; being single chose him.

He understood Dan's need to help him with his love life. His brother struggled with some personal remorse. He had Amanda, and they were about to start their lives together. Nick had no one, but truthfully he couldn't be happier for the pair. If anyone deserved to be happy, it was Dan. He had always been there for him growing up and had continued to be over the years. Nick just wished his brother understood that there was no need to feel any guilt.

Nick shook his head. "I'm sure, but I'll pass."

"Come on, don't think of it as a blind date. It won't be like the last time, I swear. Amanda and I will be there, so no pressure. Just a couple of friends having dinner. If you and Lucy should hit it off, well, great. If not, it's not a big deal."

Nick frowned. "It's a waste of time. Once she finds out about me, she'll bolt for the door. They always do."

"Lucy is not what you think. Amanda told her about your situation."

"And she still agreed to come?"

"Yup."

Nick knew everyone had skeletons in the closet. His wasn't something that could be kept hidden. It wasn't something that defined him, either, but it was very much a part of his life. After his surgery, Nick had had an ongoing fear he would be undateable, like damaged goods. There was no easy way around it, so Nick had decided early on that if he met someone he was very interested in, he would be upfront about his situation. That way it gave a girl an opportunity for a way out, and it would be early enough in the relationship that he wouldn't be too hung up on it. But Nick had been single since his last long-term relationship went up in flames; he'd gotten used to being on his own. What was wrong with that?

"Come on, buddy, what else were you going to do on a Saturday night?"

"I'm a very busy man. I've got stuff to do."

"Yeah, like what?"

"Wash my hair, read a book. Oh, clean my fridge." Nick folded up an empty cardboard box. "Wait, I'm scheduled to work!" Now Nick had the perfect excuse.

"No, you're not. I asked Yannick to take your shift."

Nick shook his head. "So what you're telling me is I have no choice?"

"Seems like it, unless you want to deal with Amanda. But I'm warning you: she's not herself these days. I don't know what's going on, but she's been so damn moody."

"Yeah, tell me about it. This morning I was using your washing machine, and she went crazy on me for mixing my darks with my whites. What's up with that?"

"I don't know. Maybe it's the stress of planning a wedding. Women. Who fuckin' understands them," Dan said under his breath. Then he gave Nick a hard nudge that almost hurt. "All right, are we doing this, or what?"

With a sharp intake of breath. "Yeah, yeah, alright" Nick said.

Dan patted him on the back. "You won't regret it."

"Something tells me I already have."

"This is going to be great." His brother beamed.

Nick wasn't convinced. He had hoped that one day he could find the right girl, the one he could trust, so that he wouldn't have to continue to tell his story. And maybe finally he'd get Dan off his case.

"Pretty good," Dan inspected the bar stool that Nick had brought in with him. The night before it had fallen apart, and Nick, who had been a tinkerer, had brought it home to repair it.

"I told you I could fix it."

"Yeah, you're a real fuckin' MacGyver." Dan smiled. "Were you able to get any work done at the studio?"

"Sort of. Nothing to write home about." Nick opened another box and stacked the bottles on the shelf behind him.

Anyone blessed with the talent of creativity knew it didn't come at your beck and call. It wasn't something you could conjure up. It came in waves and sometimes at the most inappropriate times. For Nick, it occurred at night, when his mind was still. As soon as his head would hit the pillow, his thoughts would wander. His inspiration came so fluidly, and instead of smothering the desire, he'd run down to his studio. He didn't know where the energy came from; it was like a spark that needed to get out, and through his art was where that energy went. These days he had plenty of sleepless nights, but his ability to create art seemed to have been lost.

"Do you think I've changed in some way? I've been reading up on cellular memory."

"Nah, you believe that shit? No, that has nothing to do with it." Dan's eyes softened. "Nick, you've been through a lot these past years. And you thought, what? You were just going to bounce back and expect everything to be the way it was?"

Nick ran his hands through his hair, sighing. "I thought when I decided ... when I was ready ... it would come back naturally. I never thought it was something you could lose."

Seeing his brother's frustration, Dan added, "Stop being so hard on yourself. Just give it time."

"Yeah, I know." He shrugged.

"You painted that." Dan nodded toward the large canvas.

"That's different. It's not what clients are used to seeing from me."

"Why would it be? To think of it, this would be harder to create than what you normally paint ... a bunch of splashy—splashes of color over a canvas," Dan said.

"Is that what you think of my work?" Nick frowned.

"Look, I'm not going to pretend to understand how your talent works or the business of art, because I just fucking don't. Maybe you're going to have to paint in a different way."

"George is not expecting this." Nick held out his hand to the painting, leaning against the wall. "He's expecting the kind of stuff I painted four years ago. And I don't think I'm capable. Not anymore."

George was the art director of DuPont Art, an exclusive gallery in Montreal. Nick had met him when he was nineteen, and he had given him the opportunity to exhibit his work in his gallery. It was thanks to George that his canvas *Life and Other Stories* had sold at a record price of sixty-five thousand dollars. Nick had never thought he could have a career in art, let alone make a living out of it.

"Nah, you shouldn't worry. You have a natural talent. I think you got that from Dad."

Nick sneered. "Please don't compare me to that man."

"Nick, you can't deny where you came from—pretending the man doesn't exist."

"Well, he doesn't. Not for me, anyway."

"Look, I'm not trying to justify what he did, but at some point you will have to come to terms with what happened. Just let it go."

"Are you serious? Are we having this conversation again?"

"All I'm saying is you only know one side of the story. He's trying to make amends, make things right. Why don't you give the guy a chance to explain—"

"I know enough. I was there, remember?" Nick replied. "Shit, he left Mom while she was sick. He left us with no financial support..." He paused. "Where was he when we needed him? He ran off to Calgary, making his fucking fortune. It was Mom who mustered all her strength to raise us."

Dan walked back behind the counter. "I know. He made a mistake..."

"That's not a fucking mistake." Nick scowled. "You don't do that to your family, not to the people you're supposed to love."

Dan gathered his paperwork up. "I'm not asking you to be best friends with him or even like him. I'm asking you to at least listen to what he has to say."

"Well, you can fuckin' forget about it."

"He's coming to the wedding," Dan said exasperatedly.

"Yeah, I know, with his new family. I still can't believe you invited that asshole."

"Look, don't get upset..."

"Who's getting upset? This is your life, and it's your wedding. You can invite whoever you want. Just leave me out of it."

Nick didn't want to believe that his brother wanted to have their father back in their lives, but it had only been the two of them for some time. Dan was getting married soon and would start a family shortly after that. Nick could understand the desire his brother had to belong to something bigger, because Nick wanted it too. Who wouldn't want a Victorian house with a white picket fence, a beautiful wife, and a couple of screaming kids? Shit, even going home for the holidays...a world where his mom was still alive and his parents married. It was a dream, and some dreams were simply not possible.

How could he forgive the man who had ultimately walked out on his family while his wife was fighting for her life? No, Nick couldn't let go of his anger, not yet. There was no way around it; this was his truth, his reality.

"If Mom forgave him, why can't you?"

Nick shook his head. "Please don't bring Mom into this."

"He wants to make things right with us."

"Well, he's a little too late. You want him in your life, that's your fuckin' business, but don't expect me to do the same."

"All right, you're getting upset. Let's stop talking about it." Dan picked up the folded boxes and disappeared through the door. It was clear to Nick that his brother was afraid of stressing him out. Like he was delicate.

"Yeah, let's." Nick murmured.

They didn't speak to each other for the rest of the night.

Dear girl with the red scar,

There one thing about ourselves we
keep hidden from the world, what we
desire to push from our hearts and
holler in a way we find liberating.
Do it.
I beg you, may you always find
yourself with your own eyes and heart
and when you do find the authentic
you, smile brightly. So others will
finally discover the real you.

Trust me, after all, ☺
I am Mr.universe

7

THE LONG GOODBYE

"I MISSED THIS," NINA SAID, AS THEY SAT IN A CROWDED BREAKFAST place a few blocks down from her condo.

Olivia glanced up. "What's that?"

"You without Dario."

"We've gone out before, only us..." Olivia's eyes scanned her menu.

"Not recently."

"Sure, the time we went shopping downtown and you bought those tacky curtains for your living room."

"Yes, and I was pregnant with Anthony. That was three years ago." She paused. "Hey, those curtains are not tacky, by the way!"

"Sure, if you like the Grandma's rose garden kind of thing," Olivia smirked, looking up from her menu, trying to recall more of the day in question.

"I guess I'm not considered cool enough for you or your friends."

"What's that supposed to mean?" Olivia's eyebrows gathered up.

Olivia imagined how it might seem, looking from the outside.

She had surrounded herself with Dario's friends and their significant others. They had spent a good amount of time together, many vacations and dinner dates. Olivia wondered why she had felt a need to be accepted by a group that required a Chanel bag to fit in. Looking back, it hadn't brought her joy to be around those people.

Olivia remembered one outing in particular: the girls in the group had compared their diamond rings, as if they were one of the wonders of the world.

"I've got the biggest ring! Mine is four-point-five carats and Suzie's is two-point-five." Nancy had held out her hand for everyone to see.

At that moment something had crossed her mind; she wondered if those supposed friends ever thought about more important issues, bigger problems in the world, like starving children.

No, she guessed they didn't.

When her turn had come, and Dario had presented her with a wonder of her own, she couldn't help but feel like a hypocrite. Olivia acted the part, but the truth was she was uncomfortable in her skin.

She hadn't intentionally left out her sister. Not for the reason Nina was accusing her of.

"You weren't missing anything anyways. And I thought with the baby, you wouldn't be interested in hanging around with Dario's superficial friends." She glanced up at her sister, and Olivia's stomach twisted. Perhaps her behavior was uncalled for, especially towards the people she loved most. "Honestly, if it bothered you that much, why didn't you say something?"

"I didn't want you to think I was jealous."

"Listen, I'm sorry for being such a jerk ... for not realizing sooner." She reached out to touch Nina's hand.

"All I'm saying is, it would have been nice to be invited from time to time."

Olivia placed her menu on the table. "Do you think I've changed?"

"What?"

"Do you think I'm superficial?"

Nina observed her for a moment, and the silence confirmed what Olivia suspected.

"Oh, I guess I deserve that." Olivia gave her a funny grin.

Nina laughed. "You want the truth? Dario had hold on you. Like the time when he went vegetarian and forced you to do the same."

"He didn't force me. I thought it was a healthier choice."

Nina gave her a face that read *I know you better*.

"Which reminds me, which combo has the most bacon and breakfast sausage?" Olivia glossed over her menu again.

"I don't understand why you even put yourself through that. For God's sake, Olivia, you're Italian."

"So is Dario."

"No, Dario is a reptile."

"Aren't reptiles meat eaters?"

"Whatever, I don't care. The point is, I didn't think you could live off seeds and tofu forever."

"I ate other things than tofu ... and where did you get seeds from?"

"Okay, you got my point. Shit, do you even know what you put Mom through? Or us, on Sunday dinners? She thought you were starving yourself."

"Yeah, she always thinks that, vegetarian or not."

Olivia never talked to anyone about her relationship, how much shit Dario put her through, how he manipulated her into becoming this person she didn't recognize anymore.

After some time, Nina said, "Mostly, what I saw was a repressed, empty shell of the Olivia I used to know. You seemed so unhappy."

Olivia sighed. "I was ... unhappy ... I mean, I am. There's

nothing to be happy about these days. Dario's finding every excuse not to sell the condo and Dad...well, Dad is not doing well." Olivia rubbed her eyes, wiping the tears away.

"I know, Olivia. I'm worried too, but they won't put him in jail if he has Alzheimer's."

"He's not going to jail, Nina. Because he's not guilty of anything." Olivia paused. "Why, do you think he's guilty?"

"No."

"Then why would you say something like that?"

Nina let out a long breath from her nose. "Well, if they are accusing him of something ... that means they have proof."

Olivia's shoulders dropped. As if things couldn't get any worse, ever since she'd broken the news to her parents of her failed engagement, it had resulted in a falling-out with her father.

"Don't get mad, but ... Dad's joining us this morning."

"Oh, I'm not sure if I'm ready to face him," Olivia grumbled. She had been avoiding her parents' home for the past week, only because she couldn't handle looking at her father's disapproving eyes.

"Dad caught me leaving this morning and asked me where I was going. What did you want me to say? *Don't come because your daughter is pigheaded—like you*?"

Olivia gave her sister a cheesy grin. "You could have lied."

"Well, I'm not a good liar, like some people," Nina said.

"What are you implying? I'm not a liar."

"Oh, get over yourself, Liv." Nina snapped her menu shut. "I knew something wasn't right, but you pretended that everything was just peachy. *Oh*, life is just grand!" She threw her hands up in the air. "We all suspected you've been fraying at the seams," Nina said more softly. "Dario hadn't been treating you right, for a very long time."

"Who's we?"

"All of us except for Dad. Dad is in denial, but we knew Dario was a complete asshole ... especially toward you. If only you were straight with me ... if you'd told me what was going on, I could have helped."

"What could you have done for me that I couldn't have done for myself?"

Even as children, Nina could let nothing go. One time when Olivia kept getting her shoes stolen at school by Alice Donald, a girl in her first-grade class, it was Nina who took matters into her own hands. One morning Nina cornered Alice, pulled her by her school uniform and shook her like a rag doll. Nobody bothered Olivia after that day.

Thank God for big sisters.

Olivia sank into her chair. "I'm not ready to see Dad."

"How long are you going to give him the silent treatment?"

"He's the one who's not talking," Olivia blurted out.

"And whose fault is that?"

"Not mine." Olivia shook her head. "I shouldn't have to take the blame for Dario being a dirty cheat."

"No, you're right, but it's your fault because you weren't straight with Dad." Nina added more milk to her coffee. "Listen, Olivia, if you're not willing to tell Dad the whole story, how the hell do you expect him to react? Whose side do you expect him to take?"

"But I'm his daughter."

"Tell him the truth about that reptile or let this one go. Let's not forget the amount of shit Dad's going through." Nina's eyes softened. "Just let it go."

Olivia bit her lip but felt compelled to clarify. "The only reason I didn't tell him the whole story is because I didn't want to give him any more trouble. I figured it would be better for me to take the blame. It was easier for him to think I was the one who wanted out. It's the only way Dario and Dad could continue to work together."

"I don't understand why you're still protecting Dario." Nina frowned

"I'm protecting Dad from the truth."

"Did you Google Dad's name yet?" Nina spat out.

"No."

"Go ahead, Google his name on your phone. See what they are saying about him."

Olivia glanced up and spotted their father walking toward the table. She allowed Nina to greet him first while she remained seated, leaving it up to him to make the first move. As Olivia predicted, her father leaned over and kissed the top of her head. *All is good.* She knew he couldn't be mad at her forever.

Olivia caught sight of her father's smile, a smile that reminded her of a time when things were alright, before all his troubles at work, before his diagnosis three months ago.

Isn't it right about memory? Mr. Universe had written. *You need a little glimmer of an image or a scent to ignite it, shifting you to a precise point in the past. Once you remember, images and moments dash through your mind, running their course in all directions. The sweet montage, caught on the move, moves like silk, so fragile, and it dissolves with the light, never getting back its essence. Time is constant, time doesn't get old or fade away... but it's tragic that we do.*

She hated to admit it. Her father had changed over the years. Physically, at first: his once-brown chocolate hair had turned to a light shade of gray, and the lines around his hazel eyes had become profound, heavier now.

It had been a year ago that her mother first expressed her concerns about him. She must have seen it before, but like Olivia, she had brushed it off as nothing until it could no longer be ignored.

"Mom, he's sixty-five. It's normal to forget things." Olivia didn't want to believe it at first, but then one Sunday morning at her parents' house, she had caught him standing in the hallway, looking lost and gazing around like he wasn't sure of his surroundings.

"Dad?"

His eyes had blankly caught hers. For a moment the words eluded him, as if he had forgotten how to speak.

"Dad, are you okay?"

"Yeah, sure. I was just looking for...well, I forgot what I was looking for ... those things ... you know. I can't read this damn paper." He squinted his eyes, holding the documents away from him.

"You mean your glasses? They're on top of your head, Daddy."

"Damn ... Old age is ugly, love."

Looking at him now, seeing how much he'd aged since then, Olivia wondered if her father could get any older. He had once been a vibrant man.

"How are you, love?" He picked up the menu in front of him.

"Good, Daddy."

"What have you been up to?"

"I signed a contract with a realtor," Olivia said.

He frowned. "Which agent?"

"Joanne Gadbois, from Montreal Realtors."

"Oh, Olivia, please not her! She's an idiot. You should have talked to me first. I would have recommended someone else."

She would have, if they had been talking.

"Where's Paul? That kid is always late."

"Dad, I already told you this morning ... Paul is not coming." Nina shot Olivia a knowing look.

"Oh, right..." He frowned, glancing back at the menu.

"Listen, Olivia, I talked to your mother, and we both agree that you should move back home with us once you've sold your condo."

Olivia stared at him for a long second. Moving back home had never crossed her mind. Twenty-three years living with helicopter parents was enough for anyone. "No Dad, I don't think it's a good idea."

"Listen, please." He held his hand up and stop her from continuing.

"No, Dad, actually I've been thinking about applying for a position at W. Moda. Gaby believes I have a good chance of getting a job with my experience." Olivia nervously played with her napkin on her lap.

"What experience? What do you know about working for a magazine?" he asked.

Her cousin Gabriel was a fashion photographer based in Milan. Being an only child, Gaby had grown up with Olivia and spent a lot of time with her family. Throughout the years, they'd formed a close relationship. Olivia was even a bridesmaid in his wedding when he'd married the daughter of the editor-in-chief of W. Moda. They'd spoken a few days ago, and Olivia had finally broken down and told her cousin the truth about Dario's infidelities. Gaby had told her this was a great opportunity to come to Italy and get away from it all. He had also promised to help her find an apartment and had enough pull to get her a job with the magazine. Anything was possible, If only her father would give her his blessing; then she wouldn't feel guilty about leaving. But how could she even bring herself to leave when her father was in turmoil?

"I work in the fashion industry; W. Moda is a fashion magazine. It's not much of a stretch, Dad."

"Oh, you think so?" He paused to give the waitress his order, returning his focus back to Olivia. "Okay, so tell me one thing." He gazed at her.

She recognized that look: the squinting of the eyes, the tightening of his lips and the slight head bob. The look her father gave before he crushed her dreams: *let's be realistic; this will never work out for you.*

"What position is available?"

"Gaby's mother-in-law is looking for a personal assistant. It's a year-to-year contract," Olivia said as she took a sip of her coffee.

"So you're telling me you want to move to Milan, Olivia? It's the craziest idea yet." Letting out a long breath, he added, "Look at your aunt Teresa. She's a total mess since your cousin moved to Italy. Gaby comes down, what? Once...twice a year to see his mother? Your family is here, Olivia. You will only be breaking your mother's heart."

"Geez, Dad, it's not like I will be gone forever."

"Well, I don't have forever."

"I can't believe you're giving me the guilt trip."

"No, I'm telling you I don't know how long this head of mine will function the way it should. Your mom will need you, all her children, when things get tough around here."

"I understand, I do. It's just ... It's a once-in-a-lifetime opportunity. I want a career in fashion—it's something I've wanted since the age of six. Don't you want this for me?"

"You have a career already. You're a fashion designer."

"No, I'm an assistant!" she corrected him. "All I do is get coffee for my boss. I have no creative freedom. He basically brings me samples to knock off. You can't call what I do design. That's—" She would say plagiarism, but her father might think it pertained to him. Not that she was accusing him of being a plagiarist, but the word relatively assumed some sort of criminal activity. And James Montiano's name had been associated with criminal activity enough as of late.

Her father shook his head. "But didn't you say it was an assistant position?"

Olivia sank further into her chair. "Yeah, but this is W. Moda. Do you know what this could mean?"

"No, I do not, Olivia." He shook his head, his voice assertive.

"This means access to big designer houses, fashion shows, and media. Do you realize what this can do for my career?"

Olivia needed to remind herself that she had once been a girl who only knew how to dream big. Ever since she was a child, she had sketched and made clothing for her dolls. She knew this was her destiny, something she was born to do. Olivia wanted to be a designer by Milan, Paris, or even New York standards. She wanted her very own couture house that would cater to movie stars and politicians' wives. It might have been unrealistic to some, but this was Olivia's dream. Some dreams came true if you wanted them badly enough.

"So, come up with a business plan and we will discuss more," her father said.

As tempted as she was to get her father to fund her project, it would not change Olivia's situation. She'd still be in the same spot where she stood now ... doing things someone else's way, what she had envisioned her label to be forever limited. Olivia wanted to do this on her merit.

"No, Dad, I want to get some more experience first," Olivia replied.

"Dad, she's got a point. It doesn't necessarily mean she needs to move there permanently," Nina added.

He frowned. "Do you think Gabriel's intentions were to move to Milan permanently when he left six years ago? No, Olivia. You'll only meet someone over there, and where will it leave your mother and me?"

"Well, you still have Nina and Paul," Olivia grumbled.

"Dad, I think this would be an incredible opportunity for her..."

Olivia was grateful for Nina's support, but she knew it wouldn't be enough to persuade her father.

"Maybe so, but if you're not happy with your job, Olivia, you should come to work for me and learn the ropes. Take your brother, for instance. At first he had no interest in what I do, but thankfully he came to his senses. And I hope you will too." He paused and looked around the room. "Where is Paul?"

And so it was the end of that conversation.

AFTER BREAKFAST, Olivia and her sister walked back to her car.

"Do you think it's okay for Dad to be driving?" She gave Nina a sideways glance.

Nina let out a long exhale, creating a waft of steam with her breath. "Honestly, I don't know. I asked Mom about it, and she assured me the doctors said it was okay to continue his normal activities." Nina adjusted her wool scarf around her neck and gazed down the street, sliding her hands further into her pockets. "You know, I don't want to push the subject, make him feel he's incapable, because sooner or later he will have everything taken away from him."

It was mostly silent on the drive back to Nina's house. Olivia assumed her sister felt the same way...because nobody liked to speak when there was so much stuff going on in their heads.

"Are you seriously thinking about moving back in with Mom and Dad?"

Olivia shrugged her shoulders. "Is it possible to be twenty-three and still feel like you have to do what your parents tell you?" Olivia put on her left blinker, moving the car forward, crossing the intersection.

"Try twenty-seven, married, with a kid, and I still do what they want."

"At least they don't see you as a failure. Nothing I ever do is good enough for Dad."

"That's not true." Nina frowned.

"Yeah, well, feels like it." She paused. "Maybe it wouldn't be such a bad idea to move back home. I could help Mom with Dad when things get worse."

"Olivia, if you move back home, you can kiss your life good-bye. Besides, I'm there if they need me."

"What life?" Olivia murmured.

"You'll see. You will meet someone else, hopefully someone

good this time. And maybe settle down and have a family of your own. I know it's hard with all the shit that's happening with Dad, but life doesn't stop, Olivia."

Nina opened the glove compartment, and everything came tumbling down. Laughing, she said, "Seriously, do you ever clean this car?"

"What are you looking for?"

"Gum."

"I got none. I'll pull over at a gas station and pick some up."

"No, it's all right."

Olivia looked up, catching Nina studying her.

"Olivia, if you don't want to move back home then don't—"

"Oh yeah, this coming from the woman who bought a house next door to her parents."

"Yeah, yeah ... well, you know Dad. He can be persuasive, but he means well."

"No, it's like an emotional trap. I don't want to disappoint him, so I keep making these decisions based on what Dad wants instead of what makes me happy, especially now that he's sick."

"If it makes you feel better, you're not the only one...Why do you think Paul is afraid to bring his new girlfriend home to meet our parents?"

"What? Paul is seeing someone?"

"Yeah, for the last eight months ... but there's more."

"Oh my God, he's *engaged!*"

Nina's face distorted slightly. "Ah—I can't tell you anything else. I promised Paul I wouldn't say a word, so just wait until he does. All right?"

"I can't believe he told you and not me...Paul tells me everything!"

"Well, you know I'm his favorite."

"Bullshit!" Olivia giggled.

"Don't get offended. Maybe he thought you had more shit going on in your life and didn't want to trouble you with more."

Nina peered down to find a folded paper at her feet. "What's this?" She picked up the paper off the ground.

"Oh, it must have fallen out of the glove compartment. It's nothing." Olivia snatched the paper out of Nina's hand.

"What's this about? Who's Mr. Universe?" Nina smiled.

Olivia explained how she had been randomly finding these notes everywhere, from the windshield of her car to the inside of the front pocket of her purse. Nina took the paper out of her hand and studied the note once more.

"Hey, this is Paul's handwriting."

"No, it's not," Olivia replied.

"Of course it is…"

"No, Paul is not the type to go through the trouble—"

"I'm almost certain. He's always kidding around like this. Seriously, ask him."

Dear girl with the red scarf,

The universe is always trying
to reveal something to you.
When you choose to ignore it,
it has a clever way of grabbing
your attention in the most
vigorous way. For God's sakes,
pay attention.
Trust me, after all, ☺
I am Mr. universe

8

PATH CROSSED, WORLDS COLLIDE

AFTER OLIVIA HAD DROPPED OFF HER SISTER, SHE HEADED BACK TO her place to find Dario's car still parked outside their apartment. Refusing to spend another minute with him, she decided to turn at the next light and head east. Olivia never worked on Saturdays unless it was a few weeks before a buyer's meeting. Her boss, Jack, had given her a set of keys to the office, hoping she would put in the extra hours when needed. Today would benefit them both. It gave Olivia a place to be and her boss a jump start for the next season. She didn't make it very far. Once her computer was turned on, she decided to Google her father's name.

In bold, blue letters:

JAMES MONTIANO ARRESTED *on the allegation of tax evasion.*
Montreal construction magnate, James Montiano, denies mob links.

THEN SHE GOOGLED ALZHEIMER'S.

WHAT IS ALZHEIMER'S?

OLIVIA CLICKED on the heading and continued to scroll down. The information was pretty much what the doctors had already told her family over a month ago, but she couldn't stop searching the Internet for something new, some vital information she might have missed. She was just searching for hope.

After surfing the web for an hour, she came across a home video of a woman filming her mother living with Alzheimer's. The woman asked her mother several questions about herself. Then she was asked if she had any children.

"Sure, I have children..."

"How many do you have?" the daughter asked.

After a short moment, she responded, "I don't remember."

"Do you know who I am?"

"No," she responded.

"I'm your daughter. Do you know my name?"

"I don't remember."

Olivia had had enough. She shut her laptop, then rubbed her eyes. She wondered about her father's future. Sick with worry. How was she even breathing?

IT WAS dark outside when Olivia peered out of her large office window. It had been snowing all day, but by two o'clock it had turned to rain, causing the snowy ground to become a thick sheet of ice. She glanced down at her wrist; it was already ten past five. The watch was a gift from Dario on her birthday last year. It was one of those overly expensive, high-tech wristwatches—too many gadgets to even know what to do with it. It wasn't even her style—just another reminder of how Dario had never gotten her. *How does one spend so much time with*

a person and not know them at all? she wondered. Perhaps it was time for Olivia to gather all the gifts he had given her over the years and send them back. She slid on her coat and shut off the lights. Olivia stepped onto the street; during the day had been a hustle of people and cars, but it was now completely transformed into a remote and quiet place. Before Olivia reached her car, she decided to go to the corner store and finally succumb to her urges. She gave the guy behind the counter a twenty and was waiting for her change when the sound of a familiar voice called out her name.

She looked up and smiled. "Hey, Waldo, where have you been? I didn't see you all week."

"Oh, did you miss me?" Nick's eyes fixed on her.

Olivia took her change from the guy behind the counter. "Hey, can I ask you something?"

"Sure, but it will cost you," Nick said cheerfully.

"Do you live around here?"

Nick reached for a pack of peppermint gum from behind her. "You think I'm stalking you?" He smirked.

"Well, one never knows." Olivia smiled at him.

"I live up the street." He took his change from the clerk.

She glanced back up at him while he wasn't looking. He appeared somewhat different, more handsome, even. Thankfully that sad-looking hat was missing.

"Well, look at you—all sharply dressed."

"I'm flattered you noticed." He raised his brow. "Well, I got a ... date."

"*Oh...*" was the only sound that escaped her mouth. It should have meant nothing, but Olivia was confused by the knot in her stomach.

"Well, it's a blind date. I promised myself I would never go on another one of those things, but my future sister-in-law tricked me into it," Nick said, standing near the magazine rack.

"Well, you never know. She might be the one you're looking

for." Olivia was trying hard to make it sound as honest as possible.

"Maybe ... but I doubt it." His eyes slowly dropped to her hand, clutching the pack of cigarettes, and he frowned. "Those things will kill you."

"Oh, I don't smoke," Olivia said.

A puzzled look crossed Nick's face.

"It's ... a long story." Olivia discreetly slid them into her coat pocket. "Well, I've got to go. Good luck on your date tonight."

She was out the door before he had another chance to say a word. After several attempts, Olivia finally got her frozen car door to open. She started the engine of her black sedan, then cleaned off the remaining ice on her car. She didn't get very far down the street before her phone rang.

"Olivia, where are you?"

"What is it to you, Dario?" Olivia scoffed.

"I need to see you. I thought we might be able to talk this morning, but you ran out the door before I could get a chance," Dario said.

"That's because I have nothing left to say."

"I'll be here when you get home."

"No, don't bother. Do you understand?"

Olivia thought he'd hung up, but not before seeing a set of bright lights heading toward the passenger side window.

Olivia wasn't sure whether she held her breath or her life even flashed before her eyes, because everything moved so fast.

Contact.

The sound of shattering glass and bending metal, followed by a *swish* from the airbags deploying.

Then it stopped. Everything around her went silent, except for the sounds of rapid breathing.

Inhale. Exhale. Realizing it was her own.

She was alive, thankfully in one piece. She sat there, stunned and motionless, until she detected movements and shadows around her.

"Olivia, are you okay?" asked a familiar voice.

"What the fuck is wrong with you, lady? You went through a red light. Are you fucking crazy?" shrieked another voice.

"Hey! Calm down, man."

When the disgruntled driver refused to step aside, the friendly stranger placed himself between Olivia, who was still sitting in the driver's seat, and the man who had rammed her on the passenger side.

"Back the fuck off, will you," the familiar voice said more assertively.

When the man finally walked away, her savior turned his attention back to Olivia.

"Are you hurt?" He opened her door.

She inspected herself. "I ... I don't think so."

"Are you sure?"

"My ... my head hurts—"

He looked her over.

Nick sucked in the air from his mouth. "That's a nasty gash you have on your forehead, but the ambulance is coming."

"Is it bad?"

"I promise you'll be alright. If this is some foolish attempt to stop me from going on that date, you could have just said so." He grinned.

"I thought this would get your attention." Olivia smirked. "Is he right? Did I go through a red light?"

"I didn't see what happened. What's important is that no one got seriously hurt," Nick reminded her.

"Is she okay?" A stranger's voice came from behind Nick's shoulder.

"I'm fine," Olivia said as she unbuckled her seat belt. With shaking limbs, she tried to slide out of her seat.

"Whoa, where are you going?"

"I need to get out..."

"I think you should wait until the ambulance comes."

"No, you don't understand. I can't breathe." Olivia's hand went up to her chest, her breathing rapid.

Nick searched around for someone to help them. "Olivia, don't move. I'll be right back," Nick reassured her.

Her whole body shook. This was something Olivia had never felt in her entire life, so out of control, and it frightened her. She grasped onto his coat with urgency, desperately not wanting him to leave.

"Please don't go, Nick," she begged, catching him off guard.

His eyes softened as he took her hands in his.

"Hey, I am not going anywhere, I promise." He brushed her hair out of her face, his stare ... intense. Olivia realized why she'd always avoided direct eye contact when she'd seen him around. She would pretend to text someone or look inside her purse so she didn't have to face him. It was never a question of disliking Nick; it was because of the way he provoked something inside her that she couldn't quite grasp.

"Olivia, look at me," he said, continuing to hold her hands in his. When he got her attention, he continued. "You'll be okay. Trust me."

What was it about him that made her so compelled to give in, but felt she couldn't? Like she wasn't allowed to.

"Close your eyes," Nick said.

She let out a long breath. "Okay..."

"I know this might sound lame, but it works for me when I get scared."

Her eyes flew open. "You don't seem like the type who gets scared, Montgomery."

"It might come as a surprise to you, but I'm human. Shocking, I know."

"What now?"

"Picture yourself in a place, a place quiet and safe."

When she didn't say anything, he continued.

"Are you picturing it?"

"*Shhh* ... I thought you said somewhere quiet."

He gave a little chuckle. "All right, where are you?"

"Hmm ... I have the ocean right in front of me." She smiled. "It's beautiful."

"Describe it?" he asked.

"It's spectacular, like when the sun hits the water in a certain way—it changes from turquoise to a darker blue..."

"You make me wish I were there too."

She didn't realize at what point her body had stopped shaking. Only when she reopened her eyes and met Nick's soulful ones did she realized how amazing this man was. And it was like seeing him for the first time.

"Your eyes are blue." She took a closer look. Why had she thought they were brown?

He blinked several times. "Ah, yes, they are—since birth, in fact. Are you okay?"

"Yes. No—I'm not sure of anything anymore." Olivia wondered what else about Nick Montgomery she had been wrong about. The sound of sirens in the near distance made her stomach tighten, because now they would have to be separated.

Within seconds the flashing lights appeared from behind Nick. But help was already there.

Dear girl with the red scarf,

One step usually leads to another...
keep on going. With
enough stubbornness, you will
eventually get to your destination.
Trust me, after all,
I am Mr.universe ☺

9

THIRTY-FIVE PILLS

Nick arrived at his one-bedroom apartment at eleven that night. There wasn't much to it. Open concept with only the essentials: a hand-me-down couch, a couple of stools at his kitchen counter, and a bed. Nick kicked off his shoes, turned on the evening news, and walked into the kitchen to make himself a sandwich. He had had a hell of a night, but was grateful that Olivia was going to be alright.

Nick had seen the whole thing unfold right in front of him while he was clearing the snow off his car. At first, Nick hadn't even realized who the driver of the black sedan was until he'd gotten closer to the scene. When he'd realized it was Olivia's car propelled to the other side of the road, fear had swept right over him. When the ambulance arrived, Olivia refused to go with them at first, stating the gash on her forehead was only a scratch, until Nick persuaded her. He wasn't able to ride in the ambulance, but Nick reassured her he would be there at the hospital when she arrived, even though it caused him some grief.

Hating hospitals was an understatement. The smell of sanitizer was all it took to conjure painful memories from the past. Just like that, he was back sitting next to a hospital bed ... or in

76

one. If he had to sum up all the times he'd spent in that facility, the worst was the last time he had seen his mom. He remembered how fragile she had looked, how he had been almost afraid to touch her. There were moments when Nick had thought he couldn't do it anymore, witnessing her suffering, watching her painfully slip further away. There were moments when he wished he had died first.

Nobody ever talks about the sound the heart makes just as it's about to lose something. After that, the heart goes silent.

As Nick was about to sit down at his kitchen counter, there was a knock at the door. He knew it could only be Dan, who lived in the apartment below.

"Hey, you're still up?" Nick stepped aside to let his brother through.

"I heard you come in." Dan shrugged. "So, is she okay?" He followed Nick back at the kitchen counter.

"Yeah. A little shaken up, but all right."

Nick took a bite out of his sandwich. "Do you want one?"

"No thanks, I'm good. I had an enchilada stuffed with spaghetti for supper." Dan placed a hand on his stomach. "I wasn't sure if you had eaten anything, so I brought you something from the restaurant." His brother placed the paper bag on the counter.

"Nice!" Nick removed the foil plate from the bag.

He could always count on his brother to look out for him, but even more so after he got sick. He was grateful for Amanda and his brother, but over time he had felt like the irrelevant third wheel, probably more of a nuisance for them. Not that he needed someone to take care of him.

Nick changed the plate and brought it to the microwave. He could feel Dan's eyes observing him.

"You look tired."

He rubbed his face. "Yeah, it was a hell of a night. So, Amanda must be pissed." Nick winced.

"That's putting it lightly, but what do you expect? You blew her friend off for some girl you don't even know."

"Amanda's friend must think I'm such an ass."

Dan shifted in his seat. "I told her you weren't feeling well. Maybe you should call her tomorrow and plan to meet another time."

"I never asked you to lie for me." Nick's eyes sank back down to his sandwich. He couldn't understand why he repeatedly found himself in a position he didn't want to be in, always trying to do what pleased others ... mainly his brother.

"I thought maybe I'd try to salvage it. You could set up another date."

"Ah-ha! I knew it was a date. All right, if that's what you want." Nick shrugged.

"It's not what I want. I'm only suggesting it if you don't want the door shut."

Nick wanted the door closed. Even better—nailed shut, never to be opened again. Why couldn't Dan understand that he didn't need his help? He felt sorry for standing Lucy up, but it was not like he knew the girl, and he had never wanted to go on this blind date to begin with. It wasn't his fault that a friend needed him. Friend? Or more of an acquaintance. Actually, he wasn't sure what Olivia was to him. He finished the rest of his sandwich. Three bites and it was all gone.

Dan quirked his eyebrows, watching Nick devour his meal. "I take it you didn't eat all day?"

"I'm starving. All I had was an oatmeal cookie from a hospital vending machine," Nick responded with his mouth half full, making his brother frown even more.

"You know you shouldn't do that. You need to eat to stay healthy. Don't fuckin' mess around."

"Hey, I take thirty-five pills a day. Who needs dinner?" He grinned, which infuriated Dan even more.

"You think you're funny? I'm serious."

"Okay, spare me the lecture."

"I don't have to remind you what will happen if you don't keep yourself healthy? We don't want any relapse, right?"

"You sound like Mom..." Nick mumbled, the words slipping out of his mouth.

After their had mother passed away, Dan and Nick barely spoke of her. How could they? It was too painful. His mother had been like a beautiful crystal vase, the kind the light easily mirrors through, reflecting warmth and glow on everything it touched. As beautiful as it was, it was also fragile. When it broke, it shattered, crumbling into a million pieces and sending the glass scattering across the floor...propelling everyone into the dark shadows.

So now, these days, life was grayer.

It wasn't uncommon for people to lose a parent by the time they were twenty-six, but Nick wished his mom were still around. He missed talking to her, to have her to comfort him, and Mrs. Montiano was a good reminder of what he had lost.

At the hospital, he had found himself in the company of Olivia's mother. As they waited together while Olivia was being looked over by the doctor, he had found it easy to speak to Mrs. Montiano. He certainly knew where Olivia got her looks, except her mother was more of a gentle character compared to Olivia's standoffish nature.

She had asked him about his family, and he'd openly told her it had only been Dan and himself for a while now. Whether she was genuinely sincere or simply felt sorry for him, she had extended an invitation for dinner once Olivia was feeling up to it.

Dan lowered his gaze back down to his hands. "Well, Mom is not around anymore to keep an eye on you. So don't take it personally if I express my concerns, because all I have left is you, asshole."

"Well, that's not entirely true." Nick paused from chewing on his second sandwich. "You still have Dad." He smirked.

"Okay, are you deliberately trying to piss me off? Because if you are, I'm just going to go."

"I'm just saying, if something should happen to me before the wedding, you could always ask him to be your best man. At least he could be best at something—"

Dan got up, shaking his head. "Okay, I see where this is headed."

"Where are you going?"

"Home."

"Stay, I'll stop," Nick said, and Dan sat back down. "Look, I rarely skip meals. I don't need someone to tell me exactly how to take care of myself."

The microwave chimed, and Nick removed the plate, placing it back on the counter.

"It's obvious you need someone to tell you."

Nick remained silent, it was hopeless to argue.

After several minutes of watching Nick dig into his vegetarian enchilada, Dan said, "So, are you going to tell me what happened tonight?"

"I was waiting for you to ask me that question." Nick smiled, putting his fork down into his dish and went to the fridge. He tossed a bottle of water at Dan and took one for himself.

"So what happened?"

"Like I already told you, she ran a red light and got sideswiped."

"Yeah, but how did *you* get involved in this?"

"What do you mean?" Nick shuddered.

"I mean, should I be concerned ... as in, are you stalking this girl?"

"Seriously?" Nick dropped the fork. It made a *thud* when it hit the floor. Now it was his turn to be upset.

"I find it interesting. You seem to be at the right place at the right time."

"Is that what you think of me?" Nick frowned. "I was on my

way to meet you guys when I ran into her at the corner store. I don't know what she was doing there."

"Okay, so..."

"Yeah, just pure luck, I guess."

Nick reached into his cabinet and pulled out his plastic seven-day pillbox—another thirteen white and red pills before bed. Sure, it was madness, but it was necessary to prevent any infections. There was a time when Nick couldn't even have swallowed an aspirin. It used to take endless glasses of water to flush it down. How far he'd come! "Olivia's mother invited me over for dinner next Saturday."

Dan let out a low whistle.

"It's no big deal. She wanted to thank me for helping her daughter."

"Are you going?"

"I'm thinking about it." Nick shrugged.

From the distance, a familiar word caught Nick's attention, and his eyes shot up to the TV across the room.

"Oh, shit."

"What?" Dan frowned.

"Shhh," Nick said, putting the volume up higher.

"James Montiano, the chief executive of Montiano Inc., is due to appear in court this summer. Montiano had argued against this summons, testifying that the inquiry would jeopardize his right to a fair trial ... The Supreme Court dismissed the request."

Nick studied the picture of a man he'd just met four hours earlier at the hospital. Now he was on the evening news.

"Nick? What am I missing here?" Nick turned around to glance at his brother's face. "You know this guy?"

Nick knew him alright. "Yeah. That's Olivia's ... father."

*

AFTER DAN LEFT, Nick sat down on the couch and closed his eyes and, at some point, he dozed off.

He didn't know how long he had been asleep when he began to dream, a dream that seemed too real. He was on the rooftop, but there were no stars, no moon; it was as though the world was in total darkness. Nick thought he was alone until he heard a young voice coming from behind.

"Can you help me?" the stranger asked.

Nick turned around to see a shadowy figure standing near him. He couldn't see his features, but didn't feel threatened.

"Who are you?" Nick asked

"You know who I am, Nick. Think..."

"What do you want?"

"It's time."

"For what?"

"To let go of the past and forgive your father."

"Did that prick send you to talk to me?" Nick frowned.

The young stranger ignored his question and continued. "We are built to make mistakes, and we all deserve a second chance. I should know...so don't waste it."

"What do you want from me, kid?"

"Can you relay a message for me?"

"Sure." Nick frowned.

"Can you tell my parents I'm sorry, and that I'm okay? But tell them ... tell them I love them."

Nick woke up like he had just been underwater, gasping for air. Shaken up, it took him a few moments to realize where he was.

God, he had to stop eating so late.

Dear girl with the red scarf,

Families are the greatest thing ever created, even with all their flaws and antics. There is nothing quite like a family to civilize you ... mold you into this person you've become. For better or worse. Isn't that the truth? You quickly learn that you're not the only one, you're not more special or more important than anyone else. Family is like a compass that guides us through this crazy adventure of life. No matter how far or how long we go, we can always find our way back. Everyone needs one. Not everyone has the privilege of having one. So appreciate it. It's a blessing to be loved by kindred folks that you're bonded for a lifetime.
Trust me, after all,
I am Mr. universe ☺

10

PHILOSOPHY OF FAMILY

IT WAS A FIFTEEN-MINUTE DRIVE FROM DOWNTOWN TO HER PARENTS' house, if Olivia didn't catch any traffic over the Champlain Bridge, the main route that led to the suburbs. Although the house was a beautiful Georgian-inspired home, this wasn't the house Olivia had grown up in. Her parents had built this home five years before in a newly developed gated community. After spending twenty-five years living in the same house, her parents had thought it would be nice to move out to the suburbs, still relatively close to the city and her father's office.

She reached over to retrieve the house keys from the glove compartment, and tiny pieces of folded paper came trickling out. Olivia had been finding these little notes everywhere. Most of the time they would be found under her windshield wipers. Other times they were written on her paper coffee cup or handed to her by the barista at Café Orleans. One Monday morning she even found a message written on the black menu board that hung above the counter for everyone to see.

Blush.

Olivia had found her friend Jessica smiling oddly that morning, like she was hiding something from her.

"Seriously, Olivia, do you think I would have the capability of doing something like that? Sweetness is not part of my MO." She pulled a face.

"Okay, who is it, then?"

"I don't know what you're talking about. If I knew I would tell you. You know I can't keep anything a secret."

It seemed that, whoever this Mr. Universe was, he had everyone in on the fun. No matter who Olivia asked, she couldn't persuade anyone to reveal his true identity. This person had masterminded this whole scheme ... but why? Was it someone she knew? It had to be. It could well have been Dario, but she shook that idea as fast as it came to her. No, Dario would never have the capacity or heart to do something like this, no matter how desperate he became to get her back. One thing was for sure: she looked forward to the next note that would find her.

Olivia unlocked the front door to her parents' home.

"Hey ... hello?"

The clicking of dishes and laughter came from the kitchen, and when Olivia reached the opening she was surprised to find her mother and sister, nicely dressed for what was supposed to be a casual dinner.

"Who's coming over for dinner?" On her way to the kitchen, Olivia saw her mom's fine china spread out on the dining table.

"Gee, Olivia, what are you wearing?" Her sister let out a little laugh.

"What's so funny? I always wear sweatpants on the weekends."

That had been before Dario, she reminded herself. He hated when she wore them; he had said it made her look like a welfare case, and now she was liberated, no longer needing to please him.

Olivia's brother-in-law walked past her.

"Hey, you're late ... again. Just to let you know, I set the table two weekends in a row."

Peter was in his early thirties, with dark brown hair and eyes.

He wore black-framed glasses that made him look like what he was: book smart.

"Do you want a medal?"

"Yeah, one that reads: best brother-in-law...ever—"

"You're the only one I have ... thank god." Olivia murmured.

"All right, I'll settle for your doing the dishes tonight," he replied.

Before leaving the room, Peter paused, giving Olivia a second glance.

"Hey, Liv, the nineties called, and they want their pants back." He chuckled.

"Ha, ha ... funny."

"Where did you find those? In MC Hammer's closet?" He laughed even harder.

"You're so lame, Peter. I'll have you know these are fashionable right now." Olivia placed her hands in her pockets, twirled around once.

"Well, they are very much...ugly." He picked up a tray and Olivia grabbed the garlic bread off the platter, but not before Peter slapped her hand away.

"Ah!" Olivia gasped.

"Leave some for the rest of us, Liv," Peter said.

"Olivia, you didn't eat today?" her mom observed from across the counter.

"No, I went to work this morning to catch up on some things —now I'm starving." Olivia stole a piece of bread before Peter could notice.

"You shouldn't starve yourself, Olivia. You'll get sick if you don't eat," her mom said, as Olivia rolled her eyes.

"Ma, I eat. It's just I got so wrapped up with work, that's all."

"Sure, sure. Ever since you moved out, you don't eat."

Olivia looked at her sister knowingly and smiled, because they could read each other's minds.

"Ma, believe me, if I were starving myself, would I look like this?" She pointed to her body, taking another bite out of her bread. Olivia had never known the word skinny. Come to think of it, she'd never been on a diet. She had accepted a long time ago that she had curves, and that was okay with her.

"Poor girl, look at you!" Peter said, half laughing. "You're withering away right before our eyes. For goodness' sake, Ma, get the girl a plate of pasta."

Everyone laughed. It was a relief, because smiling these days was hard, and it seemed her family couldn't catch a break.

Olivia's eyes land on her mother's disapproving look.

"What?"

"Santa Maria—Olivia! Stop being so stubborn and get changed. You still have clothes in your closet. See if you can find something decent." Her mother waved her hand in the air.

"Why? I'm comfortable like this." Olivia's face dropped, her stomach twisted in knots. "Don't tell me Dario is coming over."

It would be no surprise if her father had invited him over in some last desperate hope to patch things up. Since she had decided not to disclose any of Dario's indiscretions, they would have no reason to hold anything against him.

"No ... don't you remember that boy, Nicola, is coming over for supper?" Her mom looked her over as though she ought to have known.

"What? Nobody told me that," Olivia said.

"Oh, right! I forgot to tell you," Nina said, starting the process of making lasagna, spreading tomato sauce on the bottom of the pan.

This was an awkward situation. For the past couple of weeks, she'd been trying to avoid Nick by minimizing the chances of running into him on the streets or at Café Orleans. Nick was a nice guy, who possibly had a thing for her, and she had a difficult time getting him off her mind.

So much for a quiet family dinner, but then again it was rarely ever just that anyway.

"Go up and get ready. Nicola will be here any minute," her mother stated.

"Mama, his name is Nick, not Nicola," Nina corrected.

Olivia picked at the cheese platter that Peter was bringing to the dining room. "Ma, why did you have to invite him?"

"Why not? He saved your life. It's the least we can do," her mother said, grating the parmesan cheese.

"My life was never in any danger. He waited with me until help arrived. No big deal." But it had been. Olivia thought about the way she'd felt when Nick had held her hand, the way he'd calmed her down. She realized there was something between them, and, somewhere deep inside, she'd hoped for more. But Olivia didn't want something to play out in front of her family, not where she might be judged.

"Thank the saints Nicola was there. It was sweet of him to have waited with us at the hospital," her mother replied.

Olivia realized that Nick hadn't been obligated to be there with her overbearing family, and yet he had done what he promised. He would never leave her.

"What's for dinner?" her brother, Paul, said as he walked into the kitchen.

There was always a misconception about the middle child: neglected, with no sense of belonging. This was never the case for Paul. He was spoiled in every possible way, especially by their mother.

"Please get out of the way, Paul, so I can finish." Nina shushed him with her hands.

"I'm starving." Paul looked around to see if there was anything good to eat.

"Paul, would it kill you to wait five minutes? The food is almost ready," Nina replied.

"I am surprised, Ma, that you would invite Nick to dinner." Olivia tried to ignore the sibling rivalry that had taken place at the kitchen island.

"What do you mean?" Her mother gave her a hard look.

"Well ... he's..." Olivia knew nothing about Nick Montgomery. She knew he would feel out of place with her family and wondered why he had accepted the invitation. Okay, so maybe she had a good idea.

"What, do you mean crazy, like us?" Peter replied as he took another platter to the dining room.

Nina gave her a blank look. "But you do know him? Nick gave me the impression you two know each other..."

"What? I ... Well, I don't know him personally, no," Olivia said, not wanting to go into any more details on how she and Nick were acquainted.

"It's funny, because I could have sworn just by the way he spoke about you that you guys knew each other before the accident," Nina started.

"He seems like a good boy, and I feel for him. He lost his mama a year ago. It's just him and his brother. He's too skinny and probably has no one at home to cook him a decent meal. Truly, Olivia, I'm doing this out of the goodness of my heart," Olivia's mom said.

Olivia hadn't been aware that Nick had lost his mother last year. How could she have known? There was a knot in Olivia's stomach. She felt guilty now.

"All right, Ma, how about if Olivia brought home a guy like that?" Paul said, teasingly.

"What, like a boyfriend?" Her mother frowned.

"Yeah, Ma, like a boyfriend..." Teasingly, he looked up at Olivia.

"Well, it would be better than Dario," Nina murmured.

Their mother took a long, hard look at Paul. She opened her mouth, then closed it, as though she had changed her mind about what she wanted to say.

"Paul, please stop this nonsense, and Olivia, please get changed," her mother said, then she exhaled. "If he's truly a good person, I would not mind at all." She looked up at Olivia. "You forget that your father and I came from nothing. Olivia, I want you to have a beautiful life. I want you to find someone who loves you and respects you." She paused. "It doesn't matter if he wears old clothes but be sure he has a good heart underneath it." She brushed the hair away from Olivia's face.

"So ... what you're saying is, if I hit it off with Nick tonight, you would give me your blessing?" Olivia smiled wickedly.

"Olivia, stop. Don't be such an ass and get changed," Nina said.

Olivia's mom rolled her eyes. "Tonight, I'm not playing match-maker. I invited this young man to dinner ... to thank him. It's the right thing to do."

"No, Mom is hoping that you and Dario will get back together again," Paul added.

"Well, that's not going to happen. I would rather..." Olivia tried to find the right words. "I'd rather become a nun than marry Dario."

"Saint Olivia. That has a ring to it. You can be the patron saint of pains in the ass," Peter joked.

"Peter! Don't joke around about the saints."

"Don't be jealous, Peter. You only wish you could be like me." Olivia flung her hair back with her hand.

"No, I don't want you to be with Dario." Her mother shook her head.

"What? I thought you liked Dario," Olivia said in surprise.

"I only like the people who make my children happy, and since that was never the case..." Her mother's words trailed off. She placed the lasagna in the oven. "What do you children understand about life? You have never known what it was like to miss anything, and that's my fault. I've spoiled you. You will never know the hardships your father and I have gone through. When I was a child, I lived in a two-room, stone house ... and there were seven of us! I shared a bed with my four sisters. I had two outfits and only one pair of shoes. Look at us now," she said, waving her hand around the room. "Now we have too much. I can honestly say I was much happier when I was a child, at a time when we had nothing."

✳

"DADDY, WHAT ARE YOU DOING?" Olivia found her father sitting at his mahogany desk with an open photo album in front of him.

He glanced up. "Just reminiscing."

Olivia came around the desk. "My God, look at Uncle John's hair. I forgot he used to have a mustache."

"So many good times. Most of these pictures were taken, and I wasn't even a part of them." He sank further into his chair.

"You were working."

He nodded. "I'm so sorry, Olivia. I should have worked less. We would have had less, but at least I would have been at home more with you guys."

"Dad, you were always there when it counted. You were the one who taught us to ride a bike and swim. Remember all those summer vacations we took to Wildwood? I don't want you to feel guilty for anything. You did the best you could, and you gave us so much." She paused. "Besides, look how good we all turned out to be ... Okay, maybe not Paul." She smiled.

"You know, Olivia, there are things I've done in my life I'm not so proud of, but being the father of you three is the only thing I did right."

"I love you, Daddy. A girl couldn't ask for a better father." She wrapped her arms around his neck and rested her chin on his shoulder. He passed a finger under his glasses. She had never recalled witnessing her father cry before.

Then he glanced up at her. "I want you to promise me something."

"Anything."

"I don't want you to worry about me, no matter what happens, and I need to know you will look after your mother ... You guys have your lives to live, but your mom will take this the hardest."

There was a short silence.

"How do you know they're right? Maybe this is all a mistake and they misdiagnosed you," Olivia said.

He sighed, the kind of sigh where no hope was given. "I wish that could be possible, Olivia, but this is the reality I have to face," he said, continuing to flip through the pages, going through most of the eighties and nineties: the changes, the kids growing up, Nina's wedding, and the baby.

Olivia wished she could make time slow down, keep the ones she loved close to her instead of moving through life, knowing it was just a matter of time before the bottom fell out.

"Look at this life I worked so hard to build, and for what? Soon I won't remember a damn thing...Who will I be when I am a stranger to my family? When I lose myself, I will lose it all."

It was difficult to see her father so vulnerable. The man she had grown up thinking of as Hercules never called in sick, worked hard, and took care of his family. The man was so strong she had almost believed he was untouchable. How could this happen? Her heart ached. She didn't want to think about the future ... a future without the father she had known and loved all her life.

"I'm so sorry."

His eyes softened. "There's nothing to be sorry for, love. It will be okay." He wiped her tears away with his hands. "If I had a pick of any life, I would have chosen the same one. Made every damn bad and good decision the same way...just so I could wake up every morning and say, 'I have a family who I love and who loves me dearly. I need nothing else. My children are healthy, my grandson is good. How lucky am I?'"

"Are you afraid, Daddy?"

He closed the album and turned to her. "No, not a man like me," he said, with a half-smile. After a short silence, he added, "My fear is not for myself but for all of you. Who will look over all of you when I'm gone?"

"You did an excellent job in taking care of us. Now it's our turn to take care of you. When the time comes...I'll remember ... I'll remember for the both of us."

He smiled. "That's why I know it will be okay."

Dear girl with the red scar,

Overtime, we add layers to ourselves
like a coat. Unintentionally, we veil our
eyes from the truth because for
every layer we add on, we get lost
and tangled. We try so hard to be
everything to everyone we become
nothing to ourselves. Don't be afraid to
pull that thread and unravel yourself.
It could be frightful but why waste
your time pretending to be something
you're not? Let yourself shine. No
better tie than now.

Trust me, after all, ☺
I am Mr. Universe

11

THE ARTIST

AS SOON AS NICK STEPPED THROUGH THE DOOR, HE WAS surrounded by the Montiano family, most of whom he had met the night of the accident. After he had greeted the last member, he was disappointed to discover Olivia was nowhere in sight.

His heart sank until he looked up, and there she was, on the steps of the oak staircase. How long had she been standing there? His eyes met her big, beautiful brown ones. Her smile slightly curved up on the side, as though saying, *"You are so screwed."*

He had hoped to impress her tonight, and from the look of her, he thought he had done just that. Instead of wearing the T-shirt that Olivia loved so much, and after much of Amanda's pleading, he had gone with his button-down gray dress shirt and a black pair of pants. As the hall entrance emptied and everyone headed to the dining room, Nick stayed back to greet her at the bottom of the staircase.

"Hey, Monti."

"Mr. Montgomery." She smiled.

He could feel the heat in the palms of his hands, the sweat on the back of his neck, that uneasy feeling he got for the girl he felt something for. His heart raced, trying with every fiber in his body to slow things down, but his uneasy manner must have shown, because she frowned.

"Are you all right?" She paused. "Sorry, my family can be overbearing," Olivia said.

"You are very fortunate." He looked over her shoulder into the dining room, where Olivia's family gathered around the table.

"For what?"

"Having such a loving family." He looked past her as a father picked up his young son into his arms, a sister and brother joked around, a wife swatted her husband's hand away from the platters on the table, scolding him for not waiting for everyone to be seated at the table. He thought about how nice it must be, to be part of something larger than yourself, something as comforting as being surrounded by people who loved you. Being around the Montiano family reminded him of a time in his life when things had been good, the time when his father had been around. Up to this moment, he had forgotten what it was like.

"You won't say that after you've had a meal with us. I must warn you, though. They do get loud and crazy." Olivia smirked.

"That's okay. I like crazy." He looked her over. "How have you been doing?"

She nodded her head. "Doing well. The stitches are all gone. I'm only left with this tiny, ugly scar." She lifted her hair away from her forehead to show him. "I know what you're thinking. Say it, I look like a freak."

His eyes softened. "You don't look like a freak, Olivia. Anyhow, scars fade over time." He smiled.

Olivia looked at herself in the mirror that hung in the entrance hallway. "You sound like you know a thing or two about it." She turned back to look at him.

"Ah ... well, you can say that."

She studied him for a moment, trying to add him up. He hoped in her eyes that he added up to something good.

"I hope you like Italian food." Olivia bobbed her head toward the dining room.

She gave him a side smile that showed her dimple, and without another word she turned and walked away. Nick stood there watching her for a moment before following her into the dining room. He realized that there were two empty chairs, side by side. He was grateful to be sitting beside her and not across from her, where she would be in plain sight and he would look like an idiot, because he wouldn't be able to take his eyes off her. Nick had pulled out a chair for Olivia, and she slid into the seat. He sat next to her, pushing his chair further in, his knee—he was well aware—touching hers.

"Would you like a glass of wine, Nick?" Mrs. Montiano asked.

"No, thank you. I'll have water instead if you don't mind."

"So, Mr. Montgomery, tell me what you do?" Mr. Montiano asked from the head of the table.

Nick cleared his throat and said, "Well, I'm an artist."

"What do you mean? Like an entertainer or something?" Paul raised a brow.

"No, I paint. Mainly abstract art." He felt a pair of eyes on him, and he turned to meet Olivia's gaze.

"I thought you worked at a bar?" Olivia frowned.

"I do," he added quickly. "I support myself by working at a bar. The art thing ... well, that's for me. An artist. That's how I like to define myself." He played with his glass, aware that Olivia was taking more interest in him. Everyone passed the platter around, and her nephew's antics kept everyone unfocused on Olivia and Nick. He leaned in slightly toward her and whispered, "Are you intrigued? Do you want to know more?"

She smirked at his allusion to their first conversation at the bar. "Well, Montgomery, I want to know more, but you may keep your secrets."

He laughed and nodded.

"An artist." She said it to herself, like she wasn't sure what to make of it. "You know, I have a soft spot for the arts." Olivia tried not to look at him directly in the eyes.

"You do?" His eyebrows rose.

"What's so surprising?"

"Well, you're too young to seem to be able to appreciate the arts."

"So are you." Olivia poured water into his glass. "So, what made you want to be an artist?"

"I don't think anyone can choose to be one. I think it chooses you. I've always liked the idea that some part of an artist shows up in their work. There was this girl I once knew, who painted a series of self-portraits. In the corner of each canvas, she had this blotch of color, not very noticeable, like it was unintentionally dripped. It was meant to represent her insecurities and her secret battle with depression. Art is personal to the artist but not to the viewer. It's a way to reveal yourself without showing yourself to the world."

"Interesting ... so, what are you working on right now?" Olivia handed him a platter.

"I'm supposed to be working on a collection for a venue next year. To be honest, I had stopped for a good time, but now I am slowly trying to get back into things." He filled up his plate and handed the platter to Peter, who was sitting next to him on the other side.

"Why did you stop?" Olivia asked.

"Ah ... well, let's just say other things were going on in my life that took up most of my attention."

She took the hint that it was a subject she shouldn't explore further.

"Do you use acrylic paints or oil?" Olivia asked.

"Both," he replied.

"Abstract art, you said? It must be easier to create abstract art than figurative art, I suppose?"

He was amazed that she had taken an interest in his work.

Most girls he knew never cared what he did, much less wanted to talk about it.

"Well, not really. I would say figurative art would be easier to paint, for me, anyhow. Abstract art is something you must put together, an association of forms and color to create some meaning. As for figurative art, it's quite straightforward." He looked around the room. Several oil paintings were adorning the walls, but one caught his attention. "Look at the picture across from us. The girl in the field..."

"Yes..."

"It's easy to understand what's going on. The top of the hill there is a brown brick house; it's a beautiful summer day, which is why the young girl seems content, running around in the field filled with orange flowers growing throughout the tall grass." He looked back at Olivia to find her smiling.

"How do you know she's happy? She's too small to see her expression."

He looked back at the painting across from him. "Well, that's just it. It's how everything is put together that makes me assume she's happy: the vibrant colors, the blue sky, and the wind blowing in her hair."

Olivia smiled. "Well, it looks more like she's running away. Her hair flying behind her only means she couldn't get away fast enough."

He gave her a glance. "Well, that's the thing with art: it has a different interpretation for everyone," he replied.

"It's an ugly painting. I've told my mom many times it doesn't belong in the dining room." She took a sip of her wine.

"So where does it belong?"

"On the side of the curb," Olivia said honestly.

"Hate it that much, eh?" he asked, laughing low. "What did that painting ever do to you?"

She shrugged. "It was gifted to my mom from my ex."

"Ah..."

"So, you never told me what's the theme you're working on now." she asked.

"Well, at this moment that's what I'm trying to figure out...I seem to have hit a creative block."

"Maybe if you thought about what inspired you in the past, it could jump start the process."

At first, he looked at the ceiling, then back at her and smiled. "The universe."

Olivia's face lit up. "The universe?"

"Did I say something wrong?" He quirked a brow.

"It's funny you said that." She took another sip of her wine.

"Why?"

"I have been mysteriously receiving little notes from someone who's been signing them as Mr. Universe." She gave him a sideways glance. "You wouldn't know anything about that?"

He looked around the room to see if anyone was listening to their conversation. Lucky no one was. "No, I wouldn't." He shook his head.

He felt her observe him for a quick second. "I guess not." A disappointed look shadowed her face.

"I wish I could say it was me." He looked back on his plate. He could still feel her eyes on him. "So, you're telling me there is someone out there sending you handwritten love notes?" He frowned.

"No ... not love notes, more like inspiring words. I've been finding them tucked away in places I usually show up."

"You should be careful. You might have some stalker on your hands."

"Well, I hope not. It would be very disappointing if it were the case."

"How so?"

"I think it's incredibly sweet that someone is going out of their way, surprising me with these notes. I'm going through a tough time, and the words are incredibly uplifting." Nick couldn't look at her, because now he had caught the attention of James Montiano, who was now watching them. "So, what exactly about the universe inspires you?"

"Ah ... well, you're full of questions." He grinned.

"Well, you got me curious." She smiled.

He searched for the right words. "The universe defines every-thing. All that existed, all that will exist. The possibilities are endless. But what actually inspires me is—when you look up at the night sky, it's so wondrous. It takes you in, and you can't help but to be so captivated by her beauty." He gazed at her, making her blush, because he wasn't talking about the universe anymore.

"Well, Mr. Montgomery, perhaps when you complete some of your work, I might be interested in seeing it. I'm always in search of new art," Mr. Montiano said from across the table.

"My dad is an art collector..." Olivia added.

Nick shifted in his seat. Those brown eyes looked through a pair of silver-framed glasses and burned his skin, as if her father had known Nick's intentions, and he didn't like them. He felt intimidated by James Montiano. For one, he now knew who he was. Second, Nick had already sensed that James wasn't fond of him. He had gotten that impression the moment he met him that night at the hospital.

"I'm what you call a corporate art collector, and I am in the works to purchase a property. Once it's renovated, it will eventu-ally need artwork," James replied.

"Of course, Mr. Montiano. I will be glad for you to see them when I am done. I'll leave you my business card before I go."

"Does it actually pay well to be an artist, Nick? I mean, it is probably hard to make a living out of it," Paul asked from across the table. Olivia's eyes widened, and Nina kicked him from under the table.

"Some are lucky enough that they can. I work at a bar at night, so during the day I am free to create."

Everyone nodded and continued to eat. Nick glanced back at

Olivia, hoping to pick up where they had left off, but now she was playing with her food with her fork, trying to avoid eye contact. He was disappointed to have had their conversation cut so short, just as she had started to open up. He couldn't understand what had just happened.

"Olivia is also an artist," James added.

"No, not really, Dad." Olivia blushed.

"She's very talented." James wiped his mouth with his napkin.

"I don't doubt that." He looked back at Olivia, whose face went to a darker shade of pink.

"Olivia, you should show him some of your work." James leaned back in his chair.

Nick turned to Olivia. "Yes, I would like to see them."

"Don't listen to my father." She placed her hair behind her ear. "It's something I used to do for fun. Believe me, I'm not great at it." She took another sip of her wine, avoiding his gaze.

"I'll be the judge of that."

"You can't. I threw them out long ago." She shrugged.

It made sense to him now. Nick had been putting the pieces together, and it all started to be enough to understand what was going on. She intrigued him, and he wanted to know more. He had to find a way around the wall that she'd built. He knew it wouldn't be easy, but certainly it would be worth any trouble.

Dear girl with the red scarf,

Sometimes life throws a curve ball, knocks us to the ground. Trust me, I've tasted dirt more times than I'd like to admit. My point is we all have been there (if you're anything like me) and most likely be there again.
But you need to get up, dust yourself off, and move on. Maybe the best part about this experience is that you will keep on getting stronger and wiser. I mean this with every fiber of my being: I believe in you. Never give up or surrender to all the things your heart desires.

Trust me, after all, ☺
I am Mr.universe

12

BROTHERLY LOVE

PAUL HAD OFFERED TO HELP HER UNLOAD BOXES FROM HER PLACE and move them into her parents' basement for the time being, or at least until she could sort out her living arrangements. Though there was no urgency yet, only a few visits and no offers. Now half empty, the condo didn't feel like a home. Come to think of it, perhaps it never had.

"Shit, I don't remember you having these many boxes when you moved in last year."

Olivia looked around the room. "I'm ashamed to say this is not even half of it. There's still more stuff to pack." She smiled shyly.

"You're kidding me."

Olivia shrugged her shoulders.

Paul sighed and took off his baseball cap, tossing it on top of the boxes and reaching for his phone from his back pocket. "We will need more manpower, or else we'll be here all day."

"Who are you texting?"

"Peter. He needs to get his ass over here and help us out."

"Hercules?" Olivia mused. "I love him, but Peter wasn't much help the last time. I guess we could give him the lighter boxes to carry."

Paul laughed. "I will tell him you said that."

"What? It was Peter who admitted that strength is not his forte. Anyhow, there's no rush. I didn't say we needed to bring all of them today."

"Well, I'm here now. We could load both cars; at least that way we could get this stuff out before noon." He pressed send and looked up at Olivia. "But first I need an espresso," Paul walked toward the kitchen.

"Paul, I..."

"Oh man, don't tell me you've already packed the espresso machine?"

"No."

He gave her a dumbfounded look. "You let Dario keep it?"

"I get to live here until we sell this place. It's the least I can do."

"He's a fuckin' cheat. He shouldn't be entitled to anything." Paul irritably reached for his phone.

Olivia snapped her head up from taping up the boxes. "Nina told you?"

"She didn't need to tell me anything. I'm not blind, Olivia. I came up with my own conclusion ... The man is a fuckin' asshole."

She felt ashamed; her brother must have thought she was an idiot for staying with him.

"Are you texting Peter again?"

"Damn right. Do you want a cappuccino?" he asked without looking up from his phone.

Olivia frowned. "We haven't even started, and already you're on a coffee break."

"Cappuccino ... yes or no?"

"Yes please ... Hey, Paul, I wanted to ask you something before

I forget." Olivia placed the cap back on a black marker and walked closer to her brother.

"What's that?"

"Have you been writing notes and putting them in places for me to find?"

"Notes? What kind of notes?"

"Stop kidding around, Paul. I know it's you."

"Seriously, I have no idea what you're talking about."

Olivia reached into her glass bowl and fished out a folded paper, handing it to Paul so he could read it.

"Well, don't look at me." He shrugged and passed it back.

"I've been getting these notes for a while. I just thought it had to be someone close to me. I can't figure out who it could be."

"Maybe it's that crazy chick you hang out with."

"Jessica? No, it's not her. I already asked." Olivia went back to wrapping and piling things into a new box.

"What are you doing for Christmas?"

Olivia frowned. "It's a little early, don't you think? Who knows where I'll be in a week, let alone ten months from now." She looked up from her box to see Paul still waiting for an answer. "I don't know, why?" Olivia shrugged her shoulders.

"Because I'm planning Christmas at my place."

"You're moving out?"

He nods.

"That's great, Paul!"

"Yeah, I thought it was overdue...leaving the nest."

"You think? But I can't blame you. Having someone cooking and doing your laundry could postpone things." She paused. "But Mom said nothing to me last night."

"Because she doesn't know yet."

"So what are you planning to do? Sneak off in the middle of the night?" She laughed. Olivia understood how hard it was to talk to her parents about anything. That was why they were always the last ones to know about what was going on in their children's lives. "Did you already find a place? Because I know of a beautiful condo for sale." She smiled.

"Yeah, this place is grand, but a little out of my budget." He glanced around the room. He opened and closed his mouth, hesitating for a moment before saying, "I'm moving in with Elise."

"Elise? Is that the girl you've been dating for the last eight months?"

"Yeah, how did you know? Nina?"

"I'm thinking our big sister can't keep any secrets." Olivia smirked.

"Did she tell you ... we're expecting?"

Olivia's mouth dropped. She wasn't sure if she should worry or be happy for him. "Oh my God...Wow!"

"Yeah, I know."

Olivia's first gut instinct was that this could be a catastrophic mistake. He'd only been dating this girl for a short time, too short to know if he wanted to start a family with her. After all, she had taken five years to figure out that Dario was wrong for her.

"Wow ... but Paul, I mean you never introduced her to us."

"I know this is sudden, and it's not something we planned."

Olivia looked up at him. "Are you happy?"

"I am. I mean, after getting over the initial shock...I'm excited. Elise is great. I've never met a girl like her. I know it's working backward, but we plan to get married eventually."

She wrapped her arms around him. "Congratulations! I can't believe you're going to be a dad."

"I know. I can't believe it myself." He laughed.

Olivia could see he was genuinely happy, and that was all she had ever wanted for him.

Paul sat down on the box, and she took a seat across from him. They both sat in silence for a moment.

"I hope ... I don't fuck this up. Now I have another life that I'm responsible for." He nervously ran his hand through his hair.

"Oh, Paul, you're going to be a wonderful dad. I've got to tell you, though, I'm a little upset with you that you told Nina before me."

"Well, I didn't want you to worry about me. I mean, with your breakup and all this shit that's happening to Dad…"

"You know I'm always here for you."

"Yeah, I know. I feel like I've failed you as your big brother. I should have been looking out for you."

"What?"

"The way he treated you when he thought no one was looking. I guess I should have said something or done something. I always knew you were unhappy."

Olivia nervously laughed. "You make it sound like I was being abused. Dario never touched me or anything like that."

But that wasn't entirely true. Sure, he'd shoved her when things got heated, but he had never beaten her to a pulp. That wasn't abuse…was it?

"Olivia, you don't have to be physical to be considered abusive."

"I guess you're right. But you never failed me, Paul. I failed myself."

She looked back at him, not wanting to talk more about it.

"So, when are you planning to tell Mom and Dad?"

"Soon." He ran his hand through his hair again. "Well, I thought of bringing Elise over for dinner next weekend and taking it from there. Are you going to be there for support?" He smiled.

"You know I will." She glanced back at him. "Regardless of what you think, Dad will be happy about this…this good news is very much needed."

"If it's a boy, we'll name him after Dad."

"That's so nice, Paul. Dad will be touched." Olivia leaned her head on his shoulder, and he placed his arm around her.

They both remained silent. Olivia could feel what he was feeling; her heart was squeezed so tight that, if either of them moved, it would break. Every time she thought of her father, the tears would start to fall. Like Nina had said: life didn't stop. In five months Paul would have his baby. Whatever happened then, they had each other, and that brought Olivia some comfort.

Paul picked up his baseball cap and placed it back on his head. "So that guy Nick..."

"What about him?" Olivia wiped her eyes, already knowing what her brother would say next.

"Do I have to break his neck or something?"

Olivia laughed. "What are you talking about?"

"I watched you two last night."

"I didn't know it was a crime to talk to someone."

"The guy likes you."

"No, he doesn't. We're just friends." The truth was Olivia wasn't sure what label to put on their...whatever it was.

"I'm a guy. I should know."

"I don't know what you're talking about." Olivia could feel the blood rush to her ears.

"It's okay if you like him."

"I don't..."

"Okay, if you say so. He seems like a decent guy. I mean, I don't understand the whole artist thing, but—"

"Believe me, nothing is going on. Besides, can you imagine what Dad would say if I brought home a guy like him?"

Paul arched a brow. "First, you *did* bring a guy like that home. He was there for you."

"He was there because Mom invited him."

"Whatever." Paul adjusted his baseball cap. "You're missing the point. Look, I know Dad kind of planted this seed in our heads...that we need to be with someone who has the perfect job, the perfect family background ... but no one is perfect. Well, except for me." He smiled.

Olivia stifled a laugh.

"When it comes down to it, love is just love. It doesn't actually look like anything, except how the other person makes us feel, and, well, I guess what I'm saying is—a guy like Nick could be good too."

"Are you sure you didn't write those letters?" She shook her head. It was too weird to talk to her brother about her love life, or lack thereof. "Okay, this is so strange. Can we not talk about this? Let's get back to cleaning up the rest of my mistake."

He studied her for a moment. "All right, but can I say one more thing?"

She shrugged in defeat.

"I want you to be happy."

"And you think I could be with Nick?"

"No—yes ... What I mean is I just want you to do what makes you happy, okay?" Paul got up and moved the boxes around, leaving Olivia to her thoughts.

She looked down at her palm, still holding on to the crumpled note.

Dear girl with the red scarf,

Don't try to fill the void with artificial things. you know it will never make you happy or fulfill your life.
Stuff is just stuff.
That's all it will ever be.

Trust me, after all,
I am Mr.universe ☺

"HEY, Paul, hold on. I've changed my mind... I'm just going to donate my things."

"Donate?"

"Yeah, why are you so surprised?"

Her brother scanned the boxes. "All of them?"

Olivia took a moment to answer. "Why not?"

"You sure? I know how you feel about your designer shit."

She sighed. "It's only stuff." Olivia looked back at the boxes. "I think it's time for a change." For some strange reason, Olivia already felt lighter, as if she were liberated.

"All right, you're the boss," Paul said, picking up a box,

heading toward the entrance. Olivia rushed past him and opened the door to find Peter standing there.

"Did anyone order a cappuccino?" Peter said.

"I told you he was good for something," Paul called out from behind.

"Hmm?" Peter arched his brow.

AFTER SHE DROPPED off the boxes and Paul and Peter went their separate ways, Olivia got into her car. She didn't know why, but all she could think about on the drive back home was Nick. She'd be lying to herself if she said this was the first time she'd thought about him since they met at the bar. Sure, they seemed to have some sort of connection, but it wasn't like she was some school-girl with a big crush.

At a red light, she retrieved her phone from her purse, and, in doing so, a piece of paper fell onto her lap. As she read the note to herself, her mouth stretched out into a smile.

A sudden urge had her going right instead of straight, and five minutes later she found herself parked outside of an upscale gallery. Further down, Olivia spotted Nick's old truck parked outside. She remembered Nick telling her about a friend who had a showing tonight, and he would be helping him set up early in the day.

She sat in her car for a moment, trying to figure out what she would say if they came face-to-face because they would—that was the reason she was there.

She could just walk in and say—what?

Inside it was quiet, with no sign of Nick or anyone else. Olivia had been there before with her father. The gallery housed three floors of the most prominent artists in the world. It was Olivia's favorite gallery. It had an executive feel, with its Carrara marble floor and expensive furnishings.

When Olivia heard footsteps, she chose to look at the canvas on the wall, like she was some potential customer.

"Olivia?"

She turned and met his eyes. "Nick? Oh, what a surprise." God, she *was* a schoolgirl with a crush.

"Our worlds seem to be getting smaller by the minute. What are you doing here?"

Mostly stalking, she thought, and he smiled, like he found her amusing. The reason she was there must have shown on her face. "I was across the street. I saw you come in and, well, I guess I just wanted to say hi—so, hi."

"You were across the street?"

"Yeah, just running some errands."

Nick glanced over her shoulder, knitting his chestnut eyebrows together. "At Teasers?"

Olivia turned around and saw a big red sign, *Topless dancers,* just underneath the word *Teasers.* She thought she might die.

"Yeah, I..." Olivia sighed; she was probably red like a tomato right now. "Okay, well, it was nice seeing you, but I have to go,"

His confused face lit up, as though he'd seen right through her.

"So, bye..." Her voice rose slightly, and she did a clumsy curtsy.

What was wrong with her? God, she was such an idiot.

He gave her one of his best grins. "Olivia."

"Well, I'll see you around, Montgomery." She headed toward the door as fast as possible.

"Olivia, wait!"

She stopped and hanged a left. "Hmmm?"

"What are you doing tonight?"

"Mostly packing..." Her voice trailed off when she realized

why he had asked the particular question. "I have nothing planned, why?"

"I was wondering ... that is, if you're not running anymore errands at Teasers ... if you wanted to come to tonight's show." He smiled. "We could come together. Maybe even grab a bite before swinging by."

"Are you asking me out?" Her lips went up to one side.

He touched the bridge of his nose. "I would have to say no... since I'm clearly not your type." He grinned. "We're just two people with a soft spot for art."

She felt herself smile. "Well, since you put it that way ... how can I refuse?"

Dear girl with the red scar,

I believe we have this misconception about love that everything has to be perfect. How could it be when we deliberately show others our false side? We want to be accepted, loved and cared for. Everything wrapped up in a beautiful bow. But love is not about loving what is perfectly good in person. That's easy. Anyone can love that side of a person. it's about loving all the parts that are imperfect and ugly. Accepting that not all the puzzle pieces are in the bob but deciding to put them together never the less.

Trust me, after all,
I am Mr.universe ☺

13

THE WAY YOU LOOK TONIGHT

NICK HAD TO KEEP HIMSELF FROM PULLING OLIVIA INTO HIS ARMS, especially since they were standing so close, viewing a canvas on the wall.

Earlier they had had dinner together at a nearby restaurant, and he had found it exhilarating to learn more about her life. She talked about her career and her father's condition, the early stages of Alzheimer's. Olivia was in a difficult time of her life, and he wondered if he would ever find a comfortable space in it. He wished he could make the sadness completely disappear, erase any pain that anyone ever caused her...if only she allowed him.

"Do you enjoy working with your brother?" Olivia asked just before taking a sip of her champagne.

"It can be challenging," He grinned. "To be honest, working for my brother, it's not something I imagine doing forever." Nick cast his eyes throughout the crowded space. "I mean, I have other aspirations. I guess sometimes we have to put our wants aside to do things out of necessity—at least until you can."

"What is it you want to do?" She glanced up from her glass, waiting.

"This—" he gestured around the room—"to paint again and

one day maybe even have a gallery of my own. Maybe it's wishful thinking."

Nick had always considered himself optimistic, considering what he had been through. He had wondered if he could get back to art, which had once been his life.

"It's possible, Montgomery. It depends on how badly you want it."

He wanted Olivia—badly.

She was what he liked to call *feminine-classic*, sophisticated in a black blazer worn over a deep V-top and slim black pants. It amazed him how she was balancing her red purse-thingy under her arm without dropping it once. Standing under the spotlight, her hair glowed like it was begging him to run his fingers through it. Her eyes revealed a glimmer of wonder, so vast and deep...too big for her own good. They gave him the impression that they had taken in so much from this life, and perhaps it was the reason they seemed so empty. But not this evening. No, tonight they seemed entirely different.

"Nick," a vibrant voice called out from behind him.

He turned around to find George Sanders, the art director, extending his hand. George was the one who had given Nick his big break eight years ago, and they had remained friends ever since.

As a child, Nick had never cared to sketch or color like the other kids, so it was surprising to some that he had found art as his calling. At eighteen, he had had his first group exhibition at this gallery, and from there everything had snowballed into a promising career. His name was recognized in the art industry, and his career took him all over the world.

But, like everything else in Nick's life, things were not meant to last. Just when things were getting good, life had found a way to knock him on the ground. It wasn't something that had happened overnight. It was gradual...several chains of events. It had started when he met Chloe. She had consumed, devoured him, and when he was spit out, he had become a different man. The drama of their relationship had had a great impact on his career. Then, at twenty-four, Nick had had another setback. When he got sick, his creative energy had disappeared altogether.

But that was the past, and he wanted to focus on the future.

"Hey, George." Nick shook his hand.

"So, when are you going to come by? I want to discuss your next project."

Nick winced, not sure how to answer. He had been locked up in his studio, but hadn't created anything satisfying for viewing.

He watched George's eyes shift to Olivia. "Well, hello—who are you?"

"George, this is my friend Olivia."

George slid off his glasses from his bald head, placing them over his eyes. "Ah yes...but we've met before. You're James Montiano's beautiful daughter." He held Olivia's hand a little too long for Nick's liking.

She smiled. "I came in with my dad a few months back."

"If I recall, he bought one of the Tally DuPont pieces." George tapped his temple.

"That's right."

"Olivia, maybe you could convince my friend over here to pick up a paintbrush again." He paused. "He was once one of my best sellers. Do you know clients still ask for his work? Nick is one of the most sought-after artists of his generation."

"Correction: *was* ... I don't know, maybe I need to find some new inspiration."

"You have all the inspiration you need standing right before you." George's eyes set on Olivia, and her cheeks turned from a pale pink to a bright shade of red.

"Believe me, George, when I get something completed, you'll be the first one to know."

He didn't seem satisfied with Nick's answer, and he turned again to look at Olivia.

"This guy is the most honest and talented person I ever met." His eyes softened. "I hope he can find his way back." He tapped Nick on his shoulder. "We'll keep in touch, my friend."

When George left them, Olivia looked at Nick with curiosity. "You had an exhibit here? Nick—that's a big deal." Her face lit up.

"Well, that was long ago." He gave her a sideways glance, enjoying the fact that she was impressed.

When Nick felt a firm hand on his shoulder, he turned around.

"Thanks for coming, buddy." Nick found his friend, Luke, wearing blue jeans and a black blazer. A forest green lightweight scarf wrapped around his neck.

"Luke, I want you to meet Olivia."

Luke's eyes widened, and he had a stupid grin that Nick wished he could just wipe off. "Nice to meet you, Olivia."

"Hey, some turnout tonight," Nick said, trying to get Luke's attention.

"I know. Thanks for your help this morning."

"No problem, man..."

"I know you." Something crossed Olivia's face. "Aren't you the guy who bought my friend Jessica a drink?"

Luke shot a look at Nick. "Ah ... I think I hear George calling me. I'll be right back...Again, thanks for coming, guys." Luke walked backward before disappearing into the crowd.

She turned to Nick. "Hmm ... I think you have some explaining to do."

Nick smiled. "Ah, all right. You got me."

He should have told her that, the night Olivia walked into his brother's bar, he had thought it was a sign. Literally. Because there was a marquee sign in the shape of an arrow that hung on the wall, lit up brightly, and Olivia had stood right next to it when he first caught sight of her. It was like the universe had conveyed a little secret. *"Hey, stupid, I brought her here, so don't mess it up."* Oddly, the voice in his head sounded very similar to Dan's voice.

Out of the hundred bars that lined the streets of St-Denis, she had decided to walk into his. It seemed at first that all the stars were aligned, or so he thought.

Nick had known it was the opportunity he had been waiting for. All he needed was to get her alone, and there was Luke, who was very single. Nick didn't have to twist his arm. Luke took one look at the redhead, and voilà! It had been a win-win all around. It almost hadn't worked as he'd hoped, and he thought he'd almost blown it—thanks to his natural talent for placing his foot in his big mouth. As much as he liked it when she got fired up, he didn't intentionally want to cause it. To some miracle he had turned things around, and then there she was, coming out of her shell. He loved the way she laughed, the way her eyes sparkled, the way a dimple would appear in her cheek. She was one of the most beautiful creatures he had ever seen.

He wasn't going to deny it.

"I just wanted to hang out, get to know you better." He cast her a charming smile.

Olivia studied him for a moment, her eyes revealing more than words ever could. It was almost seductive, the way she walked away from him, gazing back so he could see her eyes, enticing him to follow.

Dear girl with the red scar,

I must advise you, don't fabricate people into something you regard as loveable. But I guess there's something far more devastating: manufacturing yourself so you're appealing to others. you need to prioritize your self-worth over inadequacy. Because you have a responsibility not to fabricate, but just to be.

Trust me, after all, ☺
I am Mr.universe

14

DAMN ELECTRIFYING HEAT

OLIVIA LED HIM AWAY FROM THE CROWD AND INTO A ROOM, cleared of everything except for a long leather bench and several artworks on the wall. She leaned against the doorway, holding her almost-finished champagne glass to her mouth. His eyes trailed across her face—her eyes were softer than they'd ever been, and Nick thought it might be an open invitation; if he were bolder, he would have tilted his body and seen where his lips would have taken him. He struggled with the urge but sat on the bench instead.

"So ... this whole thing is strange, right?" She gave him a sideways glance.

"What's that?" He playfully swirled his glass between his fingers.

"Well, we show up at the same places." She pushed herself from the wall to get a better look at the canvas nearby.

"Yeah, that's a bit weird." The side of Nick's mouth went up. "I may need a restraining order."

"Ha! That's funny." Olivia shot him an amusing look. "No, seriously, why is it we have never spoken to each other?"

"Well, I think a girl like you wouldn't give a guy like me the time of day."

"What's that supposed to mean? A girl like me?" She tilted her head to the side.

"Beautiful. Smart..."

"Rich? Spoiled brat?" She offered.

"You'd be surprised to find I'm not who you think I am." She glanced around the room before saying, "Anyhow I'm not rich. My father is."

"I didn't think you were a princess." His smile was curt. "I was only trying to say something nice." Nick knew that, under all that hard exterior, there was a gentler version of Olivia. He only wondered if there was a way to bring her out.

"I know you were." She rubbed her face. "My grandfather used to say: we're all imposters; it's fear that keeps from being who we are."

"Wise man."

She shrugged. "He was an amazing person. He passed away six years ago." A hint of sadness crossed her face.

"I'm sorry."

"Don't be. That's just life, isn't it?" She deflected her eyes back to the painting.

He was familiar with the agonizing suffering of never seeing, touching, or hearing the voice of a loved one again. It was a deep scar on the heart, but the love remained, and for that Nick was grateful.

Tonight, he didn't wish to talk about loss. He only wanted Olivia to smile. Maybe he was selfish, but when she did, it had a profound effect on him. It was his duty to keep all the bad away, giving only the best of himself.

"Hypothetically, let's just say we met here for the first time." His eyes found hers. "Would you have given me a chance?" He made a silly face, which made her laugh.

"Sure."

"I don't believe you."

She gave him a perplexed look. "I'm here, aren't I?"

"Because I told you a small part of myself, and now you're curious about me." He beamed.

He could feel Olivia's eyes studying him, like she was trying to decide something. She took another sip of her drink before getting up and walked toward the next canvas.

"The first time I saw you was at the Café Orleans—sitting in the back with a sketchbook. A pencil behind your ear, wearing a lame T-shirt and that sad-looking hat."

"Hey, I love that hat." He grinned. "But I'll let you in on a little secret: it was all a ploy so you would notice me."

She smiled. "Of course I'd noticed you, Montgomery. Any hot-blooded woman would."

He gave her a curious look, but she turned away before he could question her any further.

"So, you think I'm beautiful, Montgomery?" She kept her eyes distracted with an artwork of two young women on a beach.

"Yes, you're undeniable, breathtakingly...beautiful." Olivia's cheeks suddenly glowed to a brighter pink, but Nick didn't drop his eyes for a moment. "But that's not the reason I find myself so compelled by you."

"So what is it?" she half-whispered.

"It's something that can't be explained." He looked up at the ceiling, trying to gather his words. "It's like I've been wandering around without a purpose, and then out of the blue, I look up and there you are. I get this feeling inside—It's like a sweet déjà vu. You evoke all these sentiments and familiarity in me." He paused. "I feel like our souls knew each other before." He could tell by the look in her eyes that his bluntness had taken her by surprise. Perhaps she hadn't expected that from him, but it was the truth.

"You think we knew each other in another lifetime?"

"Maybe." He shrugged. "Think of all the drama that's going

on above our heads? The universe...It's surreal. Why couldn't it be possible for something more?" He glanced up to find her staring. "Anyhow, whatever it is...faith, destiny, or pure dumb luck, all I know is if I followed that thread, I'm almost sure it would lead me right back to you."

Her mouth slightly opened, but nothing came out. Maybe he had freaked her out. His stomach twisted in knots, and he had a feeling he he derailed the train before it took off. "Sorry, I said too much. Maybe I'm just not explaining myself correctly."

"No ... you are."

"Then what?"

"I got chills." She shuddered, like she felt the electricity running between them.

"What's that about?"

"I don't know—what you said, I guess..."

"I'm glad I have a profound effect on you," Nick said.

He could hear Olivia's heels clicking on the marble floor as she traversed to the next canvas behind him.

After a moment, she said, "Well, I guess...if I lived in the past, I'd hope it would be in the Victorian era."

"Why?"

"I would have liked to have met artists like Tissot and Renoir."

"Are those your favorite artists?" Nick swung his legs over the bench to get a better look at her as she walked to the other side of the room.

"A few ... not that I studied much about art, but I took a Costume History course back in college." She tilted her head to the side. "You know, you probably would fit right in..." She lifted her chin. "Facial hair for men was quite the trend in the Victorian period." She giggled.

"I know, right? What a pair we would make. I would be a starving artist, and you would be some duke's daughter."

"No! I wouldn't want to be a duke's daughter." She looked into her glass.

Nick was curious about Olivia, but then again, he was always curious about people. He liked to figure them out in his head before getting to know them. Like a mathematical equation: take their upbringing—or lack thereof—plus the joys, subtract the fears and pitfalls, equaling the person you found in front of you. He wasn't sure why he did that. Maybe because he was brought up on broken glass and bread crumbs. If he added all his handful of joys, subtracted his tribulations and sorrows—he should have turned out to be an entirely different human. He was trying hard to defy the odds.

Olivia was by far the most interesting girl he had ever met, because of the person she wanted to repress. There was something about her that was lonesome, yet refined. Like a fine-cut diamond that illuminated when the light hit it, he couldn't help but feel at peace, basking in the warm glow. It was a shame she didn't see what he saw.

"Then who would you be?"

"I'd rather be some starving artist's muse."

"Ah..." He evaluated her answer. If she chose to be in his life, she would never starve ... not in any shape or form. He would make sure of it. In his eyes, Olivia wasn't just any random person who had walked into his life. Whatever defined this fascinating life or the next one after it. If another parallel universe existed, whatever the belief, whatever higher power might be, there was only one truth he felt at that moment: he had found the piece of the puzzle he had been looking for. Maybe there was a danger in believing in that, but he wouldn't have it any other way.

"Why are you looking at me like that?" He watched as she came closer.

"I was just thinking."

"That might be dangerous..."

"Funny guy." She nudged him. "I was trying to picture your face ... what you look like under all that hair."

He rubbed his jaw. "What? You don't find this sexy?"

"No! Not at all." She giggled. "Sorry, the lumberjack look is just not doing it for me," she teased.

He stifled a laugh. "Smartass."

"What made you want to grow it out?" Without looking at Nick, Olivia sat back down next to him.

"Well, I don't follow trends. I'm a man who chooses substance over style."

She glanced back at him and smiled.

"Well, at first, it was pure laziness but then the girls seemed to like it, so it stuck." He gave her one of his best grins.

Olivia rolled her eyes. "It's always because of the girls."

"Well, I won't shave this for anyone. This is part of the package." He rubbed his jaw.

"Really? I bet I can get you to take it off."

"Is that so?" He raised his brows and his lips curved up.

"Yeah." She straightened herself.

"How are you supposed to do that?"

"Well, that's for me to know and you to find out." Olivia said.

This might be fun, Nick thought. It was evident the two glasses of wine and champagne were now talking. She was opening up, and he liked this side of Olivia.

"This sounds more like a bet."

"Yeah, I guess it does."

"So, what should we bet for?"

She narrowed her eyes at him. "Hmm ... What is it I want from you?"

"I could give you a few suggestions," he mused.

She ignored his remark. "All right, Montgomery, if I win you have to cook dinner for me for a week, and I'm not talking about a Mac and Cheese kind of thing."

He grunted. "I'll let you know I can cook a pretty mean meal. I have never made Mac and Cheese from a box in my entire life."

"Great! I've never had a man cook for me before." She tapped her leg.

"Not even Mr. Smarty Pants?"

She laughed. "Dario? No—no way. So, what is it you want from me?"

His eyes lingered on her full lips.

"A kiss."

She blushed. "I can get great tickets to a hockey game…"

"Just a kiss."

"Scrub your floors or do your laundry for a month." She lifted her hand in the air.

"No."

She looked perplexed. "Well, normally when you make bets, usually the prize is something big, not something easily obtained."

"Are you saying you want me to kiss you? Now?" He smiled wickedly.

"Listen, Montgomery, if there is one thing you need to know about me—" She placed her empty champagne glass on the floor, returning her eyes back to his. "I'm not the kind of girl you can kiss easily."

He liked the way she was confident, trying to hide her smile from him. "You know, those are the best ones to kiss." He beamed. "Joking aside, I know what kind of girl you are, Olivia. I think the issue here is that you don't know what type of guy I am."

"So, tell me then. Who is Nick Montgomery?"

"I could tell you, but you should never trust what someone says about themselves. It's something you need to see for yourself."

"Are you always this cryptic?" she murmured. "You're a strange man, Montgomery."

"All you need to know is I gain nothing from hurting someone. I'm not a fraud, and I hope in time you can see that."

The words were out there so suddenly that neither of them spoke for a moment. As she leaned closer, the surrounding air seemed so charged that he felt that, if he lit a match, the whole room would disintegrate.

Damn electrifying heat.

"Don't take this the wrong way. I find you very attractive," Nick said.

The corners of her lips curved up and just as he was about to kiss her, a crowd of people walked into the room.

Dear girl with the red scarf,

Don't dwell on your disasters. I
promise, if you idle in it too long, you
will never find your way back. Follow
the light out of the corn
maze instead.
Trust me, after all,
I am Mr.universe ☺

15

SAME OLD LOVE SONG

THE NEXT MORNING OLIVIA WOKE, PULLED HER HAIR UP INTO A BUN, and headed for the kitchen. She hadn't gotten much sleep, and she needed something to pick her up. As she stirred her coffee, her mind kept going back to the night before.

After she had left the gallery, Nick had walked her back to her car. They'd continued to talk for another forty-five minutes. It was surprising how easy it was to listen to his voice, discovering things about him...and maybe even about herself. There was a sense of sweetness about Nick, the way he looked at her, the way he smiled like he was fascinated when she spoke, like she mattered. Olivia couldn't remember the last time anyone had made her feel that way.

God, she hated to be disappointed.

Olivia caught her reflection in the glass window, smiling from ear to ear. She was smitten, yet felt so conflicted. Her mind was telling her she shouldn't rush into anything. Nick came from a different background; would he be able to fit in her life, or she in his? Her father would never approve, but then again, it was her life, wasn't it?

Every time she thought of Nick, she had this sensation...a

rush of excitement like butterflies dancing in her stomach. How could this have happened? It was bad timing; if only she'd met Nick after she'd gotten herself on track, selling the apartment and finally removing Dario from her life. Then Olivia could have focused on figuring out what there was between them.

On the second buzz, Olivia picked her phone off the counter. She knew who it was before looking at her screen. Who else besides her sister would call her this early in the morning?

"Hey, Nina..."

"Were you sleeping?"

"No."

"Is he there?"

"Who?" Olivia frowned.

"Nick."

"Oh yeah ... yeah, he left ten minutes ago." Olivia lied, waiting for a reaction.

"Don't tell me he slept over."

"Sure, I had a slumber party last night. *Oh*, and we braided each other's hair ... It was so much fun—relax. Nothing happened." Olivia half-laughed.

"Very funny. What you do is your own business, Liv."

"Well, mother, he didn't come over, if that's what you're thinking." Olivia could hear her sister's exasperated breath.

Nina thought sleeping with someone on the first date was not an intelligent thing to do. Mother Teresa herself could rest assured that sex was definitely the last thing Olivia had had on her mind.

Well, now she was lying to herself.

They had been raised in a traditional Catholic home. Growing up, their mother had drilled the message into them, so when it came to boys, sex, and modesty, it was a religion of its own.

"So, aren't you going to ask me how my date went? Or were

you more concerned about who I have hot, steamy sex with?" *The new Olivia should*, she thought.

"I freakin' hope you'll have sex, and lots of it. I just want you having it with the right person, that's all. Like it or not, you are on my list of concerns, Olivia. When are you going to get that?" The sounds of dishes clanking together and cartoons sounded in the background.

"What list?" Olivia asked.

"I have a list ... people I love the most. My son comes first, then it's our parents, and you and Paul."

"And what about Peter?"

"Oh yeah, sorry, P—"

Olivia heard a deep voice in the background. "What did he say?" Olivia asked.

"He said, what else is new." Nina then said to Peter, "Oh, Peter, I could never forget you. You come after Christopher." Christopher was their two-year-old Yorkie.

"You're terrible, you know that," Olivia laughed.

"Okay, so how did it go?"

"Well, I had a really good time."

Olivia studied the plant on the window ledge, frowning at its poor condition. It had been brittle and neglected, barely surviving. Then she wondered, what else had she tossed aside? Olivia had been trying so hard to make everyone around her happy, never considering what she wanted in the process. All these years she had slowly withered away, and now she hoped to revive herself to a time before Dario had broken her.

"So, are you going to see him again?"

"I want to ... the thing is ... well, people might not think we have anything in common—but we do. Last night...we clicked. It's just so easy being around him. The only thing is—Nick works at a bar. It doesn't bother me, and it shouldn't, but..."

Her sister repeated what Olivia had said back to her husband.

"What did he say?" Olivia frowned. "I'm what? Oh, for Pete's sake, Nina, just put me on the speaker. Welcome, Peter, glad you can join our session this morning. Do you need a recap of the days of Olivia's life?"

He laughed. "No, I think I'm well caught up. But, let me give you a piece of advice." Peter cleared his throat. "Look, Dario really did a number on you ... messed with your head. And at some point, we'd thought we lost you." He sighed. "I think you deserve to be happy, and if Nick can be the one to do that, then the hell with everyone and what they think. What you have to keep in mind is that you should surround yourself with people who make you feel good about yourself, and that, my dear, is a rare commodity. There's no money in the world that could get you that."

"I know, you're right."

"I'm always right. That's why I married your sister. She makes me feel special every day."

"Do I detect sarcasm, Peter?" Olivia's eyebrows went up.

"No, it's the truth. I don't need to explain your sister to you. On the exterior, she acts all tough, but on the inside she's an extraordinary woman."

"Aw, you're so sweet ... Hey ... are you Mr. Universe?"

"Mr. Who?"

"No, Olivia, it can't be Peter. Have you seen his handwriting? It's so meticulous," Nina said.

"What are you guys talking about?"

"I'll explain later. Olivia, I've got to go, but keep me posted."

"Sure. We should do this again ... sometime next week?" Olivia mused.

"The first session is free, then it's fifty dollars an hour." Peter laughed.

"With my issues, I don't think I could afford you, Pete." Olivia could hear her nephew's antics in the background.

"Anthony, get off from there!" Nina shrilled, after the sound of broken glass.

"Is everything okay?" Olivia asked.

"Ugh, I have to let you go. Your nephew just dropped his bowl of cereal all over the floor for the second time this morning. Hey, Olivia, you said you have the agent coming this morning?"

"Yeah, why?"

"Will Dario be there?"

"Of course..." Olivia half rolled her eyes.

"I don't like you being alone with him."

"I won't be. The realtor will be here."

"Okay, but call me when Dario is gone."

OLIVIA LOOKED AT THE TIME, and her stomach twisted. She needed to prepare herself mentally, because it'd been some time since she'd last seen him. And even though life was so much better without him, Olivia wasn't sure if his control over her was completely diminished. Almost like a drug, she was afraid of a relapse. As crazy as it sounded, she still didn't trust herself around Dario.

Olivia sat there for a moment, trying to remember when the shift had happened, when the thread had been pulled and her alter ego came through the seams. She was born out of necessity. It was almost essential for her survival to become this prudish, empty, superficial person. Dario wanted her cold; it was much easier to control her that way. She had spent so much time living in the small corners of Dario's life that, at the beginning of their breakup, it had felt foreign not to have her life tangled with Dario's. The changes were made quickly, cutting herself off from his friends or anything associated with him. Now the only thing left was this apartment.

The doorbell rang and when she opened it, her heart sank. She had hoped the agent would arrive first.

Dario looked her over. "You look nice."

Olivia frowned. Was he for real? She had worn her sweat-pants, purposely knowing it drove him crazy when she did.

Olivia closed the door behind him. "Joanne called, she's on her way." It made Olivia feel at ease, him knowing that.

"To be honest, I came early because I wanted to talk to you about something." He halted in front of the walnut accent table in the hallway. From the look on his face, he didn't seem amused by what caught his eyes. There they were: handwritten notes left out in the open.

"About what?"

He turned to her and acted as though he was naked under her gaze. "I fucked up ... I know I'll never get you back, never be worthy of your forgiveness." The words came out fast and rehearsed.

"It's not my forgiveness you need. I think the question is, can you forgive yourself?"

He glanced cautiously at her, and she returned his gaze.

"I hate what I did to us..." Dario looked wounded.

She wasn't sure if he meant the fact that he had cheated, or that he had been abusive.

"Look, Olivia, about what happened with Ann..." Was he about to come clean? Did he want her pity? She extended her hand to stop him from going on.

"I'm in a good place now, so whatever you want to tell me, it's all irrelevant."

"You hate me."

Olivia remembered reading a note from Mr. Universe: *The only way to forget someone is to forgive them. Hate has a way of poisoning the heart, like a nasty virus, consuming you until there is nothing left.*

No, she didn't hate him; she just wasn't sure if she was ready to forgive.

"I don't know how I became this person, this bitter, miserable human being. I knew what I did to you was wrong, but yet I kept on repeating it." His face looked grave. "I'm so sorry for everything, Olivia. If I could take it all back, I would."

"Please, stop. I don't want to hear it anymore." She diverted her eyes to her feet.

"We were happy ... once?" It was a question that made her stomach tighten.

When her life with him was so tainted with bad memories, it was hard to think of the happy times. She felt ashamed to admit that someone who had treated her badly had once been so important in her life. He had made her believe that, without him, she was nothing. But he almost had her...drowning in his web of lies. Then her cage door had opened up, and she had seen life ... her life for what it could be. She thought about his next victim. She was free of Dario, free from the humiliation and the pain, but what about the next girl?

In the beginning, she would be duped like Olivia had been, believing it was love. And with a flip of a switch, everything she thought he was would be a complete lie. But by then she would be too far in, too broken to leave. Because that was what abusers did: they manipulated, used words that cut deeper, breaking her until she was too weak to leave. Dario would blame his behavior on her ... because it was her fault for dressing a certain way; if she acted appropriately, he wouldn't lose it on her. She would dread every time they went out with friends, fearing that one of their male friends would innocently place a hand on her shoulders or kiss her in greeting, knowing that, later on that night when it was just the two of them, there would be hell, because he'd accuse her of provoking it. Sometimes it would get so bad she would question his sanity...or hers for staying with him.

So no, she was never happy.

✳

DARIO REFUSED THE OFFER; he thought it was too low, pointless to counteroffer. Olivia knew better. This was another ploy to have a hold on her life.

When the realtor left them both standing at the entrance, she was hoping he would leave, but how could she kick him out of what was technically still his?

"If you don't mind, I have to get ready for work." She held a hand out to the open door.

Nodding, he paused just before the threshold. "I...miss you, Liv." Dario uttered.

If he was trying to stir anything from the bottom of her heart, then he had failed poorly.

Olivia crossed her arms and looked down at her feet. "Honestly, I don't know how to answer that." Her voice came out harsh. "I mean, how can you even say that? After what you put me through, what you continue to put me through?"

"I said I was sorry...You don't understand how much this is killing me."

"Look, if you want to stay and go over what stuff you wish to keep, then fine. If not, I can't stay here and have this conversation again. Believe me when I say there is nothing—nothing—you can say now that will ever change my mind." She grabbed the doorknob, like she was about to shut it behind him. "Please go."

His dark eyes glanced back at the papers on the accent table. "Are you seeing someone?" His eyes met hers.

"That's none of your concern," Olivia spat out.

He studied her for a moment before replying, "Keep it all. None of it was ever my taste to begin with." Finally he left, disappearing down the corridor.

Olivia had wondered if he was talking about the furniture, or her.

Dear girl with the red scarf,

you are more BEAUTIFUL than the makeup
and clothing you wear. you are more than how
you see yourself. A BRILLIANT and
AMAZING girl that truly deserves
everything.
Trust me, after all, ☺
I am Mr.universe

16

PERFECT IMPERFECTION

HELL, WHO WAS HE KIDDING, BELIEVING HE WOULD GET ANY SLEEP when Olivia had been perched on his every thought? He was vulnerable to putting her on a pedestal before getting to know what she was really like. But it seemed with Olivia that the world had stopped spinning and everything had come into focus. It didn't happen often, finding someone that could do that for him … this exhilarating feeling. He knew that something inside him had shifted.

Nick had once been the kind of person who had plans that made no sense, and Chloe was one of them. At the beginning of their relationship, it had seemed rushed. He had met Chloe many years ago at a bar—it hadn't been hard to take notice—she was tall, bleached blonde, with a hot body, and had flirted with him all evening. By the end of the night, she'd been in his bed. Within a week, she had moved into his apartment. He'd found her exciting, unpredictable, off-balance, and at the time Nick had been drawn to that. Little had he known those attributes would become a nightmare. Nick had allowed her to take everything he loved away. She had isolated him from his family, and he had stopped painting when she accused him of not spending enough time with her.

It was always Chloe. *First. Last. Always. Chloe.* After a while, it had become a question of whether or not to stay or go. He believed in being in a committed relationship, and that's why, when things got tough, he had told himself he couldn't just walk away, because he wasn't his father.

Then, one day he got sick, and it left him hospitalized. What he had thought was a common cold ended up being a virus called myocarditis, which attacked the heart muscle. Nick was in heart failure. After several months in and out of the hospital, Chloe finally left him.

He had seen it coming, hadn't he? Nick had had enough experience with people pulling away from him to know when it was happening. Nick remembered lying in the hospital bed, after months of fighting for his life, as Chloe told him she was waiting for the right moment to tell him she needed her space to figure things out; that she still loved him, but just didn't know how to handle what Nick was going through. He had given her the time that she needed, hoping she would come back. Then he had found out while hospitalized that she was with someone else.

Nick had lost so much: his father, his heart, his girlfriend, and then his mom. A girl he had gone on a blind date with after had said to him, *"Good God, how do you get out of bed?"* It was true; Nick had been to hell and back so many times that he could have easily allowed the pain to destroy him. He realized he didn't have control over the things that had happened, but he did have a loving family, and had surrounded himself with friends. Letting go of the pain meant he had to be brave, and being brave was difficult. It was a choice he made every day; he could have easily never left his bed, but he wanted to show up and be seen in his life. What had happened in the past didn't matter now. Nick needed to be in the present.

Olivia was the present.

But Nick needed to stick to certain facts. He didn't know what his future held, because the longevity of his life was in the gray area. Olivia deserved someone who could give her the kind of life and love that could run the test of time, and that made Nick ultimately wrong for her. Nick knew he would need another heart at some point—that was his reality. He had this little mantra that he would say to himself when he would get a little down about his circumstances: *be here, stay focused, and live fearlessly.* Sometimes it was easier said than done, but there was never a moment that Nick allowed himself to feel sorry for himself. He was blessed with so many things in his life, and that was what he needed to focus on. As for Olivia, it was too early to tell her at this point. For now, he decided he'd see where things went with them.

Nick mixed new paint and stared at the large, blank canvas before him. He wasn't able to muster motivation, not one ounce of inspiration to continue his work. It seemed like there was a lack of passion for his craft, and fear crept into his mind that there was a possibility that his creativity had dried up. If that was the case, where would that leave him?

He felt his heart thump and closed his eyes, breathing in the air deeply. He wasn't empty. He could sense there was so much going on in his head and in his heart...maybe he felt disconnected with himself. The only thing he had on his mind was the brunette with the smart mouth.

He wondered if Olivia would be at work by now. Maybe they could meet for lunch. After all, last night she had volunteered her number. He took out his phone; it rang three times and went to her voice mail. His heart picked up the pace, and his palms became moist.

"Ah ... hi, Olivia. It's Nick...just calling..." He cleared his throat. "Ah ... I was just calling to see how you are...Anyway, call me back. It's Nick...Bye." He tapped his phone on his head.

Ugh, get a grip.

Within seconds the phone rang, and he was eager to press the answer button. "Hey you." His voice came out overly enthusiastic, and he squinted his eyes.

"Hey, Nick. Sorry I missed your call. I didn't hear my phone ring."

"That's okay." There was a short pause. "I know there's a waiting period before calling a girl after the first date...but I'm not the kind that follows the rules." He paused again. "It's just that I had such a good time last night..."

"So did I," Olivia said with sincerity. "Look, I will be at the Café Orleans later on. Would you like to meet up for lunch?"

"Yeah, sure."

"Okay—I'll meet you there, say, in a half an hour?"

"All right, sounds like a plan..." There was an awkward moment of silence. He was trying to find something clever to say to keep her on the line. He heard the sweet sound of her voice from the other end.

"So what are you doing?" she asked.

"Right now?" He looked back at the blank canvas.

"Yes."

"Well, I'm talking to this incredibly beautiful girl."

There was another pause.

"How's that going for you?"

He could hear the smile in her voice. "Honestly, I'm so incredibly nervous..." He chuckled.

"I make you nervous, Montgomery?"

"I..." He sighed. "You know you do." He ran his hand back and forth through his golden-brown hair. "I like you...and I don't want to mess things up. I've never met someone like you before." He placed his hands over his eyes. Maybe it was best to reveal a little less of himself, but when it came to Olivia, he couldn't help himself.

"Oh, that's so cliché..."

"Why is that?"

"Well, that's the sort of thing you say to a person when you're first getting to know them. You always think they are different and unique ... until they're not."

"Are you always this pessimistic?"

"I'm a realist," she corrected him.

"Well, you had ruin the perfect moment."

"I'm sorry, Montgomery. I just don't want you to think that highly of me. I promise, you'll be disappointed."

Nick frowned at her words. It felt like Olivia was just building another wall between them. She was trying to discourage him, intentionally or not, but Nick wasn't a guy who was scared off easily.

"I'm all kinds of imperfections," she added.

"What, you're not perfect? Hmmm, now this is going to be a problem," he said, "because I only date women who are perfect."

She laughed.

"I guess Mr. Fancy Pants really did a number on you."

She was silent.

"Look, Olivia, imperfection is not necessarily a bad thing. Everything has an imperfection...some sort of flaw that's always been there. If you look at it long and hard enough, at some point you'll find it in everything. Our imperfections make us who we are ... they give us uniqueness. Personally, I think imperfections are a beautiful thing."

She remained quiet, taking it in, or maybe she thought he was lame ... because, with Olivia, he never knew which way it was going to go.

"What are you thinking?" he asked.

"What makes you think I'm thinking of anything?" She laughed softly.

"Oh, I could hear those wheels turning in that head of yours," he said.

"Are you always like this?"

"Like what?" Nick's eyebrows gathered up.

"So ... proverbial."

"Maybe I am." He paused. "Is that a bad thing?"

"No. I rather like that about you. It's just you're..."

"What?" he said, leaning onto the desk behind him.

Olivia laughed. "I don't know. You have this raw edge, but then when I talk to you—you're not what I expect."

"Yeah, well, don't be fooled by my neglected, scruffy appearance," he said, rubbing his jaw.

"No, that's not what I meant. You're honest, thoughtful...sweet."

He chuckled. "Ugh, sweet, eh? Shoot! That's going to hurt my reputation." When she didn't make a sound on the phone, he said, "Listen, Olivia, everyone has many sides to them. And the hidden parts—those are our most vulnerable, because they are our true self. Our dreams and passions, our beliefs. We're afraid if we show it to others, we might not be accepted by them. I guess you have a way of bringing that side of me out."

"Surely, Montgomery, I can't be the only girl?"

"You're the only one I want to show parts of me."

He heard her sigh on the other end of the line. He was hoping that he'd touched a nerve—made her understand how, for a very short time, she had impacted his life in the most extraordinary way ... he felt alive, and that was something he hadn't felt in a long time.

"Hmmm, maybe this is too soon to have this conversation... You know I recently got out of a long-term relationship, and I wanted you to understand I don't want to rush into another one." She paused. "So I hope you can understand..."

He had expected to take things slow. Which he agreed with, because he didn't need another hole in his heart.

"And since we're being honest with one another, I have the tendency to rush into things. That's probably why nothing ever works out for me." He rubbed his jaw.

"Okay, Montgomery, how is this supposed to work? If you

rush into relationships and I take things slow ... how do you expect we'll find ourselves on the same page?"

"Well, I guess I will have to realize that you're worth the wait, and you will have to know I'm worth jumping into with your eyes closed. Somewhere in between is where we'll find ourselves."

Dear girl with the red scarf,

There is always a danger
when you give someone the
power to hurt you. Demand
your dreams to be broken and
allow them to tell you who
you are. these are the kind
of people you should stay
clear from. cast them away
as far as you can.
Trust me, after all, ☺
I am Mr.universe

17

SOMEWHERE WITH YOU

"You're unbelievable. It's only been two months and you're sleeping with someone else," Dario barked.

An awful tightness had come over Olivia's chest. This was just like Dario, to hurt her with his words, but she didn't feel the need to clarify why Nick was in her apartment. They had been on their way out to dinner when Dario surprised them at her front door, claiming he needed to get something in the office. When Dario asked to speak to her in private, Nick offered to wait in the lobby.

"Like I said, I was on my way out..."

"What are you doing with that guy? I can't believe you're belittling yourself after you had someone like me."

"Oh, you're so full of yourself," She crossed her arms, deciding he wasn't worth her breath. "It's none of your business. Just get what you came for and go." Olivia walked out of the room, but Dario followed right behind.

"I accepted we're not getting back together—fine! But what do you see in that guy?" He pointed his thumb at the door, which Nick waited patiently behind.

"I don't need you to tell me who I can or cannot see..."

"It's clear you do, especially when you're about to ruin your life."

Olivia raised her eyebrows. "Ruin my life?" She let out a laugh. "Nick is amazing, which is more than I can say about you."

"The guy is a loser," Dario murmured, walking back to what had once been his office. Furious, Olivia followed.

"He's not a loser! You don't even know him."

Dario frantically looked through his drawer. "And you do? How long have you known him?"

She remained silent as the muscles of her jaw tightened.

"Just what I thought. Open your eyes, Liv. What do you think he wants from you? Can't you see he's just using you? He sees this place. He knows your daddy is rich. He's only taking you for a ride..."

"Yeah, I know, right? He's nothing like you," she nodded vigorously. "I haven't known him long, but I know he's not using me."

"You realize people like him don't fit in with people like us, Olivia?"

She smirked. "People like us? Well, I'm tired of people like us —guys like you..."

"Well, this might be hard for you to understand, but I still care. I don't want to see you get hurt."

"That's very noble, since you're the one who cheated on me."

He threw the papers he had in his hands back on the mahogany desk. "I never cheated on you. How many times do I have to tell you that? I didn't do anything wrong."

"But you admitted it the other day." Olivia's voice went up.

"When?"

"You said you were sorry for fucking things up."

"Yeah, for not being a better boyfriend, but I never told you I cheated on you."

She put her hands up. "I don't know what kind of game you're playing! It doesn't matter to me. Just get out!" Olivia walked toward the front door.

She didn't have to subject herself to his abuse any longer, and felt at ease knowing Nick was a couple of feet away. But just before Olivia got the door open, Dario placed his hand, holding the door shut.

"I know what you're up to. You're just using him to make me jealous ... You only want to get back at me for what you think I did."

"Ha! Don't flatter yourself,"

"Alright, Olivia." Dario shook his head, his eyes peering down at her. "But this is still my home, so I'd appreciate it if you didn't allow him or anyone else in here again."

Before she could say anything more, Dario walked out, nudging Nick's shoulder before continuing down the hall. She didn't know how Nick just stood there, calmly watching Dario disappear, because his eyes told a different story. They only softened when he turned to look at her.

"Are you okay?" He walked back into the apartment.

"I'm sorry. He's normally not so..." She rubbed her forehead.

"Dipshit? Don't make excuses for him."

"How much did you hear?" Olivia bit her bottom lip.

"Enough."

"Listen, I understand if you want to cancel our plans." Olivia's eyes softened.

"Why? Because of Mr. Fancy Pants? No, forget him," Nick shook his head. "It will take more than your ex saying a few stupid words about me to ruin our night."

She played with the seam of her scarf. "Maybe we should do this another time. I won't be much company."

"Well, a girl still needs to eat, right?"

Olivia knew he was going to pick up on it. She didn't want Nick to go. But Olivia had been embarrassed of what he might think of her, to have been associated with an ogre like Dario.

"I kind of lost my appetite." Her eyes diverted to her boots.

She was sure Nick wouldn't want to see her again, so she was giving him the opportunity to walk away.

"Roshambo."

She glanced up at him, trying to hide her smile. "No. I don't think so."

"Come on. If you win, you can go back to your lonely apartment and sulk over a container of Häagen-Dazs, thinking about all the fun you've missed out on tonight."

She laughed. "I don't have any ice cream in my freezer."

"Even more reason to come out." His eyes twinkled.

He raised his fist, Olivia rolled her eyes and within seconds Nick had Olivia repeating the syllables in unison: *"Ro. Sham. Bo."* She made a rock, and Nick made scissors with his fingers.

"You're not lucky at this game." She hinted a smile.

"All right, so in my head it played out differently. Forget roshambo. I still want to take you out." His eyes leveled with hers. "I don't care where we go, as long it's somewhere with you,"

She had never quite met a man like Nick Montgomery. With him, everything seemed so simple. It was easy to be herself around him.

"So, Monti? Would you like to get lost somewhere in this crazy city with me tonight?"

She eyed her watch. "We lost our reservation."

"I have a place we can go." He smiled.

"I CAN'T BELIEVE you've never been to Griffin town." Nick held the door open for her as they walked out into the moonlight.

Walking away from the restaurant, Olivia looked up at him and shrugged. "I had no idea this was here. The only thing I imagined was a bunch of run-down buildings—"

"Yeah, I grew up a few blocks down."

"Oh ... I didn't mean..."

"No, it's okay ... It used to be a dump, but it's changed drastically in the last couple of years. A few cafés and restaurants are now established in the district. It's now one of my favorite neighborhoods."

"Really? Why? Other than growing up here..."

"I guess I feel like I could relate. It's quite extraordinary how a place that was once so run-down can all of a sudden reinvent itself, breathing life into a corners that have been dormant for so long, becoming one of the most vibrant neighborhoods in the city."

"But it takes people to invest, and it takes people to want to come in a place to spend their money."

"Exactly, but it all starts with a dream and some sort of belief." Nick stopped at an empty building with a sign in the window that read: *loft for rent*. "This is it."

"This is what?" Olivia stood right beside him.

"One day I'm going to open up my very own gallery, right here." Nick stretched out his arms.

Olivia smiled at his enthusiasm. The glee in his eyes made her believe this was more than just a dream. She could relate to what it was like, to want something so badly. And so she wished it even more for him.

"So aren't you glad you came out? You have to admit that was the best hamburger you've ever had."

"It was all right." Olivia shrugged.

"Oh, come on, I saw how you wolfed down that hamburger. It never had a chance."

She laughed and nudged him. "I did not!"

As they approached the corner, Olivia frowned.

"Where are we going? You parked the car down there."

"I thought we'd go for a walk since it's not too cold."

"A walk?"

"Yeah, you know ... an activity that consists of one step after another." He demonstrated. "Preferably more enjoyable done with someone else."

When he saw her hesitate, he said, "Come on, let's wander."

"Is it safe to walk ... here?"

Nick peered around, then returned his gaze back to Olivia. "What are you worried about? I thought you said you had a black belt in jiu-jitsu?"

"I do ... My dad made sure I knew how to defend myself." Oddly enough, she had the means to protect herself, yet nothing had shielded her from Dario.

Nick pulled his collar higher, digging his hands deeper into his pockets. "Good, now I feel much better, knowing you're able to save me from any dangerous men lurking in dark corners."

Olivia smiled, enjoying the comfort of silence for a moment as they walked side by side.

He gave her a sideways glance. "Not that it's any of my business, but I just wanted you to know, if you ever want to talk ... I'm here."

She was conscious of how he watched her, as if the answer meant something to him. Nick wanted her to feel she could trust him, and somewhere within her very confused heart she wanted to. Olivia wondered what he was trying to get at ... the situation with Dario that had happened earlier, or the way she had been victimized for the last five years. Could she really call herself a victim?

Yes, sure, Dario had unpredictable mood swings, but he had never physically hurt her.

She couldn't talk about it, not to anyone, because it went beyond admitting it to her family or her friends—even Nick, for that matter. Because once she said it out loud, dragging this huge secret into the light, then she would have to admit she'd let down the most important person ... herself.

Where would that leave her?

"Would it be all right if we talk about it another time? I don't want to ruin a perfect night." She peered up at the night sky.

Nick nodded.

They came up to a bench overlooking a frozen canal. Across, in the far distance, Olivia could see the Five Roses sign sitting on the roof of the old Ogilvie flour mill.

"So tell me about your family." Olivia wanted to know, since he had mentioned nothing about them.

"Well, let's just say I had a very different upbringing than yours. My dad left us when I was young." He cleared his throat. "One day he went out for a pack of cigarettes and literally never came back."

"*Oh*, how awful. It must have been so hard for you." Olivia frowned.

"Yeah, it was, but more for my mom, who had to raise two boys on her own." He ran his fingers inside his collar, like it was getting tighter by the minute. "It's strange to say, but sometimes I think it's hard to hate the guy. In the short time we had with him, Dan and I had a happy childhood." He paused. "I remember when we were kids. We'd spend hours in the garage with my dad, watching him fixing up some old car."

"So your dad was a mechanic?"

"Well, it was more of a hobby than anything else. Sometimes he would pick up old, run-down vintage muscle cars. You know, the ones you'd find in open fields with the grass growing on the inside." He smiled at the memory. "He would build them back up to their former glory and keep them for a short time until my mother would force him to sell them."

"Have you ever seen your dad again?"

"No, but my brother still keeps in touch with him." He looked across the canal. "I heard he's had a successful business building new homes somewhere in Calgary for the past fifteen years."

"Oh, he's a contractor like my dad."

"Yeah, I guess ... sort of." Nick said.

"I can't imagine what it would be like to have someone you love just walk away like that."

"At first I thought it was something I did. Then I realized he was the adult, and fathers aren't supposed to leave their children."

"Well, from what I see, you turned out okay—except you're fashionably challenged." Olivia winked. She looked down at his poor choice of footwear: black high-top Converse sneakers, half soaked by the wet snow.

Her eyes met his gleaming ones. "You're jealous. I'll give you permission to copy it."

"What's that?" Her eyebrows peek.

"My style,"

She stifled a laugh. When her eyes met his, Olivia could tell he wanted to say something else.

"Can I trust you?" Nick's eyes softened. There was a certain vulnerability and openness about his question that made Olivia wonder if she was worthy of such trust. She could hear it in the tone of his voice that he had been disappointed before. "I mean, I know we haven't spent a lot of time together, but I want you to know everything about me."

Olivia sat quietly under the lamppost light, and beside her, she saw a man who desired to be understood. At that moment, she feared he might tell her something that might alter the way she viewed him. The truth was Olivia wanted for none of the feelings stirring within her to change.

"I'm not blaming things on my father, but here's the truth: sometimes life makes you feel things you're not even sure how to process, and I guess with time it led me to do a lot of stupid stuff I'm not proud of."

Nick swallowed.

"I was fourteen when I got mixed up with the wrong crowd. I started cutting class. I did everything from stealing money from my mom to doing drugs. It wasn't until I got arrested for trying to break into a hardware store that my mother had to do something drastic."

"So what happened?" Olivia's eyebrows peaked.

"Well, my mother sent me to live with my paternal grandmother in the eastern townships. I had no car and no money, no way of getting back to the city. Being away gave me the time to grasp what I was going through. I could just as easily blame my father for my problems, for my bad behavior, but that would have been too easy. I was so angry with him, I hated him for what he had done to our family, but I had to own it—what I was doing to myself and to others wasn't fair, either. Over time I figured I had two choices: fuel my pain and go down into a blind hole, or find something positive to do with my life. That's how the artist in me was born—"

She wasn't afraid of the excess baggage he carried with him. Olivia was just worried she could never relate to a man who had been through so much.

"Listen, I just want you to know that's not me...not anymore. I don't usually share this much of myself with anyone. I hope this doesn't change your mind about me."

Olivia took a moment before she spoke. "Honestly, it's not a deal breaker. And since that was the past, I won't hold it against you." She smiled.

"No, I'm not that person anymore."

"I can see that. It takes a very mature person to overcome something like that. It only makes me admire you more."

"Well, a man only matures with every single scar that is engraved on his heart." Nick tapped Olivia's foot with his.

"You should write that down," Olivia smiled. "You talk like you have many?"

"Only a few. Perhaps some are not mine."

Olivia wasn't sure what he meant, but let it slide. She studied him in silence, wondering what to expect from Nick. It came to her only when his eyes diverted away from the canal back to hers.

Even though it was dark outside, his eyes were so transparent that it reminded her of a clear pool of water she wanted to get lost in. He had revealed something that wasn't easy to share, taking a chance and hoping there would be no judgment which meant he trusted her.

Olivia opened and closed her mouth, not sure what to say next. What could she say? Then she realized all she could offer him was her honesty.

"That night when I walked into your bar, I had just found out that my fiancé, Dario, had been cheating on me for the past three months."

His eyes softened.

"That's not the worst part..." She shook her head. "The worst part is, I let him treat me like shit for most of our relationship." She paused. "I never imagined myself to be the kind of girl who allows someone to mistreat them. I never thought I was weak."

He devoured the air as though he felt her pain. "Sometimes we want things so badly we're willing to walk through shards of broken glass to get it. That desire to be loved ... it's so blinding. It's easy to be misguided. I don't think you're weak, Olivia. You should never feel ashamed, not for wanting to be loved."

Olivia looked away, because for a moment she thought she might cry. He placed a hand on hers, and she looked up.

"Do you know what happens after the glass breaks?"

She shook her head.

"You clean it up ... and life moves forward."

MARCH

Dear girl with the red scar,

I have this little mantra that I'm
going to share with you: know who
you are, know what you want and
know what you already have. if you
do not have the answers to these
questions, then it's time to take a
step back and look at your life with
a new set of eyes.

Trust me, after all, ☺
I am Mr.universe

18

UNINVITED

THE LAST PERSON NICK EXPECTED TO FIND AT HIS FRONT DOOR WAS be James Montiano, with a pair of cold, gray eyes peering back at him. It was a look Nick recognized well, the kind his mother used to give him when he did something questionable.

"Nick, did I catch you at a bad time? I found myself in the area and thought maybe since I was here I could see your work."

Nick hesitated, because he was on his way out, wanting to get cleaned up before meeting Olivia for lunch. He hoped it would be quick and painless.

"No, not at all. Come in." Nick closed the door behind him. He wasn't stupid; he knew this surprise visit had nothing to do with his art. "Have you something in mind, James? I do commission work as well."

James wore a black wool coat on top of a navy suit, like he'd walked out of a board meeting. Nick pitied men who followed convention, confining themselves behind a desk. That kind of profession would be a menace to Nick's sanity. He couldn't think of a duller pursuit in life, but he would never consider James Montiano a dull man.

"Mr. Montiano." He brushed past Nick. "Only those who are close call me James."

Nick's brows elevated.

He watched as James slid on his silver-framed glasses, making his way around the room.

Nick had rapidly outgrown the tiny studio in the last few weeks, filling the space up with new paintings, all of which now leaned against the once-white wall. He'd finally broken through the dry spell.

Peering around his studio, he cringed at the dirty rags and empty spray cans scattered on the floor. They were a testament to his productive night. Nick wondered if Olivia had had anything to do with it, because she was never far from his thoughts. It seemed she was the spark of fire he had needed.

"Don't mind the mess. I would have tidied up if I knew you were coming." Nick continued to clean his hands with a rag.

"Don't worry, son. I'm not here to judge. I'm more interested in your work than anything else."

James took his time pacing around the room, which played with Nick's patience.

"Nice little place you have. What's the square footage?" James's eyes bounced around the space.

"Ah ... man, I don't know." Nick exhaled the breath he'd been holding. "About three hundred square feet ... roughly." He rubbed the back of his neck.

James nodded. "You must pay a pretty penny to rent this place."

"Jesus, yeah it doesn't come cheap, that's for sure." Nick sat on the edge of his desk behind him.

"What does this place run you? About five dollars a square foot?" James pulled his glasses off, swinging them around.

"Something like that." Nick frowned, wondering what the interrogation was leading up to. "It's convenient for me. I live in the apartment upstairs."

"Upstairs?" Something in James' voice made him think he wasn't thrilled about that idea. Nick was smart enough to know that this visit somewhat related to Olivia.

"My daughter Olivia works just up the street." His eyes glared in such a manner that Nick knew he was searching for some kind of confirmation. When James studied the canvas Nick had been working on, he got the evidence he needed. "But you already knew that, didn't you?"

Nick glanced at his fingers and picked at the paint on his cuticles. "Sure, I remember her telling me," Nick said. "How did you know where to find me?"

"You left me your business card. Don't you remember?" James smiled, but not a friendly smile.

"Ah ... yes it slipped my mind." He wished he hadn't.

The air grew dark, and Nick felt unpleasantly tense. He felt intimidated by James, not because of who the media portrayed him to be, but because he was Olivia's father. Nick had never had issues with in-laws—got along fine with Chloe's dad, but then again, he was never around. Nick knew James was a man who understood the weight of providing for his family. And he could appreciate that; it was something he'd never known, but desired. It seemed reasonable to expect that a man like James would think Nick wouldn't be suitable for his daughter. That made James Montiano the gatekeeper, and Nick was at a disadvantage.

"Huh ... this strikingly resembles my daughter..." James took a step back to appreciate the painting.

He wasn't sure if Olivia had told her father anything about him, but then again there wasn't much to tell. So far, their relationship was platonic.

"Well, it's not finished yet." Nick placed his hand on the back of his neck, feeling warmth and dampness.

James studied the canvas once more. "You're very talented."

"Thank you."

"A close friend of mine has a gallery on La Montagne Street ... Les Atelier Belmont. Have you heard of it?

It was one of the best exclusive galleries in the city, and it was tough for an artist to get representation there, even with Nick's past credentials.

"I think he would be interested in seeing your work. I could put in a good word for you."

Nick's eyes lit up. "Yes, that would be great." Nick thought maybe he was wrong about James. Maybe there was hope just yet. "That would really help me get my career back on track."

Coming from someone like James, who had connections, it would make a hell of a difference in his career. But Nick couldn't help but wonder why he was being so generous. He knew people like James always had an angle, a way of getting things from people. And Nick knew what it was.

"Well, it shouldn't be so hard. You've made a name for yourself in the art world, Mr. Montgomery."

"No, I wouldn't say that." Nick was being modest.

James arched his eyebrows in question. "At eighteen—you took a traditional academic training approach, traveling to the world's greatest museums to study the masters' paintings up close. After a year of travel, you came back to Montreal," He removed his glasses, keeping them open in his hands. "At twenty, you had your first showing at Galleries Le Roy, which led to other viewings all over the world." James slowly paced around the room. "You also sold your work to private and public collectors—hanging alongside works of such as Dali and Picasso. Yes, I would call that accomplished, wouldn't you?" He touched the bridge of his nose.

"Wow, that's impressive. You really did your homework."

"I make it my business to know who my children surround themselves with, Mr. Montgomery."

James placed his glasses back on his face.

"But there is one thing I don't quite understand. Your career took shape, and you simply faded into the background. In your choice of profession, it takes time to gain a comfortable income. A year of traveling would be expensive, especially for someone who had no real source of income."

"Get to the point."

"What I'm trying to understand is how you supported yourself all that time … all this time?"

"No offense, but I don't think it's any of your concern."

"Olivia is, and since she's decided on you…" He glared back at Nick.

"Are you accusing me of doing something illicit?" Nick sucked the air between his teeth.

"I don't know. You tell me?"

Was Nick being accused by a crook? Fucking brilliant. He quickly reminded himself that this was the father of the girl he liked. He needed to be the bigger man.

"Look, I don't owe you any explanations on how I support myself, so let's cut to the chase, James…I know you're not interested in my work. Why are you here?"

"On the contrary. I am very interested in your work. What I'm concerned about is you spending time with my daughter." He paused. "Understand this: it's a delicate time in her life right now. I know when she comes to her senses she'll go back to her fiancé —five years? You don't throw that away, Mr. Montgomery."

Nick clenched his jaw, deciding it was best to stay silent. He knew that if he talked it wouldn't help his cause.

"To be honest, what worries me is that my daughter doesn't know the full truth. You're hiding something, and I want to know what it is."

"I have no secrets. If you want to know something, then fucking ask me—"

"What's your business with my daughter?"

Nick shrugged. "Only Olivia can answer that."

"But I'm asking you!"

Nick diverted his eyes back to his hands.

"Does my daughter know about your interesting past?"

Nick's eyes flashed back up. "Listen, I don't know what kind of dirt you think you've got on me, but Olivia knows about everything she needs to." Nick cleared his throat, knowing it wasn't entirely true, but James didn't need to know that. He sat on the edge of his desk, thinking of a way to make James believe he wasn't the bad guy. "Olivia is an amazing girl, and I respect your daughter. I would do nothing to hurt her."

"Olivia is vulnerable and impulsive, which leads her to make the worst choices."

"Well, you give her less credit than she deserves. She's not as defenseless as you think." Nick's brows peaked.

"Mr. Montgomery, maybe you'll know it for yourself one day, and I wish that for you, but a father knows what's best for their children, and you, my boy, are definitely not what she needs."

"Maybe you should let Olivia decide what's best for herself."

James laughed. "I know men like you who look for an opportunity like Olivia, taking advantage of her money and connections." He paused. "Mr. Montgomery, stay on my good side and there will be endless opportunities I will pass your way. Go against me, and, well...you will find many closed doors."

"Is that a threat?"

"Oh, you bet your life it is, Mr. Montgomery!" He glared. "What kind of future can you offer Olivia? She's not a simple girl with simple needs. She will want more. What are you going to do then?"

Nick could feel his heart beating, and it took everything to stay in control. When he laid down the facts in his head, he knew if he acted out of anger there would be repercussions. He quickly decided he wouldn't give James any more reason to dislike him. No matter what James did or said, Nick would refrain from stepping over the line.

"I don't plan to work at a bar forever."

"Mr. Montgomery, dreams won't feed you." James' voice softened.

"I care very much for Olivia..."

"Well, now I'm glad to hear we're on the same page. You're a smart man, Mr. Montgomery. If you cherish her as you say you do, then I know you'll do the logical thing. Don't take it the wrong way, son. It's not that I have anything against you. I'm only protecting what's mine. Trust me, I'm doing you a favor by telling you...you need to let her go."

Nick needed to look at it through James' eyes. He knew Olivia's father was acting out of fear—the fear of not being there for his children. James was fighting against time, putting everything in its place before his illness robbed him not only of his life but also of fatherhood. No matter how old their children were, fathers took care of them. Nick didn't need to dig deep to understand this. Toward the end of his mother's life, she had expressed the same urgency. She agonized over whether Nick would take care of himself after she was gone.

As for Olivia, it was already too late. Nick was in too deep, and James Montiano would have to do his worst.

"I'll take the one that resembles my daughter ... You may decide on the amount, and when you have a price, contact my secretary." James slid his business card on Nick's desk, and then he was out the door.

Half an hour later, Olivia called and canceled their lunch date. She blamed it on a last-minute meeting at work, but Nick knew better. This was the work of the gatekeeper.

Dear girl with the red scarf,

I believe we all have this misconception about love. That's supposed to complete you and that it should be faultless. The truth is, there will be times love will be ugly, push you to unreasonable bounds—even break you. That said, love may be many things to people but it's whom we choose to ride this crazy roller coaster with that make this adventure so crucial.

Trust me, after all, ☺
I am Mr.universe

19

DAUGHTER TO A
FATHER

IT WAS ONE THING TO CANCEL HER PLANS WITH NICK, BUT ANOTHER to have to lie to him. But Olivia had a good reason. When her father had called wanting to meet up for lunch, she really couldn't say no. If Nick tagged along, then she would have to explain her relationship, which at the moment she wasn't sure of.

So a little white lie was much easier, to avoid unnecessary awkwardness.

Growing up, her father was the one who had hidden her from the world, shielded her from all its brutes and ugliness. He was her father, and she trusted that he knew what was best. But lately, she felt they'd been living in different worlds...partially because she saw the slight changes in him. Or maybe it was within herself?

"Is everything okay?" her father asked from across the table.

"Sure." She didn't feel that was true as she played with the tip of her ponytail.

"You don't come and talk to me anymore." His eyes scanned the menu.

He was right. Since she had broken it off with Dario, she had tried to avoid alone time with her dad for fear of this exact moment. She knew it was just a matter of time before she needed to face the music.

James placed the menu beside him, catching her gaze. "Do you remember when you were six, you discovered this old rusty bike inside that green barn?"

Her grandfather had had a farm, but technically it hadn't been a functional one since the 70s. Her grandfather had purchased the property intending to grow vegetables for himself and their family. It was a way of life in his old country, a hobby in the new one. She remembered as a child driving over the Mercier Bridge, and half an hour of winding country roads. You knew when you were close because you could see the forest-green barns from a distance.

"Sure, Daddy, I remember."

"It was too big for you to ride, barely touching the pedals, but you were so determined to get on that bike and ride it."

"I don't know how many times we went down that dirt road." She smiled at the fond memories of summer days at her grandparents' country place.

"Yes, you didn't need my help. You needed my support, but you wanted your freedom," he replied.

"By the end of the summer, I rode it on my own." Olivia played with the edge of her napkin.

"Yes, you did. I even bought you a new bike, but you didn't care much for it. All you wanted was that old thing." He grinned. "You've always been that way, huh, Liv?"

She shrugged her shoulders. "I loved it." It had been special to her because it was attached to the few memories she had of her dad. Growing up, he had been busy building his business. Olivia had no resentment toward him; she had just missed him growing up.

He waved his hand in the air. "Ah, that thing was a piece of junk." He sighed. "How is it going with selling the apartment?"

"Slow. I've had visits and one offer that Dario refused. I told him I wanted to lower the price, but he doesn't want to hear it." She leaned closer. "Listen, Dad, do you think you can talk to him for me? He'll listen to you."

"I will try, but he's like you—very stubborn." He slightly raised his eyes from his menu.

Dario was nothing like her, but she didn't clarify that.

"What's the story about this hippie?"

She felt her heart pounding in her rib cage. It was clear now why he had wanted to meet for lunch.

"Nick is not a hippie, Dad." Olivia frowned.

She imagined Dario would have spared no time to report to her father. Throughout their relationship, Olivia had always felt there was a competition with Dario for her father's devotion.

"Nick." His eyebrows crashed together. "Was at your apartment?"

Olivia blushed, not wanting her father to think something had happened in the Biblical sense, because it hadn't.

"I don't know why he felt the need to tell you. It's really none of his business."

"Dario did nothing wrong by telling me. He still cares for you; I wish you could see that."

"Dad, I already know what you'll say, so let's stop right here." She rubbed her forehead.

"Please, Olivia, don't tell me you're dating this ... boy?" He cast her a questioning look, then said, "It's none of my business, but what about Dario?"

"What about him?" Olivia's voice went up.

"I thought you might patch things up."

Olivia knew her father too well; when he started his sentence with *"it's none of my business,"* he really meant, *"this is my business."*

"There is no hope of us getting back together—ever."

"And you think this thing with—Nick will go anywhere?"

"I don't know." She squared her shoulders. "But he's good to me."

James studied her for a moment before saying, "I know right now this boy may seem heroic in your eyes. He came to your aid, and I am grateful for that, but don't believe in this daydream. Being an artist is a hobby, not a career, Olivia. How long do you think it will last before you realize he's not for you?" When she didn't respond, he added, "In the meantime, Dario has been suffering. He's hoping that you will come to your senses."

She rolled her eyes, hoping he was miserable. That would have given her some satisfaction for everything he'd done, but as long Dario kept his job, his life would be perfectly fine. If her father knew the truth about him, they wouldn't be having this conversation.

Of course, it was her fault that he didn't.

"And what? Take him back? No, Dad, that's not possible."

"It would be if you didn't have that boy Nick hanging around." He snapped his eyes back at her.

"Please, you don't know the whole story. Believe me, Nick has nothing to do with me and Dario not being together."

"So tell me, then ... because I can't understand how you decide to spend the rest of your life with someone and then wake up, deciding it's finished," James said.

She opened her mouth, then closed it. Olivia wanted to tell him that Dario was a creep and Nick was someone good—a person she needed in her life; that if he gave him a chance, he would see it too, but all she could say was, "Please, Dad. I'm not a baby. I can take care of myself."

"That may be so, but you're still my little girl," he replied gently. "He's not like you, Olivia. Nick will never fit in."

"You're just saying that because he doesn't come from money," she murmured.

"Open your eyes, Olivia. Did you ever think about how he makes his living?"

"He's an artist and works at his brother's bar."

"Right, he works at a bar and has a new apartment, plus a

studio. I don't see how this adds up. You don't know what kind of stuff he's mixed up in."

"That's not Nick. Besides, I don't need anyone to support me. I can support myself."

James placed his glasses on the table. "There is more than just that, Olivia."

"Really, like what?"

"Well, my love, you have different backgrounds—different traditions."

"Look, you and Mom had also come from different financial backgrounds, and you have been married over forty years."

"Yes, that was the only thing, but imagine if we had had more going against us. We would never have survived."

Olivia sighed, leaning back in her chair. "Did you ever think maybe you could be wrong about someone?" Her first thought was Dario, and how her father had him on a pedestal.

"No, I've lived longer than you, Olivia. Unlike you, I have the talent of foreseeing the future. If you go down the path with this boy, Nick, you will only bring heartache not only to yourself but possibly to Nick too." He played with his glasses. "Have you given a thought to his feelings?"

She remained silent, not sure how to respond. He was right. She had been so occupied with her own feelings, it had never crossed her mind that perhaps she would be the one to hurt him.

"Nick is just like that rusty old bike, Olivia. It was never for you, and eventually you outgrew it. You'll outgrow Nick, too," he said as she shifted in her chair.

She looked at him for a moment, then said, "He's just a friend, Dad. That's all he's ever been." Something from the back of her mind told her she wasn't really being truthful, at least to herself.

"Okay." Satisfied with her answer, he placed his glasses back on and continued to look at his menu. "I told Dario that you had more sense than that."

"Dad, please don't mention his name anymore." Her stomach turned.

"I don't know what happened between the two of you, but I wish you would give him another chance."

Her father continued to talk from across the table, but her mind drifted back to that gold bike. It had been in the far back of the big barn where her grandfather kept his tractors. She had spotted it in the corner with all sorts of things piled on top of it, so she had gotten her grandfather to retrieve it.

"Daddy thinks its garbage," she had told her grandfather.

"Forget your father. He doesn't see the true value of things like you and me." With a wink, he had cleaned it up the best he could. She had loved that bike; its defects had added to its charm. Then she realized Nick was like the old bike: she'd seen his true value, and Dario was the new, superficial, pink bike with tassels at the end of the handlebars. She sat there quietly wondering what was best for her. Olivia wasn't sure which side of the scale would tip.

Dear girl with the red scar,

You can't search for love. Love pursues you. Nor can you force it. You have to be patient ... wait patiently for it. And just when you think it's not possible, it happens unexpectedly. Just at the right time, with the right person. So let love find you.

Trust me, after all, ☺
I am Mr.universe

20

JUST FRIENDS

OLIVIA HATED WEDNESDAYS—ACTUALLY, SHE JUST HATED COMING into work. She didn't dislike what she did—she just wasn't content with the company she worked for. Especially when she knew what kind of day they had lined up: meetings with suppliers, fittings, and coming up with the next collection. Of course, that was part of the job, only the pay was lacking and there was still no talk about the promotion her boss had promised her months ago.

"Hey, I need a big favor." Jessica flew into Olivia's office.

"What's up?" Olivia glanced up from the pile of swatches that were scattered all over her desk.

"My fit model canceled on me, and I was wondering...if you could ask your boyfriend to come in and try some of my samples?"

"Nick? He's not my boyfriend, and no, I don't think that's a good idea."

"*Oh*—Friends with benefits? You naughty girl, you." Jessica had a twinkle in her eyes.

"What? No! Just friends."

"You're so lame." Jessica sighed.

Olivia rolled her eyes.

"Please, I really need to send these specs out today. If not, I'll be late for production." She gave Olivia her big brown puppy eyes.

"Why didn't you schedule this ahead?"

"I did. My dimwit assistant had sent out the wrong size specs. Thank God the production manager in China caught the mistake on time. It would have been a brutal disaster. Everything would have come in two sizes small, and Jack would have had my head on a silver platter." Jessica plopped into the chair in front of her. "I need to fix it before Jack finds out that this happened again. Call Nick, see if he can help me out. *Please!*" Jessica clung the samples to her chest. "I can't find anyone else, and Nick lives down the street. I know he'll do anything for you."

Olivia frowned. She never remembered telling her anything specific about Nick, especially that he lived nearby.

"How about the guy in the graphics department? What's his name? Derick?"

"Too small..." Jessica shook her head.

Olivia snapped her fingers. "Oh, Steven!"

"Too big." Jessica smiled wickedly.

"I don't even want to know." Olivia exhaled a long breath before saying yes.

"Thank you! I owe you big time!"

Where had she heard that before? Oh, right. Last week when Jessica had left work early and conveniently forgotten to print out her catalog, the one that Jack wanted on his desk that afternoon. It seemed Jessica had been taking advantage of their relationship, but what was Olivia to do? She valued their friendship, and friends helped each other out, didn't they? But it was clear to Olivia: it'd been one-sided.

"Don't get excited just yet. I haven't called him."

Jessica waved her hand in the air, already knowing Nick would come. "Oh, did I tell you what Jack said to me the other day?"

"No."

"He said you're talented and he's satisfied with your work so far." She smiled. "Looks like somebody's getting promoted." Jessica sang out the words and winked just before she fled the room.

A permanent smile planted on Olivia's face. It would be a dream come true if she was given the honor of head designer for one of D.S. Design's labels. She just needed to keep the faith.

✳

THE ELEVATOR DOORS OPENED, and she was greeted by Nick's bright eyes.

"Thank you so much for doing this for me on such a short notice..."

"I would have gotten here sooner, but I was in the middle of something when you called," Nick said.

"Oh, I'm sorry. I shouldn't have bothered you."

"No, I'm happy to come. I wanted to see you."

Olivia blushed. The last time she had spoken to him was on Monday, when she canceled their plans to meet. At first, she suspected he might be upset with her, because the tone of his voice had seemed a little uneasy, like he was holding something back. Whatever it was, it was gone now.

"Hey, do you want to see my office?" She was the first one to break away from their gaze.

"Sure." He followed her through the glass doors. Her office was at the end of a narrow hallway.

"Welcome to my home away from home." She spun with her

arms in the air. "Sorry it looks chaotic, I'm in the middle of working on two seasons at once."

Nick viewed the samples on the rack along the wall.

"Did you design these?"

"Yes."

"So, you're a designer?"

"I'm an assistant to the CEO of the company. It's not the same thing."

Nick seemed confused.

"I do all the work but get no recognition for it...or the pay." Olivia raised her brows.

"Right." Nick nodded his head. "How does that work?"

"It doesn't. Hopefully, I should be promoted soon," Olivia said, placing the receiver to her ear, dialing Jessica's extension.

"Maybe I should have asked this before." He browsed around the room. "It's guy stuff you wanted me to try on, right?"

"Shoot, didn't I tell you it was for a bikini?" Olivia smiled devilishly. "Come, the samples are in the other room." She accompanied Nick to Jessica's much brighter, larger office.

"Nick! You're such a sweetheart, thank you! Olivia, can you show him the samples he needs to try on? Now, where's my idiot assistant..." Jessica picked up her phone, then hung up. "I'll be right back." She frantically walked out the door.

"Is it always crazy like this?" Nick frowned.

"Well, you're lucky my boss isn't here, because there would most likely be some screaming going on."

"Should I even ask?" Several lines appeared on his forehead.

"I'll fill you in later." She half-smiled.

She went to the clothing rack and pulled out some short-sleeve shirts and polo tops from Jessica's summer collection.

"So here they are." Olivia handed him the hangers. "You can change in here if you like."

Nick peered around the room. "Is there a bathroom I could use?"

It had never occurred to Olivia that Nick might be shy. She was accustomed to models readily pulling off their shirts, changing right in front of her or anyone else in the room. They'd even get down to their boxers without batting an eyelash.

"Oh yeah, sure. There's a bathroom just out of the office to your right."

"Thanks."

"No, thank you. You're doing me a huge favor."

Clarification: Jessica.

"Hey, want to grab a bite later?"

She nodded, and with a smile Nick vanished out the door.

Olivia's eyes snapped up when the sounds of laughter flowed from Jessica's office. Luckily for Olivia, the printer was conveniently in the perfect spot, and while waiting for her sketches to be printed out, she had a clear view of her friend's working area. She didn't know why it bothered her that Jessica's assistant Racheal was standing so close to Nick, her hands all over his arms and chest, pinning the fabric of the sample he wore. It was obvious she was flirting with him, but was Nick flirting back? She couldn't see his face, but his tone suggested that he was being friendly, and nothing more.

Olivia was never possessive, and besides, Nick could do whatever he wanted. It wasn't like they were committed to each other.

When she got to her office, she found Jessica rummaging through her sample cards.

"Hey, have you seen the swatch that Brian from Fabrictex brought over last week? You know, the one with the Lurex thread?"

"Yeah, it's right here." Olivia pulled it from the bottom of the pile and handed it over.

"What's wrong?" Jessica's eyes focused on Olivia.

"Nothing." Without meeting Jessica's eyes, she placed her stack of papers on her desk.

"Ah ... just curious, was the view from the printer any good?" Jessica's red lips went up on one side.

"The printer was broken ... I was trying to get it to work."

"Funny, it was fine when I used it this morning."

Olivia sank into her chair, and before she could clarify things, Racheal glided into the room with a smile that Olivia wished she could wipe off.

"So, Olivia, what's the story between you and Nick?"

"What do you mean?" Olivia's eyes focused on the opened drawer, retrieving a pencil from the bottom of the compartment.

"Are you dating him?" Racheal watched Olivia as she sharpened her pencil, and only when Olivia was satisfied with a perfect point did she meet Racheal's eyes.

"Ah—No ... Well, he's a friend." Olivia could sense Jessica's eyes on her.

"Oh great, then you don't mind if I ask him out? I think there's a real strong connection, and I want to get to know him better."

"Yeah, *pfft*—sure, go ahead. He's very much single. Yup, he's free to date whoever he wants."

She couldn't believe the words that were coming out of her mouth, but there they were. When Racheal walked out, Olivia turned to see Jessica wearing a serious expression.

"What?"

"Wow, so that's how you look when your pants are on fire?"

"I wasn't lying. We're not dating." Olivia's voice was tight, and she felt the heat rise in her cheeks.

"You told me you liked him," Jessica said matter-of-factly.

"No, I said I liked being around him ... as a *friend*."

"I don't understand." Jessica looked perplexed. "It's none of my business, but Nick is an amazing guy. And you're purposely messing things up."

"You barely know him. You met him, what? Two times?" Olivia's lead snapped on the blank paper. "You're my friend. Shouldn't you be on my side?" Olivia rotated the shaft vigorously into the metal sharpener.

Jessica's face scrunched up, like she was struggling with something internally.

"Look, I will tell you something, but you can't tell Nick..."

Just before Jessica could say what it was, Racheal strolled back into the room so fast that it made the papers fly off Olivia's desk.

"What's the deal?"

"Huh?" Olivia honestly had no clue to what the issue was.

"I thought you told me you and Nick were only friends."

"Yeah, we are..."

"He said he was seeing someone."

"*Oh*?"

"Yeah, you!" Racheal gave her a cheesy grin. "What kind of a sick joke are you playing? Thanks for allowing me to make a fool of myself." She brusquely walked back out.

"My, my, my, what a web we weave. You shouldn't be playing games, Olivia, especially if you like the guy."

"I'm not."

Then the light flooded into Jessica's eyes. "You were testing him, right? You wanted to see if he would say yes. Olivia, not all men are like Dario."

"No, it wasn't that."

But she was right. Olivia was playing a game, and jealousy had gotten the best of her. And if she was jealous, then she had to admit Nick meant something.

"Hey, don't get offended, but I don't think it's fair to make a man chase you just because you're afraid to be alone. So get your shit together, will you? If you like him, then tell him." Jessica paused a few steps from the entrance, holding a pile of swatches. "Oh, by the way, Nick was a perfect fit. I guess it was meant to be."

Jessica disappeared through the doorway, but not before a folded paper fell out of the sample pile she was carrying.

Olivia already knew what it was, even before it touched the floor.

Dear girl with the red scarf,

There is no point in stressing about things you have no control over. Instead, stress on the details of your life that you do.

Trust me, after all,
I am Mr.universe ☺

21

LIFELINE

"Give me your hand," Nick said, inside the near-empty Café Orleans. Olivia sat across from him, wondering what Racheal had told him about her embarrassing indiscretion. She would be honest if Nick would question her about it, but he said nothing.

"No way, the last time you drew on my wrist it took nearly a week for your artwork to wash off."

"Come on. I don't need a pen for what I'm going to do." He gave her a sexy smile and, without hesitation, Olivia complied. He leaned in closer, turning her palm upward. With a finger, he followed the lines on her hand.

"That tickles." She giggled.

"See this line..." His eyes were soft and expressive. "This is your lifeline."

"How would you know?"

"Long ago, I met this woman at an art gallery. She took one look at me and felt compelled to do a reading of my palm."

"Of course she did." Olivia smiled.

"You never have to be jealous, not with me." His eyes were fixed on Olivia. She knew he meant what had happened earlier with Racheal.

"I'm not jealous."

Something about his face revealed to her that he knew better. Olivia wondered if he was disappointed in the fact that she viewed them only as friends. If he was, Nick didn't show it.

He held Olivia's hand closer to his body, tilting it toward the light coming from the window. He continued tracing the lines inside of her palm. Chills ran up the length of her arms, all the way to the back of her neck, and she wondered if he was aware of her reaction, because if he was, he would know she liked it.

"See this line over here ... This will tell you how long or short your life will be," he said, his eyes fixed on hers. "Yours is long."

"Well, that's good to know. What about you?"

Olivia was skeptical of those things, but she was curious, especially when Nick hesitated. When he finally held out his hand to her, she realized it had meant something to him.

"My lifeline is short. It breaks in certain places ... It means..." His eyes remained focused on his hand, not capable of continuing with words.

She realized there was something raw about him suddenly. He had been through something that he wasn't ready to talk about.

The thought of Nick having a short life saddened her.

"Is that what she told you? You can't believe that kind of crap. No, Montgomery, I believe nobody has the power to tell us what our future holds."

He studied her for a moment as though he might debate it, but for some reason Nick let it slide. "Maybe you're right." The gleam in his eyes insinuated something she couldn't fully understand, but it was his demeanor that caused some concern.

"Give me your hand," Olivia demanded.

"Is it my turn now?"

She took a closer look at his inner hand, pretending she knew what she was doing. "Wow, this is interesting." Olivia traced the lines with her finger. It made him shift in his chair.

"What?"

"Well, this line over here…"

"Jesus, if you continue, you will put me to sleep."

"I see—you're about to lose a bet."

"Is that so?" He chuckled, straightening in his chair.

"Yeah, big time. And this line over here means you will make an extraordinary meal for an exceptional, smart, beautiful brunette." Her eyes danced.

"Really? I wonder who she could be." Nick peered around the room.

Olivia narrowed her eyes and nudged his hand away.

"Tell me something. Do you see a passionate kiss with this beautiful woman?" His face completely changed, and he wasn't being playful this time.

She could feel the heat rise in her cheeks. Without a thought, she said, "Nope. Sorry, no kiss." Olivia giggled.

"Exceptional, eh?" He smiled.

"Don't forget beautiful and smart."

Nick got up from his chair, slid on his black windbreaker. "Hmm, more like a smartass, but I think I like your reading better. It's a shame, though. I would have liked to have kissed her."

❋

OUTSIDE, Nick accompanied her back to her office, but before doing so he swiftly stepped towards a homeless man taking shelter between the walls of her building. Olivia recognized him. It was the man who had given her the first handwritten note.

"Hey, John." Nick handed him the brown bag, containing a few items she'd seenNick purchase at the café.

"Mademoiselle, I see you've found your man," John said to her.

Olivia turned to Nick, but he ignored the comment.

"How are you, John?"

"Thriving."

The homeless man took a long look. "Is this your girl?"

Nick glanced at Olivia and smiled. "Not yet ... but I'm working on it."

John pointed his finger in Nick's direction. "This guy has a big heart, too big for his own good." John opened the bag, taking out the plastic-wrapped sandwich. "Did you know Nick has been going up and down these streets for months, trying to figure out how to approach you?"

"Ah ... John!" Nick laughed nervously.

"That's how we met. He was distracted by your beauty; he didn't see me lying here and almost toppled on top of me. So it's really thanks to you, mademoiselle, that we met." He smiled.

"Okay, John, that's enough. I'm grateful for your input, but I don't want you to scare her off."

"Did I embarrass you, Nick? What can I say? Love ... it's always about love," John said.

Olivia sensed Nick's uneasiness. She never saw him blush, and she found it endearing.

"I got to go, John, but I'll be around later...okay?" Nick nodded and followed Olivia to the front door of her office building.

Olivia gave him a sideways glance. "Did that actually happen? How you two met?"

"Well, not exactly." He smiled, but it was the kind of smile that meant he wasn't willing to convey the truth.

"I always wonder how someone gets to that point. Did he always live this way?" Olivia diverted her eyes back to John, who was now eating his sandwich.

"Well, it's a series of unfortunate happenings. See, for John, he lost his parents at a very young age and was in and out of foster care. One day he had enough and decided life on the streets was best for him. He felt it was the only way to have his freedom."

"Wow ... How old is he?"

"Forty-two."

"He seems much older."

"Life out here can do that."

"I see you care about him."

"Well, John is my friend. It's important to have people in your life who matter. It's not important where they come from." Nick shrugged.

Olivia caught herself staring at Nick. The more she saw, the more she liked about him. He definitely had his priorities in the right place. That was another thing she found attractive about him. At that moment, it was easy to fall for someone like Nick. Olivia just wasn't sure if she would allow herself to.

Dear girl with the red scar,

There is no reason to hold on to history, it only deprives us of a future we deserve. Let the past live in the past because there are better things ahead waiting for you. When you're ready to let go, that's where you'll find me, waiting for you with open arms.
Trust me, after all,
I am Mr. Universe ☺

22

SOMEBODY TO YOU

NICK SHUFFLED THE THICK, WET SNOW WITH HIS FEET, MAKING A neat pile in front of him, stopping when the cold water seeped inside his black high-top Converse sneakers. The breeze was cold, but the air had changed, the scent of spring lingering not too far. Maybe it was some ironic humor that had him waiting here for Olivia to arrive, standing in front of a rustic double-heart sculpture outside the modern building. They had spent a substantial amount of time together, but he felt he wasn't getting any closer to her. She was holding back.

Was he stuck in the friend zone? His brother had thought so.

"Stop playing it safe!" Dan scowled.

"I'm not—Olivia is not a girl who rushes into things. She's not Chloe."

"Well, that's a fucking good thing. I don't get it. It's either you're in a relationship or you're not. If you didn't grab that ass, then you're stuck in fuckin' besties purgatory." Dan leaned over, placing his mug on the coffee table. "Be clear about your intentions."

"And grabbing her ass would be a way of showing his intentions?" Amanda placed a coaster under Dan's mug. "What are you, a caveman?"

"Yeah, sure ... it worked for you." Dan extended a loving hand, but she slapped it away.

"For once I agree with your brother." Amanda slid next to Dan on the sofa.

Nick arched a brow.

"No—not the ass-grabbing part." She slapped Dan even harder this time.

"Ouch ... see the abuse!"

"Maybe you're unconsciously sending signals you're not attracted to her in that way," Amanda said.

"She knows I'm wildly attracted to her at least, I hope." Nick brows crashed together.

"Okay, so there is chemistry between you two?" Amanda inched closer to the edge of her seat, lacing her fingers together as if she were the love guru and the session was about to begin.

"I like to think so..."

"She showed you signs that she's attracted to you, right?"

Nick winced.

"Does she flirt with you?"

"Well, what do you mean?" Nick said, and Amanda let out a long breath.

"Have you guys kissed?"

"Well ... no."

"Seriously?" Amanda's eyes opened wider.

"Look, I'm not going to be a jerk about this...I mean, I really like her and I don't want to mess things up. I know she's been through something, and if she needs time to figure things out, then I will respect that."

"God, I'm marrying the wrong brother." Amanda's eyes shifted to Dan's.

Dan rolled his eyes. "Oh, stop being such a wimp. Do you

want a relationship with this girl, or do you want to play patty-cake?"

Amanda placed her hand in front of Dan's mouth. "How are you two even related?" Letting out a long breath, she continued. "You shouldn't hold back because it's safe, and you don't want to ruin what you already have." Her eyes softened. "I get it, but your feelings matter too, Nick. Be yourself. Show her that you're serious about this. She'll see a genuine stand-up guy, which I already know you are."

Amanda's eyes fixed on Nick.

"Have you told her about ... ?"

"My issues ... no. I'm trying to figure out where I stand in all this before I jump that hurdle."

"Just be clear. If you like her, don't hide your intentions. Girls sense when a guy is not straight with them, and that's what scares them off," Amanda said.

"Maybe you're right."

"I know I am."

Dan stifled a laugh just as Nick looked down at his watch. "I better go before I'm late for my date. Thanks for breakfast and the advice, Mandy." Nick leaned in to plant a kiss on the top of her head.

"Have a good time on your date ... Have fun braiding hair or building sand castles or whatever girls do with their besties."

"You're such an ass," Nick called out.

"I love you too, brother. Just remember one thing: stop fucking playing patty-cake."

✳

"Hey, Montgomery."

Finally.

Nick turned to find her walking down the stairs, heading straight for him.

The light came up from behind Olivia, making the vision of her appear angelic. She pulled a strand of hair away from her face, revealing her beautiful, elephantine eyes. His gaze might have made her uncomfortable, because she was the first to break away from his stare, hiding her rosy cheeks from him.

All this time they spent together, he had been plotting, scheming, and contemplating, only to sit just outside her door. Nick wondered if he would ever get the courage to turn the doorknob.

"You're late." He teasingly glanced up from his black strap watch.

"Technically, I'm not." She pulled two tickets out of her back pocket and waved them in the air, smiling brightly like she had beat him at a game.

"I've been in line for the past twenty minutes," she said with a big smile. "What's the matter? You thought I stood you up?" Olivia squinted her eyes.

"No, not necessarily," He hesitated. "Okay, maybe a little."

"Come on, Montgomery. Let's go see what's so special about this place."

A particular conversation he had had a few weeks ago with Olivia had brought them downtown. Olivia told him that Montreal had nothing to offer. He had decided he was going to prove her wrong, so he thought the museum was a good place to start.

The Montreal Museum of Fine Arts spanned four buildings and was linked to the underground. Each building housed different art: the first pavilion housed world cultures, the second decorative arts, and the last two buildings housed international, Quebecois, and Canadian art. He was dumbfounded when she told him that she'd never been to the museum.

"How is that even possible?"

"I never had anyone to go with." She shrugged.

"Well, now you have me." Nick smiled.

❋

INSIDE, Olivia handed him his ticket.

"But I invited you out."

"It's okay to let a girl pay sometimes. Don't worry, I won't think less of you." Olivia beamed.

"All right, Monti, but I got lunch, okay?" He took one ticket out of her hand. "By the way ... thank you."

"You're welcome. So where do we start?" Olivia unfolded the museum map.

"We won't need that. I know this place like the back of my hand."

"Okay, lead the way, Montgomery." Olivia folded the map back into a rectangle.

A crowd was taking pictures with their phones, and murmured sounds filled the room. They walked into a space with sculptures scattered all around. Some were displayed in glass cases, but there was one familiar statue at the center of the room.

"I wonder what he's thinking." Nick smiled at Olivia.

"Whatever it is, he doesn't seem too happy about it."

The bronze cast of Rodin's *The Thinker* sat upon a large lacquered box. It was much smaller in person than in the photographs Nick had used to look at when he was a kid.

"Rodin originally created the statue to represent Dante, the author of the *Divine Comedy,* but it came to represent the creative mind at work. This is how I brainstorm every morning." He winked.

Olivia smiled back. "Naked and constipated?"

He chuckled.

✻

"Do you recognize her?" He stepped aside, allowing Olivia to get a better view. It was less crowded where they stood. Only a handful of art students in the corner, scribbling away in their notebooks.

"Is that what I think it is? Tissot?"

He fixed his eyes on the painting, a large rectangle canvas of a woman, wearing a black feathered hat and crinoline dress, nestled inside the bottom branch of a tree, whose autumn leaves were just about to fall off.

"Yes, ma'am. James Jacque Joseph Tissot, titled *October 1877*." He stuck his hands farther in his denim pockets.

"I didn't know this was here." Olivia's voice went up and her face glowed more beautifully than he'd ever anticipated.

When she'd first mentioned to him that Tissot was one of her favorite painters, he was surprised that she'd never been to the Montreal Museum, because if she had, Olivia would certainly have been aware that one of the artist's artworks had a permanent residence there.

"She's so beautiful."

"Yes, she is." His eyes remained on Olivia. "With art, I believe anything created with profound heart is captured beautifully."

She tilted her head. "So are you going to tell me the rest?"

"What makes you think I know more?"

She smiled like she knew better. "You're the connoisseur and I'm only the spectator."

He nodded toward the painting. "The woman in the painting was Tissot's mistress and muse. She was known to him as *mavourneen*, an Irish term meaning *my love, my darling*."

She glanced back at the one-hundred-and-thirty-eight-year-old canvas. "What happened to them?" Olivia looked at him in a way that made Nick want to kiss her so badly.

"Their story had a sad ending. Kathleen, Tissot's mistress,

overdosed on laudanum, saving her lover from the pain of watching her slowly die of tuberculosis. After her death, Tissot was brokenhearted and started a whole separate career as a religious painter."

"How depressing." Olivia looked back at the painting. "Who can imagine something so breathtaking can have such sad history tied to it." Her eyes found his again. "I never heard anything so romantic."

*

"WHAT SURPRISES ME IS, you seem to have this optimistic outlook on love. How's that possible after everything that has happened to you?" Olivia said, after Nick confided in her about the last relationship he had had.

In reality, Olivia didn't know half of it. He had had to leave out the essential reason why Chloe had left. Not that it was right in keeping it from her; the only thing that prevented him from fully revealing himself was good old-fashioned fear. He'd lost so much already. Nick had to be certain that he could trust her, because the moment she knew the truth, there was a possibility that she'd walk away ... because they always did.

He'd be honest with her someday, just not today.

"Well, hate can leave a long, nasty stain on your heart if you let it. You need to let go of the venom if you want to forget someone." He glanced back at Olivia. Her eyes were distant. Maybe she was even thinking about her own situation.

"You make it sound easy."

"No, it's never easy, but there's a short supply of infinities in life. You need to ask yourself how you want to live them out. It pretty much sucks if you're going to wallow in self-pity...and for what? For a person who pretty much doesn't give a damn about you to begin with? No thank you."

"Have you ever seen her again?"

"Nope."

She must have seen something in his eyes, because she asked, "Do you ever wish that you could rewind your life, go back to that moment where you're about to make the biggest mistake? I know I do."

He sighed. "No, I wouldn't change a thing. My time with Chloe was not something I regret. Sure, I only had myself to blame, but I came to realize that even though it was a lousy relationship, something good came from it. It put me on this path and here I am with you." He smiled. "I know something now."

"What is it?" She turned to face him.

"That you shouldn't have to settle for less than what you have to offer. My relationship with Chloe was stressful, mentally and emotionally. Love shouldn't make you feel like that. I mean, sure, every relationship has issues—that's the reality of it—but it shouldn't have to make life so dysfunctional. Love should build you up, not tear you apart. And if you are lucky enough to find someone you're willing to go to hell and back for...to love like crazy, and who loves you the same way..." He glanced at her. "I guess what I'm trying to say is, I want the kind of love you just can't live without. I want someone who will be there for me in the worst possible moments of my life. Because that's when it counts. That's when you know it's real."

Olivia broke away from his gaze, fiddling with the label on a bottle of water.

"I don't think I ever had that. I don't want to sound pessimistic, but personally, I don't think it exists."

"Just because you haven't found it yet doesn't mean it doesn't exist, Olivia. Do you want to know how to find that kind of love? Forget about your head and lead with your heart. After everything I've been through, I am willing to risk it all over again ... the heartache, the heartbreak. How can you go through life and never dive in? How else are you expecting to find it?"

"Well, I like to proceed with caution at least, I try to." Olivia gave him a tight smile.

He nodded. "I think we all hope that love won't overlook us, but if you're too careful, you might miss out on something very special."

"I wish there was a way of knowing you're not wasting your time with someone." She searched his face, and Nick knew she was afraid, because he was, too.

"Yeah, life would be too easy. You know, I came to the conclusion that the people we allow in our lives fall into two categories: they can either be a kick in the fuckin' gut—life lesson—or a blessing."

"Which one am I, Montgomery?" she asked, as someone was trying to get around them.

He shot his perfectly soulful eyes at her. "I think you might be a bit of both."

"I thought you said there were only two categories?" She knitted her brows together.

"Trust me, kid, you're in a class of your own." He smiled.

Olivia nudged him playfully, pushing her hair out of her eyes to look at him.

"Want to see something cool?"

Before she could answer, he slid his hand in hers, keeping Olivia close to him as he guided her through the crowd, passing the Monet and the Picasso from one room to another until they came into a dark space. A visual art film played on a screen that made up the whole length of the wall. It was spectacular to the eye, a roller coaster of lights bouncing off the screen onto their faces and bodies.

This was not the reason he had brought her here. He was almost afraid to break the silence between them, afraid that, if he said one more thing, he might do something impulsive. Nick found himself at a point he couldn't turn back from. His mind raced a million miles a minute, and he could feel his heart pulsing in his veins. And there, under the glow of the light, she stood beside him, unaware of the fire she'd started inside him.

He liked the way she looked at him. It gave him a sense of belonging. Nick had surrendered, and she had no idea. He didn't know what it was, the light, the loud beautiful haunting music, but he just wanted to get lost, tangled and caught up in something with her. It was some rare delight to feel this surge of life, like if he left the room without capturing the moment, he certainly would die.

When he realized he was still holding on to her hand, he pushed her back against the wall in one swift movement. At first, she was surprised by his assertiveness, and with a smile her desires became apparent. Her face was only inches from his, and he found a burdensome confession in her wondrous eyes, a brief affirmation that she'd been burning too.

With his T-shirt crumpled between her fingers, her eyes slowly trailed down his face, stopping at his mouth.

"What about the bet?" she whispered.

At that point, it was already too late. He'd lost before it even started. Anything Olivia would have asked him to do, he would have done. Anything she wanted, he would have given. And there in the darkness, just like he'd imagined, his mouth crashed down on hers, allowing the world around them to evaporate.

Dear girl with the red scarf,

Sometimes love is not what the heart expects. Sometimes it's even better.

Trust me, after all, ☺
I am Mr.universe

23

PLAY UNTIL
SOMETHING BREAKS

"Can I paint you?" Nick whispered as his fingers delicately traced the outline of Olivia's cheekbone, trailing down to her lips.

His words washed over her like warm water. How could she deny him? It was the most provocative thing anyone had ever asked, to be captured on a canvas like some beautiful creature.

In a short time, Olivia had come to know the essence of Nick Montgomery. Nick's passion was his art, and how he created it enthralled her. The way he used his left hand, positioning his pencil in an unconventional manner, somehow naturally flowing across the unbleached cloth. She loved the way his skin creased just above his brow when his focus was fully on the task. His eyes, devoted to her, slowly studied her features, trailing from one to another like a road map, giving each part of her all his attention.

In the beginning, there was nothing about Nick that would have lured her in or made her want him.

Then, out of nowhere, there was. She did.

Badly.

Flat out wanted him.

"Be still, will you?" He chuckled.

Olivia kept making faces, trying to throw him off as he sketched her features onto the canvas.

"And if I don't want to?" she taunted him.

"I'm sure I could find a way to keep you still." He flashed a wicked grin.

Since that kiss at the museum weeks ago, their relationship had transitioned from friends to lovers. But to be lovers, they would have to do more than just kissing. Was Olivia ready to take it to the next step? She desired Nick to kiss her passionately until they were both breathless.

"Oh, really? And how are you going to do that?"

With an intense look in his eyes, Nick got up from his stool, lifted her chin and kissed her tenderly. She knew it wouldn't go any further, because Nick wasn't the kind of guy who moved faster than she was prepared to. But as of lately, all she thought about was Nick undressing her.

There was a knock at the door that wouldn't go away.

"Hold ... that thought..." Nick unwillingly pulled away.

He staggered toward the front door like he was drunk, and it made her laugh.

Olivia glanced away; her eyes brushed over the canvas leaning up against the wall. She remembered the first time Nick had brought her to his studio, how bare it was. Now the room was filled with artworks Nick had created in a short time. All beautifully rich with color, capable of stirring a magnitude of emotions. She wondered if they would ever see the light of day.

"Hey ... um, there's something I wanted to ask you."

"Okay..." Nick shot her a curious look before setting the brown box on his desk, retrieving a cutting tool from his drawer and sliding it across the top of the package.

"A while back you said you were a washed-up artist. What did you mean by that?"

"Well," he lowered his eyebrows consciously. "Isn't that self-explanatory? I used to have a career, and now I don't. Hence the washed-up part."

"But you're trying to revive it, right?"

"Well, I hope to have a showing at George's gallery next year."

"Why next year? You have all this amazing stuff. Have you shown these to George yet?"

"Hmmm, not yet. He doesn't even know I have some work completed."

She frowned. "Why not? He's been waiting for you to bring him something."

He shrugged. "I'm not ready. I don't think they're any good."

"You're messing with me, right?"

He walked back to his stool, directing his eyes to the canvas.

"You never told me why you stopped."

He shifted uncomfortably in his seat, putting his arms across his chest. "I guess for the longest time, I felt blocked."

"How come?" She frowned.

"For many reasons. I was uninspired, I guess."

"And now?" She smiled, lifting her hands to signify the canvases lining the walls. "I think it's safe to say you're over it."

He smiled back. "Maybe I have you to thank."

"Me?"

"Yeah, you had something to do with it."

"No, I don't think so." Olivia shook her head.

"Of course you did."

"I think something made you retreat. You armed yourself... that way you would never be exposed—never get hurt again. You closed yourself from feeling things, everything that's essential to create." She paused. "As much as I wish I was your reason— somehow you learned how to be vulnerable again."

He looked away. She knew there was so much more to Nick, and he was holding back something very crucial. He had told Olivia that he had lost his mother last year. She could imagine just that loss alone could have caused Nick's creativity to die, but she didn't want to bring that up unless he wanted to.

"So what should I do?"

"Get back into that ring, Montgomery. Throw these babies out there and see what happens." She walked toward him and plucked the pencil from his fingers.

"How did you get so smart?" Nick pulled her into his arms, and she wrapped her fingers around his neck.

"*Ah* ... I've always been intelligent, Montgomery." She constricts her eyes. "It's you that smartened up." She giggled when he playfully ran his fingers along her rib cage.

"Admit it, I'm a good influence on you." He nuzzled his lips against her neck.

"You? Hmm ... It's mostly my inspirational guru."

He rolled his eyes. "Mr. Universe? When I find out who this asshole is, I will pulverize him."

She laughed. "How do you know it's not a she?"

"I don't." He tugged her in for a kiss.

Olivia's phone buzzed within her purse. "I need to answer it—my dad had a doctor's appointment today, and I told my mom to call me when she got back," she murmured between kisses. His arms slipped away, and she rushed to get her phone.

"Hey, Nina." She looked up at Nick. "Uh. Yeah. I'm out with a friend," she said, hoping Nick didn't catch it.

"Yeah, no, I haven't heard from mom yet. Can I call you back?" She glanced up, catching Nick running a hand through his hair.

When she walked back to where Nick was sitting, she noticed his demeanor had changed. When he finally looked up at her, she saw the hurt in his eyes.

"How's your dad?"

"I don't know. It was my sister."

He got up abruptly, walking back to his desk. He removed the tubes of paints from the box he'd just received, placing them on the shelf behind him.

"Is something wrong?" she asked, already knowing the answer.

"What are we doing here?"

"What do you mean?"

"Have you told your sister about us?"

"I haven't told anyone about us." Olivia wanted to be honest with him.

"Are you ashamed to be with me?" Nick was avoiding her eyes.

"No, of course not," she sputtered. "Look, my family is still hung up on the whole Dario fiasco. And I'm not sure where this will go. I don't want to disappoint them any more than I already have."

"Oh, I get it ... because being with me would be a disappointment?" His words were rushed.

"No, that's not what I meant. We're getting to know each other." She shrugged. "What's the point of telling them if it doesn't work out between us?"

Nick's shoulders slumped, and his eyes reflected a mix of confusion and agitation.

"You're upset with me?"

His eyes met hers in a flash. "Fuck yeah. I don't understand how you don't know where we're going with this...when we spend every minute possible together."

"Yes, I know, and I enjoy my time with you, I do..."

"But..." He snorted a condescending laugh.

"No, there is no *but*. You're an amazing guy, honest and fun to be around. Do you know how much I appreciate that? I'm just not ready to define what we have right now."

He smirked. "No, what you're saying is that you're just not prepared to commit to anything."

"That's not true. I know what I want, it's just..."

"You're not sure it's with me? It should be easy, Olivia. You're either in this all the way, or you're not."

She crossed her arms. "You're being unfair about this, Nick. I don't understand why you're upset. Haven't I been honest with you from the start? I'm sorry, but I can't rush into things like you do."

"Right ... you just gotten out of a long term relationship. That's just an excuse. You think I don't see it? It's easy for you to put me at a distance, but what you don't realize you're making it much harder for me to get close to you. I don't know what happened to you, but when I look into those eyes I see someone who's just too scared to let anyone in. God, Olivia, you have to believe you're worthy to be loved."

"I'm not afraid..."

"Yes, you are—and always choosing to do what other people expect from you, living by these rules because if you don't, you're afraid of making people around you unhappy. You're not responsible for their happiness. You're responsible for yours."

"It's not as easy as that, Nick. My family is going through a terrible time. I can't just drop this on them."

"It's just more excuses you're hiding behind." He continued placing his art supplies on the shelf above.

"They're not excuses. It's the truth. You can't always think about yourself. Maybe if you had parents, you would understand."

She felt terrible, but it just came out of her mouth before she could take it back.

He stopped midair, pushing the box aside.

"I'm sorry. I shouldn't have said that..." She looked down at the floor.

Nick walked closer, but not near enough to touch her. "So maybe I didn't have such a great start in life. Maybe I'll never give you the life that Dario or your father can give, but you can be damn sure what I can offer is more than any man will ever provide ... all my heart and soul." He placed a hand on his chest so forcefully, a last resort to make her understand. "And I'm a fucking fool to believe I might be enough for you."

"You are enough." Olivia's eyes went soft.

"Then why do I feel like I'm not? You're still not sure about us ... and I can't just wait around for you to figure it out. I know what I want ... If this is not for you, then just be straight."

What she felt for Nick was indescribable and overwhelming, because once she whispered those three little words, there would be nowhere to hide. Her heart couldn't take another wreck. How could she be sure Nick could be trusted? What could she say to him to make him understand that she couldn't make the leap, not just yet?

"I don't want to lose you."

Unsatisfied with her answer, he walked back to his chair, pulling on his jacket. "All I've wanted was to be more than some-body to you ... more than just a friend. Not someone to fill your days when you have nothing better to do," he said, his expression mournfully relaxed.

"Where are you going?"

"I need air."

"Stay ... Can we just talk more about this? I don't know what you want me to say." She extended her arms to the side.

"You just said it." He studied her face, but not like before. His stare didn't make her feel like the eighth wonder of the world, but rather the biggest jerk on the planet.

"You've made up your mind. I ... I would like it if you're not here when I get back."

There was a lump that formed in her throat, preventing her from talking. She had promised herself after Dario that no other man would ever see her cry, so she held on to that lump until Nick disappeared through the door, leaving her alone.

Had they just broken up?

JUNE

Dear girl with the red scarf,

In life, there will always be an obstacle to overcome. Some question that needs an answer, a fire that needs smothering, a mountain to climb... well, you get the gist. That's life, I guess. But along the way, we forget that life is more than struggles and challenges. Sometimes we forget the rhythm of our hearts. Listen to it. It won't misguide you.

Trust me, after all,
I am Mr.universe ☺

24

THE RAIN YOU CAN'T CONTROL

THERE IS SOMETHING TO BE SAID ABOUT THE LIGHT, HOW IT CAN SEEP *through the smallest cracks. Even when you believe it's not possible, the tiniest of lights can brighten the sourest of souls. When it's gone, the lack of its presence is so visible you wonder where it could have gone, or how you were able to let it slip away, Mr. Universe wrote.*

Olivia sat in the dark, haggard in her chair with a cup of coffee at hand, her eyes fixed on the morning light filtering through the drapes. The light made her think of Nick. Then again, everything reminded her of him.

"*The most important things you need to know about art are the light, shadow, and value. It's what gives the composition depth and movement," he'd told her one afternoon, while a hauntingly beautiful Peruvian folk tune played on the radio. He looked directly at her. Under his gaze was where she desired to thrive forever. Olivia felt something stir within; there was something more going on than she liked to admit. She was aware of the way he moved his body, the way his heather-gray T-shirt fit in all the right places. How his expressive eyes wandered all over her when he thought she wasn't looking. She'd never felt so alive than she had sitting across from him in his white studio, under the natural light.*

"Are you even listening?"

She liked it when he was serious; how she missed the lines that formed just above his eyebrows.

"Light and shadow—got it." Olivia smiled shyly. If Nick only knew she had this desire to eliminate the space between them, to let the barriers fall. The unsettling way she wanted him surprised herself.

But Olivia had never considered herself forward. She was never the kind of girl who went for it, but with Nick she wanted to change all that.

"What's the matter with you?"

"What?" She coolly diverted her eyes elsewhere.

He studied her for a moment before mixing the paint. "I don't know ... You seem distracted."

"No." Her voice went up a notch.

He brushed his hair out of his eyes. "Is there something you wanted to say to me?" Nick Montgomery had a way of seeing right through her when others simply saw around her.

"I ... I was wondering ... when can I start to paint?"

He smiled, but she detected a hint of disappointment. "Patience, little grasshopper."

He placed his hand under the natural light coming through the window above them.

"Now pay attention. Before you begin any work, you need to know the basics. You need to understand light, or lack thereof. See where the light hits my hand?" His soulful eyes found hers. "The closer to the light, my skin is lighter, and farther away my skin is darker."

Olivia was an illustrator but had never painted before. Watching Nick, she suddenly had the urge to do so. Luckily, she had a reluctant teacher to show her. She didn't know what it was at that moment that she found so endearing. Maybe she saw something in him that she recognized in herself. That gleam of joy, of finally having a connection with another human being, having someone with which to share what you passionately loved. It made her wonder if Nick had been lonely, too.

He had made a space for her in every part of his life, even in his studio. He had prepared a corner with a new easel and paint brushes, including her very own set of keys. He had once explained that painting for him was very therapeutic; that was when he was at complete peace within himself. She wondered what he would say if he knew she'd sparked that pack of cigarettes she carried with her and smoked each of them on the last day she'd seen him. That was a total mistake; she'd felt awful after that, but not as awful as losing Nick.

It was difficult to forget a man like Nick, especially when he was always there when she needed him. Olivia had once told him that she was so scared for her father, and she remembered how he had held her quietly before whispering, "I know, my love." Simple words, but it was comforting to have someone to understand and be there when life regularly caused her to fall.

He did everything to prove himself, gave her every reason to trust him. When she didn't get the designing position, Nick was the first to show up at her front door with a container of Häagen-Dazs. He had built her up, given her a shoulder to cry on, and yet she kept a safe distance from him. It was a shame her heart got startled so easily.

She marveled at the way Nick Montgomery had come into her life, so close with ease. He had come through the holes, turning everything cold and bleak into something bright and beautiful. She had never thought it would be possible: the boy who grew up in Griffin town and wore a lame T-shirt and Converse high-tops in the snow; who worked at a bar at night so he could paint during the day; who got excited about light and darkness; who came into her life unexpectedly and quietly and was gone before she had time to recognize what exactly she felt for him.

The last time Olivia saw Nick was over a month ago when he left her in the dust, drowning in her pride. She had never thought she would miss him so profusely...but now she understood the significance of light and darkness. Nick Montgomery had shone his light her way. Without him she was living in the absence of light.

Olivia got up to open the drapes and watched the people come and go, cars driving by, but it was a gray truck that caught her eye. A smile crossed her face. Nick was parked outside her apartment. At first she watched him fiddle with something in his truck bed. With one swift movement, he pulled out a red bicycle.

"What is he up to?" she whispered to herself.

She quickly pulled on a sweater from her closet, slid on her shoes, and took a quick glance in the mirror before going. When she got down to the street level, she found Nick standing by his truck, surprised to see her outside of the building.

"Hey," he said, as if nothing had passed between them, closing the door of his truck.

"What are you doing here, Nick?" She swaddled her sweater tightly around her and stepped onto the sidewalk where he stood, balancing a bike in each hand.

He stared across the street, then quickly turned back to meet her eyes. "I was going to tell you I was across the street running some errands, but as you can see there isn't a strip joint in sight." He flashed her a teasing smile. She rolled her eyes. Nick looked her over. "I missed you," he said, matter-of-factly.

Olivia was bothered by her heart's betrayal, allowing his words to affect her in some way. She could have declared that she had missed him, too, but decided to stay silent, letting him squirm a bit longer. After all, it was Nick who had walked out on her, refused to take her calls or see her. She was still very much hurt and angry with him.

"I hope I didn't catch you at a bad time?"

"No, I was packing."

"Still?"

"Yeah, well, you know I come with a lot of baggage." Olivia moved to allow the pedestrians through, but when she stepped forward, she almost tripped over herself, and Nick's hand steadied her. She was too close for comfort, close enough to see his expression twinge with pain, like he wasn't sure what to do next: pull her in or walk away. Either way, her feelings were battered, so she decided for them both and took a step back, creating a decent space between them.

"So I guess you finally sold the apartment?"

"No, but I got another reasonable offer."

"Have you accepted?"

"I would have, but Dario is purposely holding out."

"You mean purposely holding on to you?"

She shrugged coolly, knowing he was right.

"I wanted to call you many times. I'm sorry I was such an ass..."

"Oh, you were more than an asshole, Montgomery, you were a pompous prick."

"I guess I earned that."

She shrugged and brushed the hair from her face. "What's this?" Her eyes fell on the bike, particularly on the gold-colored one.

"Call it a peace offering. It's not new, but it does the job. I cleaned it up, gave it a new coat of paint, and greased up the chains. She's all yours and ready to go," he said as his eyes met hers.

"You did this for me?"

He cleared his throat. "You once told me about your bike. I know how bummed out you were about losing it. I can't get that one back, so I got you this one instead."

"But that was so long ago." She smiled.

There was an overwhelming warm spot near her heart. Over the years, during her time with Dario, he had surprised her with beautiful expensive gifts, but nothing had ever moved her like this. Because it was more than just a piece of metal, more than a romantic gesture. Nick had taken his time to listen, to figure her out.

She examined the bike and climbed onto the seat. "Thank you. That's the nicest thing anyone has ever done for me." Olivia was deeply touched, and he smiled.

"Like I said, it's not new, and it's probably not exactly what you used to have, but I thought it might do the trick."

There was no doubt that Nick Montgomery had found his way to her heart.

Her eyes gleamed at him. "It's perfect. Where did you find it?"

"I found this darling at Notre Dame. I spotted it through a glass window, and it made me think of you."

Olivia laughed. "I'm glad an old bike reminds you of me."

"That's not the only thing that reminds me of you."

"Well, Mr. Montgomery, I should hope not." She beamed the brightest smile, her eyes fixed on him.

"Look, it even has a working bell," he said, ringing it twice. "Like I said, it's not new."

"It's perfect. I love it, thank you. I can't believe you went through the trouble. I mean, I didn't think you were listening."

He frowned. "Why wouldn't I be?"

"Because no one ever really cares what I have to say." She laughed.

"I care." He brushed another strand of hair from her eyes.

All her life Olivia had felt that nobody cared to take the time to know the real Olivia Montiano. The people Olivia surrounded herself with were only friends with her because her father was rich, and then had come Dario. He had never made her feel like she had anything valuable to say, tuning her out when she wanted to share a part of herself. Nick had come into her life and changed all that. That was the thing about Nick Montgomery: he was always listening.

"So, what do you say, Monti? Wanna test her out?" He got on

the red bike and weaved onto the road and back, creating circles around her. "Let's get lost…"

"Now?" she said, looking up at the dark clouds rolling in overhead. "But it's supposed to rain."

"What are you afraid of? It's just a bit of water." He smiled.

"But I haven't ridden a bicycle in years."

"Nobody forgets how to ride a bike, Olivia. We'll go slow."

She wondered if he meant something more.

"Come on, Monti. Let's hope you can ride a bike better than you drive a car," he said, zooming past her.

THEY HEADED toward the park of Mount Royal and rode their bikes past Beaver Lake, past the Heritage building, the Smith house, and all the way up to the summit.

"I think it's safe to say it would be better for everyone if you took your bike to work." He winked at her.

"Ha, funny." She looked at the people who had gathered around. Some were locals, and some were tourists. What she enjoyed the most was the view of downtown Montreal.

Nick waited for her to get settled on the steps of the Chalet du Mont Royal before handing her a vanilla ice cream cone.

"Wasn't that fun?"

"Yes, it was. But I don't know how I'm going to get back. My legs are so tired."

"What's the rush?"

Olivia shrugged and smiled at him.

"Is there somewhere you have to be?"

"Do you?" She acted nonchalant, not wanting to give Nick the satisfaction of knowing that she was easily available.

He smiled appreciatively. "Great, we both have nowhere to be. So there's no rush."

He glanced down and frowned.

"You better start working on that ice cream before it drips."

Olivia licked her ice cream, making more of a mess of herself. She laughed, and Nick handed her more napkins to help her clean off her sweater.

"You know what else I haven't done in ages?" She looked up at Nick, who sat one step above her.

"What's that?"

"Ping-pong."

He made a funny face, like she had said something revolting.

"Come on, who doesn't like ping-pong?"

"Just to let you know, I'm silently judging you."

Olivia glanced at his gray polo shirt with the happy faces scattered all over it. "Don't you dare be judging me, Montgomery. Where did you find this lame top?" She playfully ran her hand across his chest, feeling him stiffen under her touch. His smile slowly faded, and out of nowhere, there was a particular affliction overshadowing his face. "Don't worry, Montgomery, my hands are clean." She put her hand up to show him.

"No, it's not that." His voice had become heavier. "There something I've wanted to tell you." Something in his tone caused her some concern. Then she thought that maybe he didn't want things to go back to the way they were. Maybe he'd realized during their time apart that he'd rather be just friends. Or worse … there was someone else. She was afraid of what he was about to say. Whatever it was, it wasn't good. She could feel the presence of it, this thick air hovering above them. Olivia didn't know if it was the ice cream or this familiar feeling of complete disappointment, because the tugging in her stomach began to grow.

Aware of his stare, she glanced up to find his eyes on her, and for a moment Olivia wished he would kiss her and make this awful feeling go away. She wasn't ready to lose Nick again.

Then it started to rain.

Actually, it poured.

Dear girl with the red scarf,

Have you ever seen a shooting star?
They are small chunks of rocks that
collide with the earth's atmosphere. These
rocks are sucked in by the earth's
gravitation pull. They heat up and glow
as they race through the air, and then
it burn out. Well, it's a lot like love. We
don't know how long it will last. God knows
it sure will make a beautiful spectacle
while it last.

Trust me, after all, ☺
I am Mr.universe.

25

SHINE YOUR LIGHT
MY WAY

NICK OPENED THE DOOR TO HIS STUDIO, AND THEY BOTH FUMBLED in, laughing, soaking wet from the rain.

"Didn't I call it?" Olivia beamed at him as she took the elastic out of her hair, allowing the damp strands to fall around her shoulders.

He stood there watching for a moment, not able to move. Even with her mascara running down her face and her hair beginning to frizz, she was still by far the most beautiful creature he'd laid ever eyes on. It was quite simple, wasn't it? This great affection he had for Olivia was so overwhelming that he had chosen to walk away instead of being brutally honest with himself.

He was in love with her.

She was magic, a direct light—the kind that seeped through in places that didn't exist inside him anymore. The light he had thought he'd lost forever. But Nick realized that we don't lose the light, we absorb it; and with Olivia he wanted to absorb every small speck of it. Nick didn't know how he had done it, to stay away for so long; he'd tried to keep busy within the walls of his studio, putting her out of his thoughts, but she wasn't easy to dismiss.

Not a girl like Olivia.

Nick knew now: he had overreacted, and maybe he should have handled it differently, but his actions reflected his fear. After Chloe left, he had never wanted to give anyone the power to ruin him, but now he had. Nick had opened the door, allowing Olivia to come in within the margins of his life. The thing was, she meant more to him than he could have ever imagined, all he could have hoped for. So when she couldn't be honest about what he meant to her, it seemed the music had stopped, and his heart had instantly ceased to exist. Olivia wasn't on the same page; maybe she never would be; so it was much easier to break it off than to be broken. Either way, he was mangled by his own demise.

A vicious circle indeed.

*

"You look like shit," *Dan said when Nick walked into the bar.*

"Trust me, I feel better than I look."

His brother peered at him suspiciously. "I take it you haven't patched things up?"

"Nope." Nick settled on the stool in front of him. "We're not together."

"Wanna talk?"

"Nope."

"Look, Olivia came by earlier, hoping to find you here." Dan pulled something from his pocket. "She left you these." He slid the keys across the counter.

"She was here ... looking for me?"

"No, knucklehead. She was here looking for the Pope." Dan's eyes

softened. "Look, it's clear she cares about you. Why don't you try to work things out?"

"What did she say? No wait—forget it, I don't want to know. I'm not going to wait around for her to decide what she wants."

"But I don't understand. You knew she wanted to take things slow?"

"Yeah?"

"So, what exactly are you mad about?"

"Hey, weren't you the one who told me to stop playing patty-cake?"

"And you said I give bad advice." Dan arched his brows.

When Nick remained silent, Dan asked again, "So what's got your fuckin' underwear in a bunch?"

"Why does it have to be so hard? I just want her in my life." Nick looked down at his hands. "I was delusional...she's still tied up with her ex, and hides behind all these fuckin' excuses. I thought this could work. I really did."

"The way I see it, you're the one hiding behind excuses," Dan said, and only continued when Nick met his eyes. "Look, I know Chloe did a number on you, I get it, but you haven't been completely honest. If anyone should be upset—it should be Olivia."

"What?"

"Well, have you guys talked about the thirty-five pills?"

Nick felt the blood drain from his face. "Did you tell her about it?"

"No, Nick. I'll leave that up to you. She really cares about you. At least give her a chance to explain herself."

Nick sat quietly.

"You know I'm terrible with this sappy shit, and it's not like we ever learned it by example. I don't know about you, but I'm fed up with living like you always have to be one step ahead of everyone else ... leave them before they leave you." Dan's eyes half-squinted.

His brother was right. This entire time, Nick had been feeding into his vulnerability, and Olivia deserved better than that. He had been hiding his condition from her, not purposely at first. She was never around when he took his medication, and he didn't look sick, so it was *easy to pretend everything was normal, because, for once in a very long time, with Olivia, he felt like a normal human being.*

"Don't be an ass, Nick. Not everything works at your pace." Dan looked down at his receipts and bank statements lying in front of him on the counter, shuffling them back and forth. "Hey, I'm curious about something, though," he said, without looking up.

"What's that?"

"Are you gasping for air?"

Nick gave him a perplexed look. "What are you talking about?"

"I imagine it would be hard, with your head up your ass." Dan gave him the biggest dumb smile.

Later, one morning, Nick found himself walking down the street. Something caught his eyes in a window display that reminded him about a bicycle Olivia had once had. The thought of her smile brought him back to that moment, how her face lit up when she spoke about it. He wondered if he could recreate it, somehow making her glow like that again. Olivia was used to getting expensive gifts when her ex-boyfriend had been terrible, but Nick's intentions weren't the same. Nick wasn't a manipulator. He wanted to make her happy and would do anything to get her back. That was the thing, when someone was bound to a higher emotion. Love magnetized. He knew what he had for Olivia was real; it kept pulling him back.

It was exceptional if it went both ways.

*

"Why are you looking at me like that?" Olivia blushed.

"You don't want me to look at you?" Nick placed his keys on his desk.

"No, I do, just not in this condition." She looked down at herself. "I'm a mess."

"Not to me."

She looked away, self-conscious, turning her attention to the canvases around the room. "So, are you going to show me the reason you brought me here?" Olivia's eyes grew darker.

Nick tried to swallow the knot in his throat.

What was the reason?

It took everything in him not to watch as she removed her soaked sweater, placing it on the back of a chair. He was conscious of how her damp cotton tee clung to every curve. Rubbing the side of his face, he inhaled one slow breath, taking in her fragrance and awakening everything inside of him.

He knew they weren't going to pick up where they'd left off. If Olivia wanted him, she would have to say it. She would have to make the first move.

Right ... the reason suddenly came to him. Nick motioned for her to follow to the other side of the room.

"So, what do you think?" Nick showed her a large canvas lying on his worktable.

"Very organic. Is it a flower?" She turned her eyes up.

"Yeah, I guess it came out looking that way," he said, bashfully.

He had never realized the softer side of himself, because his past work had always been edgy. There was no way to describe how Nick processed his work. It came from within; it was seeing things and feeling them, bringing them to life with one brush-stroke at a time.

"I like that you use the dark blue at the top, and how it fades gradually at the bottom. Using magenta streaming through the empty spaces ... beautifully done," she said, as he watched her.

"Am I saying something wrong?" She smiled.

He loved it when she took an interest in his work. He folded his arms across his chest, mustering all his strength to keep from placing his hands in her hair, on her waist—pulling her closer.

"There's no wrong way to analyze art. It's meant to inspire without understanding, almost like classical music." He exhaled through his nose. "And, well ... I guess I was thinking of you, when I was working on it." He pointed back to the canvas.

"Am I your muse, Montgomery?" she taunted.

She had no fuckin' idea. "All the time."

He brought his arms around her waist, holding her there, and for a moment he thought he might kiss her, and would have if she didn't pull away so abruptly. Nick deserved it. He had caused her pain by shutting her out.

"I have to go," she said, walking back toward the chair to gather her things.

"What? I thought you said you didn't have plans."

"No, you told me you had nowhere to be. I, on the other hand, said nothing."

There was an elephant in the room he desired to destroy. He needed to tell her, and if she left, he would never find the courage again.

"Roshambo." He smiled. "I win, you stay with me a little longer."

Her lips twitched to one side. "Okay."

"Roshambo," they said in unison.

He smiled more brightly.

"Okay I'll stay ... for a little while longer."

He watched as she looked through his collage of sketches posted on the wall above his desk, ideas he had for his next project. This was not the first time Olivia had hung around in his studio, but lately he realized she had become more comfortable, making herself more at home. This satisfied him, because art was a big part of his life, and he spent a significant amount of time in these four walls. If she couldn't accept that, then there was no way of it going further.

"What's this?" She detached the lined paper from his board, bringing it closer.

He realized what it was. "Nothing, it's just my bucket list. It's dumb." He tried to take it out of her hands, but she pulled away.

"It's not stupid."

"Olivia, c'mon, hand it over."

"No."

When Nick finally gave up, she settled on the edge of his desk and read it out loud.

"*Walk through Japan's tunnel of lights. Open my art gallery ...* That's something you should do." She gave him a sideways glance. "*Help a stranger for no personal benefit.*"

She glanced up at him.

"You should probably cross that out. *See the Northern Lights. Live in another country for one year. Volunteer at a charity. Go on a spiritual holiday. Say yes to everything for a whole day.*

"Hmm..." A smile appeared on her face. "You'll give me a heads-up when you do?"

Nick glanced at her with curiosity. "What was it you wanted me to say yes to?" Nick asked as he peeled off a layer, removing his polo shirt, revealing a half-damp cotton tee underneath.

Her smile slightly faded "I—I'm sure—I could think of something." She swallowed. "Whatever it is, I'm sure I'll agree to it." Nick used his happy face polo to dry his hair and face.

She gave it a thought, fanning herself with the paper. "It's hot in here, isn't it? Maybe we should open a window." She glanced back down at the paper.

"*Olivia...*" Her eyes slowly veered from the list and smiled at him.

Nick could feel the blood rushing to his ears, making him feel like a bashful schoolboy.

She tilted her head to the side, grinning. "Wow, I never saw you blush before." He playfully tried to grab her, but she was too fast for him.

"I don't blush." He cast his eyes away from her.

"So, is this Olivia on your list ... me?" she taunted, still holding the note in her hand, slowly walking around the room as Nick followed in pursuit.

"Who else would it be?"

"Well, one can never be sure."

"Nope, you're my one and only."

Her smile told Nick that she was pleased. "Well, at least I should be flattered that I am the only girl on that bucket list," she said. "Or I think I am..." Olivia looked back at the paper.

"Give me that."

Nick shook his head, pinning his list back on the board.

"So what's this about?" She leaned on the edge of his desk.

She wasn't going to let it go, because Nick knew Olivia Montiano was a very persuasive girl. He had added her name to the bucket list long ago, after he had seen saw her at the café. They had crossed paths, but she would never look at him and always found a way to avoid eye contact. Olivia was damn good at it. It was around the time he found her standing at the corner of Chabanel when she'd finally looked up at him. Her eyes were so captivating, disclosing some notion that this was where his heart should stay. It was something he had never experienced before, and it sent chills right through him. He knew the moment he walked away from Olivia that it would be impossible to shake the feeling of her.

"You should know better than to ask that question, especially if you're not ready to hear the answer."

"What's that supposed to mean?" Her eyes slowly expanded, and he could see the lightbulb going off. "Do you think I'm some conquest?" she asked, raising her eyebrows.

"No." He laughed bashfully.

"Was I supposed to be another notch on your belt?" she said, smiling.

"No, it wasn't meant like that." He cleared his throat. "I wanted to get to know you, that's all."

"So why haven't you crossed off my name?"

He turned to look at her. "Olivia, you're not some conquest or another notch on my belt. If I crossed your name off my list, it would mean I was done, and I'm not done with you. I don't think I will ever be. You've changed the rhythm of my heart, and it saddens me that you still don't understand that."

Olivia was something he wanted to continue for a lifetime, even if it was a short one. He pinned back his sketches that had come loose on his board.

"What is it that you want from me, Nick?" she asked in a half-whisper, sending heat all the way to his nerve endings.

"Everything."

"That's a lot to ask from one person."

"I guess it is. But I'm prepared to give you my everything. My heart, my soul, my life...days, nights. I lay it all down for you to take." His voice was almost a whisper, barely making a sound. "Take it, because you have no fuckin' idea what you're doing to me."

She took a quick step, closing the space between them, placing her hands on the back of his neck and through his hair. It took him a slight second to respond, unsure of what was happening. Nick was conscious of her warm body on his, her lips possessively devouring and yearning for more. Then, instinctively, his arms went around her waist, hands moving wherever they wanted to go, effortlessly and without control.

His lips caught up quickly, like there was energy rising in him, reviving his heart, breathing air into his lungs, and all of a sudden, he was alive again. He wanted more of her, to completely lose himself in her hands and her body, but he knew he couldn't allow it to go any further, not until she knew the truth about him.

"Olivia," he murmured against her mouth. "Olivia, wait ... there's something I need to tell you."

"What? Is there someone else?"

"No." He smiled at the absurdity. No one could ever take her spot.

He pulled a chair from under his desk and motioned for her to sit down. "I need to explain something to you." He rubbed his eyes before continuing, knowing once the words came out of his mouth that things would change for them.

"I was severely sick a few years back...I got a viral infection that caused heart failure. I've been living with a new heart for three years."

She opened her mouth in wonder. "I don't understand..."

He grabbed his T-shirt at the back of the neck and yanked it over his head, revealing his scar. He didn't do it to get pity from her, but compassion. Nick wanted her to understand the seriousness of his situation and what it would mean if she chose to stay with him. A heart transplant was not a cure but a lifesaving treatment. Every day he lived with uncertainty; his future always at the risk of dramatic change, fear of a setback always looming in the distance. Another infection or rejection could put him back in a hospital bed.

This was his reality, but it didn't have to be hers.

She got up and walked closer, his eyes never leaving her face. Her fingers traced the light pink scar that ran down the midpoint of his chest, and she glanced up, meeting his gaze. He saw the question in her eyes.

"Why didn't you tell me? I mean, this is usually the stuff you tell somebody you're supposed to care about."

"I know. I was wrong, but I wasn't trying to keep it from you, not in the beginning. It's just the further we got involved, the harder it got to tell you. I was so scared of losing you."

"Scared?" Her eyes were bright. "But I'm not Chloe."

"I know. I know you're not." He regretted not seeing it sooner, not believing in them. He looked back down at her, drowning in her silence. "Say something, please," he begged, barely getting the words out.

Olivia looked at him for a moment before saying, "Well, it's just ... I never wanted anything bad to happen to you, and it hurts me, because it already did."

He leaned his head in to touch hers. "I hope you find a way to forgive me, because I need you in my life," he said, his feelings out of control.

"I'm not going anywhere, Nick."

Somehow, he already knew that.

She leaned in and kissed him, but not like the other times. Nick felt something different and, as the heat rose in him, he felt her hands go to his waistband and unzip.

"What are you doing?" Nick said, hoarsely.

"I'm undressing you." The corner of her lip went up and her eyes filled with heat.

"Here, now?"

"I wanted you to help me cross a wish off my bucket list. Something I wanted to do from the first time you brought me in here."

"And what was that?" Nick grinned.

"I wanted you to take me, on that table." She nodded in the direction across the room.

"I think I can help you with that. Well, then let's get to work."

Dear girl with the red scarf,

Here some rules for escaping from those who wrong you.

1. We should never go back to those who broke us. They were too casual handling your heart the first time, why would you give them another chance to do it all over again?

2. Remember, people don't change, unless they want to.

3. If you wish to forget someone, you have to let go of the hate. Hate has a way of leaving a big stain on your heart and will devour you.

4. Take no souvenirs, just leave it all behind. If you take it with you ... you will never escape them and give them the power, let it go. Believe me, you won't need it where you're going.

5. People don't always love you the way you hope they will, but be sure you do. Trust me, after all, ☺

I am Mr.Universe

26

A PROMISE OF
SOMEONE NEW

OLIVIA WAS WORRIED. IT WASN'T LIKE HER FATHER NOT TO SHOW UP for their lunch date. If anything had come up at the last minute, he would have called. Since he was diagnosed with Alzheimer's, there had been some noticeable progressions of the disease, like forgetting things or misplacing items. It had seemed like nothing at first, but eventually the qualities of his character she adored, that made up her father, was going to be compromised.

Olivia was so furious with herself. Why hadn't she just been more assertive with him? She should have gone against his wishes by picking him up instead of meeting him at the restaurant. She was worried that maybe he was driving around the city, confused and lost.

After several failed attempts to reach him and only getting her father's voice mail, it fueled her guilt even more. She scrolled to Dario's number on her phone, hesitating for a second before her finger landed on his name. Even though her stomach twisted just at the thought of having to speak to him, she had hope that maybe they were together.

"Hey, Dario, it's me. Sorry to bother you." Her stomach tightened.

"You're not, what's up?"

The sound of a rumbling engine made her believe he was somewhere on the road.

"Is my father with you?"

"No. Why? Is something wrong?"

"Well, we were supposed to meet for lunch, but he never showed up and I can't seem to reach him." She paused. "I'm scared. What if something happened to him?"

"Okay, let's not panic. I'm sure he's okay. He had said something about checking on things at the Sherbrook project. I'm sure he's there."

"Maybe," she said with hope.

"Where are you?"

"I'm just about to leave Rouge Tomate."

"Look, I'm nearby. Stay put. I'll come and get you."

As soon as Olivia closed her phone, she knew it was a bad idea. She had spoken without thinking. Why on earth hadn't she just told him to meet her there? It was not like she didn't have her car. But Olivia had been preoccupied, and it seemed to have clouded her judgment.

There was so much history between them that she didn't know how to act around him. Olivia got an uneasy vibe around the man she felt resentful toward. In his car she tried not to look directly into his eyes, not because she feared him, but because there were too many painful memories sewn up to those eyes. She had seen him at his worst, an innocent bystander to his quick temper, often making her feel inadequate so he could feel significant.

Now Olivia had nothing to fear. Her life belonged to her.

If only she'd realized that before.

"You are the only one who gives others the power to hurt you," Mr. Universe wrote. *"And holding on to hate only continues to provide them with the power, even after they are gone. You need to let go of the hate if you want to forget about someone."*

She wasn't sure if she was ready to let go, but she desired to put it all behind her.

"Don't worry, your father is fine. There is some logical reason he didn't show up."

"It's just not like him. You work closely together. I'm sure you've noticed changes in him, right?" She gave him a quick glance. "How was he this morning?"

"I noticed nothing unusual." Dario slightly took his eyes off the road to look at her. "Whatever you think of me, Olivia, you must know I respect your dad. He's done a lot for me, and I could never forget that. He's been the only father I've known. Yeah, sure, I've noticed a few differences here and there, a little less sharp than he used to be. It hurts me that your family have to go through this."

Dario had lost his father to an illness when he was a boy. As he once put it, the man wasn't such a good husband, let alone a father. Over their five years together, Olivia's dad had taken Dario under his wing, showing him the ropes of his company. No matter the strain on their relationship, the one Dario had with her father was solid. After they had broken up, she didn't give it much thought, that it might be hard for him not to be a part of her family anymore.

"I'm glad you called me. I want you to feel that no matter what I'm still here for you, at least as a friend."

She could feel Dario's eyes on her, but she didn't look his way.

"What is it that's so different about you?"

Maybe Olivia should have asked the same.

"I don't straighten my hair anymore." She looked out the window, deciding to keep conversation to a bare minimum.

"No, that's not it." After a short moment, he gave up. "Well, it looks beautiful."

"Was that a compliment?"

He frowned. "Yes, why?"

"Well, because it's coming from you."

He was making it hard for her to hate him. For once he was being nice to her, helping her find her dad.

"It was never easy getting compliments from you. Criticism... Well, that's another story. I should know." She finally got the courage to look him in the eye, and he shifted his eyes back to the road.

Olivia wondered if he felt remorse for all the stuff he had put her through, if he had any regret. Then again, would it have mattered?

"You're right. I'm sorry. I should have treated you better."

Olivia sat there and said nothing.

"How's work?" Dario was never one to care about other people's interests, unless they involved him.

"Good."

"Are you still seeing that guy?"

There it was, the question she had been waiting for.

"His name is Nick, and yes."

She felt a tinge of guilt that she hadn't called Nick. He definitely would not be happy about this, but her father was her primary concern right now.

"You don't have to report everything to my father, you know."

"I never say anything to James, Olivia."

"Oh, of course not!"

"Look, I only told your father that I saw...whatever his name was at *our* apartment. Only because I was worried about you."

"Worried about me, or worried about yourself?"

He positioned himself farther back in his seat. "I know I wasn't the greatest boyfriend."

She snorted a laugh.

"Let me finish." Dario downshifted to second gear. "I was horrible at it. I'm seeing someone...to help me sort my shit out."

She glanced up at him. "You mean a therapist?"

"Yeah." His hand slightly loosened the knot in his tie.

Olivia thought about the first morning, when she'd opened

her eyes to discover Dario wasn't lying beside her. At first the reality of being single had caused her chest to tighten but that had lasted three seconds. Life without Dario opened up all kinds of possibilities. It was as though the cage door had opened up and she saw life for what it could be.

Good.

Living her life on her terms.

All along it had been that simple. By subtracting that one person from her life, suddenly life took on a whole new meaning.

"I've got no excuses on how I behaved, and I'm truly sorry. You deserve better ... better than someone like me. I know it's hard to believe. I only want to see you happy."

Olivia studied him for a few short seconds, not sure if she could bring herself to believe him. Perhaps time apart had changed him. Maybe seeing a therapist helped him in some way. She'd changed, so why couldn't he?

"Well, I am happy."

"Good. Can we try to put everything behind us? Can we, at least for your dad's sake? Can we try to be nice without being at each other's throats? I mean, I remember a time when we didn't completely despise each other," Dario said.

It was hard to think of it. Dario had never known anything about her: how she loved to read books, how she loved to laugh. God, she had used to love to laugh. She loved stupid things like the sound of a small engine plane flying high across the summer sky. The silly things, the important things, everything that made Olivia, well...Olivia. He made her feel that, without him, she was nothing. Olivia had allowed him to push her into complete isolation and retreat within herself. If her fiancé, the one who claimed to love her, deemed her unworthy, then how would anyone else find her anything else?

Olivia had never realized how lonely she was until Nick came along. He had showed her that good guys did exist. He had never tried to stop her from being herself. In fact, he'd encouraged it.

He had taught her that, within love, there was freedom to flourish. She never needed to hide who she was. Nick had proven to be a man worth sticking by.

"*Maybe you need to find your tribe,*" *Nick had said once, as he folded his laundry, placing it in a neat pile, as Olivia sat on the table beside him.*

"*What?*"

"*You know, surround yourself with people who have the same interests as you.*"

"*Well, I have you.*"

"*No, I'm your main man,*" *he said with pride.* "*I don't count. You should have someone other than your family and me...other people, you can go to when you feel the need to complain about me.*" *He smiled.*

She snorted. "*I have nothing to complain about.*"

"*Not now, but you will. Trust me.*" *He grinned.* "*We don't live together yet—*"

She tilted her head to the side. "*Is this your way of getting rid of me?*"

"*Is that what you think?*" *He stopped folding his clothes and placed his hands on his hips.* "*Whatever this is inside me, this need for you...I want you all to myself, to steal every minute from you. But we both know we would get nothing done, and I know you have other dreams that don't always include me. What kind of a boyfriend would I be if I don't push you toward them?*" *He paused.* "*Getting out there, meeting people, this is how you grow, Olivia.*"

"*In case you haven't noticed, it's not like it's easy for me to come out of my shell.*"

She'd lost many friends along the way. Some had just faded into the background, or some she had pushed away because Dario didn't want her to hang around them. Jessica was the only one who had stuck around.

He went back to his pile of clothes and continued to fold.

"*Okay, where do you suggest I go about finding this tribe?*"

"*How about joining some club?*" *Nick suggested.*

She wrinkled her nose.

"Like a book club or take a cooking class." He smiled.

She shook her head at him. "Cooking class? Oh, that would benefit you."

He smiled, knowing that she was a horrible cook. "That's what you call a win-win situation."

She laughed.

"I know you're afraid of what people might think of you, and that makes it harder for you to get out there...out of your comfort zone, but other people have insecurities too." He looked her over. "What did that asshole do to you?" When she said nothing, he continued. "All right, I want you to tell me three good things about yourself."

"I don't know." She bashfully looked around, searching for an answer. "It's hard to talk about me."

"Hmmm ... all right, Monti, I'll tell you." He launched the last piece of clothing onto the pile and walked over to stand in front of her. "For one, you're intelligent...too smart, in fact." He placed her hair behind her, looking at her intently. "It makes me wonder what you're doing with a guy like myself."

Olivia reached out and playfully pulled him closer by his belt loops. "You're a goddess."

She laughed shyly, looking away so he wouldn't see her blush. "Goddess? Now that's a first..."

"I'm serious. You're beautiful in so many ways, with this huge heart that I love so deeply. It's a shame you don't see yourself through my eyes. You don't give yourself the credit that you deserve."

She played with the buttons of his shirt, feeling a big lump in her throat, promising herself not to cry.

"Believe me when I say, Olivia Montiano, what I have here in front of me is the most amazing human being I have ever had the privilege of knowing, who's worthy of all sorts of love."

In a very short time, she had had to build herself up, and Nick had shined the light on her, showing the way and making her realize what she wanted out of life. They existed in this calm space; he loved her into a better version of herself.

Wasn't this what love felt like? Love was supposed to build you up, not tear you apart. Dario had acted out of fear, and she had almost allowed it to destroy her.

She could see there was an internal struggle within Dario as he sat next to her. It was evident that she made him feel uncomfortable, and for some odd reason that amused her. Maybe it was hard for him to see her happy, or maybe it was difficult for him to see she had outgrown him and moved on.

"You're someone else. Everything is so different about you."

"People do change, Dario."

"Yeah, it seems like it." He put the car in park. "Wait right here. I'm going to see if your father is inside."

She watched him disappear through the front door, hoping her father was there.

Dear girl with the red scarf,

Beware. A wolf is always a wolf
even if he's dressed in nice threads.
People don't change as easily as you
think. If they made you cry
before, then they'll do it again. You
can't change them, but it doesn't
mean you have to accept them or
their behavior.
Trust me, after all,
I am Mr.universe ☺

27

THINGS DON'T CHANGE
UNLESS YOU DO

"Your father isn't here. He's with Paul back at the office," Dario said through the open door of his sports car.

"How do you know?"

"I just spoke to him."

Olivia was so relieved her father was safe and all right. "Did Paul say anything else?"

"No. They were in the middle of a meeting. He just forgot, I guess."

"Well, I'm glad he's with my brother. We should head back."

"Since we're here, do you want to come up and see my new place?"

She had almost forgotten that Dario had purchased one of the one hundred and eighty-five units that her father's company was developing. "Another time? I have to get back to work."

"It will only be a minute. I could use a designer's expertise on which colors to paint. You did an excellent job at our place." His eyes softened. When she hesitated, he said, "I promise to get you back in time. Scout's honor."

"All right." Why that came out of her mouth, she didn't know. There was a part of her that wanted to repay him for helping her out. She knew that there was a possibility that this might be more of a mistake than it already was.

They went up into an elevator, and the doors opened on the twentieth floor. Men were working in the hallway, so she felt at ease knowing they weren't alone.

"It's supposed to be ready for September, but you know how things go. Welcome to mi casa." He opened the door, allowing her to go in first.

"Of course, the penthouse." She shook her head.

"You know me. Go big or go home."

There wasn't much to see, except that the walls were up and the hardwood floors had already been laid down. The cabinets were installed in the kitchen, but the countertop and sink were missing.

"So, what do you think?"

"It's a big apartment. I love the natural light." Olivia marveled at the large windows that ran along the length of the main room.

"Yeah, about 2,002 square feet. It even has a patio." He opened the door, and she stepped out. There was a nice, warm breeze. To the left, the view of skyscrapers, and she could see the canal close to where they were. Right below, on a tin roof, were big, white, bold letters: LOVE ME. Dario caught her eyes, and she went back inside. He followed behind.

"Do you have samples or paint chips?"

"I do." He pulled out a small box from one of the cabinets and placed it on a worktable next to the window. "These are the colors I was looking at." He placed several paint chips on the table.

"I would go with owl gray in the living area and silver fox in the kitchen. Seeing as they flow one room to another." She handed the samples back to him.

He smiled at her, but she didn't smile back. "Thank you. You made it easy for me. The painters will be in here next week, and I...seem a little lost without you."

He lunged and kissed her, catching her off guard. She put her hands up and gently pushed him back. For a moment he looked into her eyes.

"Please don't." She placed her hand on her mouth. Maybe he hadn't changed after all. He was still plotting, like Dario always did, to get her exactly where he wanted, but this time around she knew better than to fall for his tricks.

"I'm sorry. I don't know what I was thinking."

"This was a mistake, coming here." She took her purse from the table.

"I love you." He held her arm, stopping her from going.

She glanced up at him. "I don't know what you want me to say."

"You can say you love me too?"

"But then that would be a lie."

He looked down. "I will never get you back."

She wasn't sure exactly what he felt remorse for, and at this point she really didn't care.

"Look, Olivia..."

Olivia extended her hand to stop him from continuing. "Dario, I've moved on." She paused. "You still work for my father, and I'm seeing someone. What just happened can never happen again. Do you understand?"

He nodded. "You hate me."

She remained silent. Olivia wasn't the same girl he had dated. No, this girl could see past the blinders. He was looking for pity, bringing the spotlight once again on himself. If Olivia hated him, then she had to justify she still felt something for him ... even if it was only hate.

"The thing is, Dario, you wanted me the way you wanted me. What I needed never mattered to you."

He looked back at her like the light had just hit him. "It's him, isn't it? That's what changed. He's the one making you happy? That's why you're so different."

He had it wrong, and for once she had it right. Olivia had placed herself first, and that was what had changed about her.

"You're in love with him and not with me."

"Dario, trust me when I say, I sincerely hope you will find someone who will make you happy."

There was no bad karma wished upon him; she just didn't care one way or the other.

"How about if I don't want someone else?"

"You're not in love with me. I don't think you ever were. You always want what you can't have."

"Maybe..."

"Look, Dario, it took us five years to realize that we don't make sense together."

"I guess there is nothing I can say or do to convince you that I'm not a monster."

"You're not a monster, Dario, but I do think that you've been hurting. I'm glad you've realized you need help."

"Where do we go from here?"

"For starters, we need to sell that apartment, so sign those papers the next offer we get. You owe it to both of us to move on. It's time to let go."

He looked at her. "All right, I will."

"Promise me something else."

"What?"

"That you'll treat the next girl better than you did me."

Dear girl with the red scarf,

Sometimes I like to throw things into the universe and see what happens. You's be surprised what you get back when you do. Somehow, if we just take even the tiniest chance, we get back so much more than we could ever imagine. Go on, throw the chips in the air, and let them fall where they may. Isn't life all about taking chances?
Trust me, after all,
I am Mr.universe

28

HOUSE BUILT OUT OF STONE

NICK DROVE UP THE SECLUDED GRAVEL ROAD THAT LED TO HIS grandmother's home. This stone house had been in the family for two generations, sat on three acres, and was surrounded by trees. Located in the Victorian village of Knowlton, it was an hour drive from the city. The original part of the house dated back to 1859, but an addition had been added twenty years ago when his grandfather was alive. After his father had left, his family moved around often. There was no stability or place he felt any connection to. This house was the only thing that was consistent in his life, a sense of home. It was where he had spent most of his childhood summers and where he took refuge during a time in his youth when he couldn't see past his reflection in the broken glass.

It was here that he had unraveled himself, discovered his hidden talents, so this was where the artist in him was born and the self-destructive boy had come to pass.

Nick shut the engine off and glanced at Olivia, who was checking herself in the mirror.

"I don't know why I'm so nervous."

"Don't be. Trust me, she's going to adore you."

She cast her eyes at him, not buying it.

He smiled. "Stop worrying. She's going to see how happy you make me, and with that alone she'll love you."

When her eyes met his, she smiled.

"Ready to go?"

Nick adjusted his olive-colored fedora hat. Olivia placed her hand on her forehead to block the sun from her eyes.

"I love these Victorian homes. They have so much character." Olivia walked around the car to where Nick stood.

He straightened her washed-out jean jacket and frowned. "Aren't you going to be hot with this on today?"

"No, I'll be fine."

Nick looked down at her pink Converse sneakers and smiled. Nostalgia hit him, missing her crazy, stupid heels and sad eyes. That was where it had all begun. Now in front of him stood not a new Olivia but a whole person. He took her by the hand and led her toward the walkway.

"Nick, isn't that your brother's car?" she asked.

He jerked his gaze further down the gravel road, tossing his head back and letting out an exasperated, long breath. His brother had told him he wasn't able to come up this weekend, and secretly Nick had been relieved. He loved his brother, but sometimes Dan had no filter. Things with Olivia were fresh and delicate. He didn't want to give her any reason to overthink their relationship.

"So much for a quiet weekend," Nick murmured to himself.

She laughed. "I like Dan. He's fun to be around."

"My brother, Dan?"

"Yeah, why is that so hard to believe?"

He smiled. "Dan can be rough around the edges, but I know he means well."

She started to walk in front of him, but Nick held her back. "I wanted to show you something first before we go in."

He guided her down a path that brought them to the lake, and they stopped once they came to a wooden deck. Nick took in the view of the calm lake before settling down on the wooden planks, tugging Olivia with him, folding her within his arms.

He had come to live with his grandmother eleven years ago. Before that he had been a reckless teenager, fueling the weekends with hard drinking and drugs. It had led him to make horrible decisions, crazy and dangerous choices. It was all self-indulgent. He had never once thought of the consequences or how it would affect the people he loved. If it wasn't for his family, which never gave up on him, he wouldn't have found himself in the present. In his life there had been many dark moments.

But now he lived in the light.

He glanced down at Olivia, who was staring out on the lake. If time should stop, this was where he wanted it to, with Olivia in his arms. His life had been a brighter place since Olivia Montiano had crossed his path. Because he had finally found someone who understood him and accepted him the way he was.

"My mom brought us here every summer," he said softly. "Even after my dad left. I guess she wanted us to feel that things could still be normal, that we hadn't lost everything." He looked across the lake. "See that tree over there? My dad installed this big tractor tire that we used to swing from and fall into the water."

"It's so quiet. I could sit here all day." She leaned further into him. He watched the water floating by, and it gave the sensation he was floating down with it too. That was what it was like to be loved by Olivia: a smooth current of serenity.

"Doesn't sound like a bad idea." He kissed the top of her head.

"What are you thinking about?" Oliva asked after a silent moment.

"How much I miss my mom," he said, staring at the lake. "I keep thinking she's going to come through those screen doors. I can still hear her voice calling out to us, like when Dan and I were boys." Nick looked back at the stone house.

"What was she like?" Olivia asked.

"Strong, pretty, a lot like you."

She removed herself from his arms to look up at him.

"It's unreal to think she was once here on this very deck, and now she's not. No longer existing. I can't help but wonder how that's possible. How someone you love so much can be taken away from you, leaving you to live with a big hole in your world."

Nick looked down at his hands, because if he looked at her, his eyes would fill with tears. He knew what was ahead for her, the pain she'd have to deal with. In her case it would be slow and heartbreaking. One day she would lose her father. It was a pain he wished he could bear for her, but Nick knew too well when it came to loss that everyone had their own cross to bear.

"I wonder sometimes—am I still considered a son of someone who's no longer here? I don't know, it's fuckin' hard to wrap your mind around it."

"Nick, you have to remember her presence is still here, around you. She lives in your heart and your memories. You will always belong to her, and she to you. And that's how you have to take it. Thinking otherwise would be too depressing. I'll never get the privilege to know what she was like, but I know what it's like to love you, and I believe she loved you too much to see you live like that."

She brushed his hair away from his eyes, under the brim of his hat.

"I wish you could have met her."

"I did. I see her in your eyes."

He gave her a quick smile. Just when he thought he had nothing left to give, nothing to offer, it was her heart that helped him grow, awaking his soul. And just like that, there seemed to be enough in him, enough for the both of them. He reached over for her.

"Get a room, you lovebirds!" a deep voice yelled from behind them.

Nick groaned. "So much for that," he murmured between kisses.

Nick stood up and held out his hand to her. He looked up the hill to see his brother, Dan, making his way toward them.

"Remind me next time not to tell Dan where we go."

Nana, a short woman with whitish-blond hair, greeted them at the back porch. She was dressed in a nautical shift dress. It was hard to believe that someone who looked so prim and proper had often done cocaine at parties in her early twenties. It had been the late sixties and something she had only disclosed to Nick. Perhaps he had gotten his wild streak from her. There was an old adage, *"You are who you are,"* but his grandmother was proof that some people did change. His nana had once told him, *"For people like you and me, it seems empathy came later. When you finally realize that every decision you make has an impact on others around you, it is with empathy that you realize you can't continue the way you're living. In life, there is nothing wrong with making things as fun as you can, but do it without hurting anyone else along the way."*

"I'm so happy to see you, love," she said as she flung her arms around Nick and hugged him tightly.

"Nana, this is Olivia."

She reached out for Olivia. "It's such a pleasure to meet you, finally! Nicky always talks about you." She pulled Olivia into her arms for an embrace, then turned back to Nick. "Nicky, she's lovelier than I imagined," she said, as if Olivia wasn't in the room.

"You have a beautiful home, Mrs. Montgomery," Olivia said.

"Please, call me Nana. They all do around here." She smiled.

With a full heart, Nick wrapped his arm around Olivia's shoulder from behind and kissed her temple.

"I'll help Dan outside with the barbecue before he makes a mess of things."

"Yes, love, please help your brother. It will give us a chance to get to know one another."

"Hmm, maybe I should stay..."

"Go!" She waved her hands at him.

He looked over at Olivia. Only when she smiled confidently did he go out the back door.

Dear girl with the red scarf,

Love was never meant to be
conquered. You have to surrender
to it.

Trust me, after all,
I am Mr.universe ☺

29

INFINITY

Inside, the interior décor was a mix of country and retro; the place felt very much lived and loved. The kitchen was filled with all sorts of porcelain roosters, every shape and color. Calling Mrs. Montgomery a collector would be an understatement.

"So, Nick tells me you're a designer?" Mrs. Montgomery asked from across the kitchen table.

"Not yet. I'm an assistant to the owner of the company I work for."

Olivia didn't look straight at her, but she could feel Mrs. Montgomery's eyes, studying her, making her feel like she was trying to pass a test.

"Olivia, I can't tell you how happy I am to know that Nick is painting again." She put her hands together. "It's evident that my grandson is happy with you. You've brought him some stability in his life." Her eyes sparkled, and Olivia now saw where Nick got his blue eyes from.

"Well, I'm glad we found each other." Olivia took a sip of her iced tea before looking up to meet Mrs. Montgomery's eyes. When she did, her smile slightly faded.

"I assume Nick told you about his health? You do understand the seriousness of his condition?"

Olivia sympathized with her concerns. After all, Chloe had left. Why wouldn't Olivia do the same? But Olivia wasn't Chloe. She grasped that Nick lived with uncertainty that things could go wrong at any time, but Olivia was in it for the long run. Whatever the universe brought them, she wasn't going to walk away.

Not from the man she loved.

"Yes, I'm well aware," Olivia replied.

"My poor boy has been through so much already. I just want to make sure you understand."

"Mrs. Montgomery, the last thing I would want to do is hurt Nick more than he already has been. He holds a very special place in my life, and I'm grateful to have him there."

A smile graced Mrs. Montgomery, and she raised her glass to her lips. Olivia's eyes caught a tiny tattoo on the corner of her hand.

Mrs. Montgomery looked down at her hand and giggled. "I got this long ago when only criminals got tattoos."

Olivia found it intriguing that someone who seemed so put together could have had such a colorful past. Nick had once told her that his grandmother was carefree in her youth, which Olivia could appreciate. Very few people do things in their life that they want to; the rest do what others expect. Olivia knew this all too well.

"I'm sorry. I didn't mean to stare."

"No, it's okay, I get asked about it a lot. Shocking, isn't it, for an old lady such as myself?" She laughed. "I was once young and foolish, and oh, what I put my parents through!" She shook her head. "That's what it means to be human. Our emotions drive us in all sorts of directions, and we are prone to make mistakes— just some are permanent."

She lifted her hand to show her tattoo. Now she sounded more like her Mr. Universe. Olivia was still finding his notes.

"Don't get me wrong, it's not something I regret, because experience should never be looked down upon, but appreciated. It's with experience you grow and, my dear, how I've grown." She patted Olivia's hand.

"Is it the infinity symbol?" Olivia asked.

"Yes, at the time it appealed to me because it represented something without bounds, countless, never-ending possibilities in life." Mrs. Montgomery got up and placed her empty glass in the sink.

Olivia looked across at the fireplace. Old pictures adorned the mantel. She walked over to get a better look.

"This was Nick when he was eight." Mrs. Montgomery handed Olivia the picture frame.

In the photograph Nick and his brother were playing by the lake.

"Are these Nick's parents?" Olivia said, her eyes set on the next one.

"Yes."

"They look so happy. It makes you wonder what happened."

"Well, at the beginning of every love story, we think it's going to last forever, but when things get difficult, it's hard to know where the arrow is going to land."

Olivia thought about her parents, on how her mother had spent years growing their family while her father worked long hours. It just seemed so unfair now. Her father was close to retirement. They should be spending time together; her mother shouldn't have to become her father's caretaker and watch the man she loved slowly disappear.

There were no guarantees in life, none whatsoever.

"Olivia, if you saw them together you would say they loved each other deeply. Somehow they just couldn't keep it together." She frowned, playing with her string of pearls. "I don't know how much Nick told you about his parents."

Olivia shook her head. "Not much. All I know is he hasn't spoken to his dad in years."

She nodded. "Nick never forgave his father for walking out on them."

Olivia didn't blame Nick for not wanting anything to do with his father. What kind of a man would walk away from his family, leaving two small children and a sick wife to support them on her own? It was one thing for any marriage to be over, but the manner in which it was done ... no longer wanting to be a part of his children's lives. It was heartbreaking.

"It was difficult for everyone. My son stepped out, and I stepped in. His decisions put me at such disadvantage. I love my son, and I love my grandsons."

"Yes, I imagine it would be. Why do you think he left?"

She exhaled a long breath. "When Beth, Nick's mother, was first diagnosed with cancer, it seemed to put more of a strain on their already stressful relationship. At the beginning of her treatment, he had been supportive, but then something changed."

Olivia handed her back the frame, and Mrs. Montgomery placed it back on the mantel.

"I read somewhere that some men can't cope with the fear someone they love might not survive. So they just get up and leave rather than face the pain. Greg didn't leave because he didn't love his family; he left because he couldn't cope with the fear that she wouldn't survive."

"But she did survive the first time?" Olivia asked.

"After a brief period, he wanted to come back, but Beth wouldn't have it, not allowing him to even see the boys." Mrs. Montgomery walked towards the window and watched the boys outside. "After a while Greg just couldn't live in the same city, knowing he couldn't see them. It tore him apart, so he moved away."

"Do Nick or Dan know about this?" Olivia asked.

"No, Beth didn't want them to know, and I had to respect her wishes. You understand, I didn't want her to shut me out as well, so I closed my mouth."

"But now she's gone, so why not tell them? Don't they deserve to know the truth?"

"I cannot be the one to betray her memory. How do you think they will feel knowing their mother was the reason for keeping them apart from their father?"

"But I don't understand. Doesn't Dan still keep contact with him?"

"Yes, he does, but at a minimum. Ever since Nick was hospitalized, Greg flew back and forth from Calgary to Montreal until Nick got his new heart. Dan and Greg had reconciled to some degree, but Nick refused to see him."

She paused and looked out the door, making sure Nick was still outside, before continuing.

"But there's more. Beth not only denied Greg a relationship with his sons, she also refused any financial help from him. Over the years, Greg made good money and put some aside for the boys. Even though Beth never accepted it, the money was there for them. That's how Dan has the bar and Nick has his condo."

"But I don't understand, you said..."

"The boys think they're borrowing the money from me and paying me back slowly, but it's their own money they're using."

Olivia shook her head. "Why wouldn't you tell the truth?"

"Nick wouldn't take the money if I did."

"So why are you telling me this?"

"I feel you can help me straighten this mess. See, my dear, if there is one thing you need to know about my grandson, it's that he is quite proud. When he decides to close that door, you can be sure he won't ever open it again."

Olivia looked away, trying to process this whole secret that had been shared; now there were two things she was keeping from Nick.

"I'm an old woman with a shortage of time. There is nothing more I would love than to see my son and his boys together."

"So what is it that you want me to do?"

"I think Nick would listen to you."

"Me?" Olivia shook her head. "No, Nick won't listen, not to me or anyone."

"What won't I listen to?" Nick said as he appeared in the doorway.

"Moving to Knowlton." She smiled with ease.

"Nana, as much as I love it here, you know I need to be in the city."

"I know, but it would be nice for my grandsons to be close by." She winked at Olivia.

"I'm going to get my bag from the car," Olivia said.

"Wait, I'll go and get it," Nick said.

"No, stay. You have a lot of catching up to do with your grandmother." She gave Nick a quick kiss on the cheek before heading down the hall. From the distance, she could still hear them talking.

"She's wonderful, Nick."

"Olivia is, isn't she? Someday I'm going to marry that girl. That way, every time she leaves the room, I'll know she'll come right back to me."

Dear girl with the red scarf,

People are always going to tell
you what they want to tell you,
but it's your heart you need to
listen to.

Trust me, after all,
I am Mr.Universe
☺

30

BLOW OUT THE
CANDLES

THE MUSIC OF A LIVE BAND FLOWED FROM OLIVIA'S PARENTS' backyard. What did Nick know about Italian music except for Frank Sinatra and Dean Martin?

"Was Dean Martin Italian?"

"Yes, his parents were." Olivia frowned. "But they're not Italian singers, they're American." She smiled.

He shrugged. "I like this tune." Nick pulled her into his arms and began swaying from side to side, but the song didn't sound like music that you could slow dance to. He didn't care. It was just an excuse for his hands to caress her curves. It was a good thing they were alone on the side of the house, hidden by the trees, far from anyone's eyes.

She smiled as she sang a few words to him. Nick had no idea what they meant, but it sounded sexy.

"That's pretty good." He smiled at her.

She laughed. "Yeah? Should I quit my day job?" She looked stunning in a white cotton dress. He liked it when she wore her hair in a ponytail. All the small hairs stood up as though she were charged with a current. "Are you ready to meet the rest of the gang?"

"You sure this is what you want?" he said, holding on to Olivia's hands.

She searched his eyes. If she looked carefully enough, she'd see how terrified he was of losing her. If Olivia's father didn't accept him, that would be a definite possibility.

"More than anything else. We're together, and my family is a big part of my life, but so are you. If you guys love me, then you'll find a way to get along."

"One big happy family, huh?" Nick's hands naturally went around her waist.

She kissed him before they walked into full view of everyone. He knew by the number of cars parked in front of the house and street there was going to be several people, but this was insane. He could barely get around without bumping into anyone or stopping to be introduced to some cousin of a cousin.

"An artist? That's interesting."

"Yes, I mostly paint abstract art."

"How old are you?"

"Twenty-six."

"Oh, you're a little younger than Dario."

It was going to be a long night. Where was the alcohol? Ha! Nick had given up alcohol long before he went into heart failure. Besides, it wasn't recommended, and on page six of the "Life After a Transplant" pamphlet, under the heading COMMIT TO A HEALTHY LIFESTYLE, it said: no alcohol. He was even the proud owner of a medical alert bracelet that he refused to wear because he hated when people kept asking him questions about it. The night wouldn't be half bad if he wasn't constantly being compared to Dario by people with high social standings.

"Where's the birthday boy?" Nick asked when he was reunited with Olivia.

At some point they had gotten separated in the crowd.

"My dad? That's a good question. He was just here a minute ago." She glanced around.

Nick had never told her about the time her father came to his studio. There was no point. It was one time only, and he'd never seen him again. He didn't want to cause any friction between Olivia and her father. Whatever issues they had were between Nick and James.

"Here, let me take them off your hands," Nick said as he reached for the gift boxes piled up in her arms. "Where do you want me to bring them?"

"You can place them anywhere inside."

✳

IN THE HOUSE Nick found James standing in the shadows, watching the party from the kitchen window.

"Mr. Montiano, is everything okay?"

"Nick?" James met his eyes. "It's just this confusion ... the music ... It's bothering me."

"Is there anything I can get you? Should I get Olivia?"

"No, no. I'm fine. I just need a minute."

He motioned for him to sit at the kitchen table. Nick was a bit apprehensive since their last conversation.

"Some party." Nick sat in a chair across from him.

"You think? This was my wife's idea. I'm not much for this kind of thing. I would have been happy with a plate of pasta, surrounded by my family."

He made Nick smile.

James looked out his patio door. "Sixty-six years. Where does the time go?" He shook his head.

"Sixty-six? You don't look a day over twenty-five." Nick smiled.

James waved his hand in the air. "A young twenty-two." He smiled back at Nick.

For a moment it seemed the awkwardness had disappeared.

"I met my wife, Lorena, in 1967 when I was nineteen. I was sitting in my car, waiting for my mother to finish work, when I saw her come from around the corner...What a vision! She left me breathless. I don't know what it was, but at that precise moment I thought to myself, 'I need that girl in my life.'" He smiled and looked at Nick. "Well, needless to say I got the girl and the kids came much later. It was devastating for Lorena when we first learned we weren't able to have children. I was thirty-six when we had Nina. Paul and Olivia came later. I guess the doctors were wrong."

James removed his glasses and carefully folded them.

"We have been married for forty-four years. There were some ups and downs, but through it all we managed to stay together. See, it lasted this long because I believe we were cut from the same cloth. Same beliefs, same heritage, same values." He paused to look at Nick, who remained quiet in his chair. "I suppose you think this has nothing to do with you, but it all has to do with you and Olivia. Everything is so easy for you young ones. Everyone thinks it's forever until things get tough. See, love can only get you so far. There are other things to sustain a relationship: trust, security, safety, and dependability. If you don't start with that, then what are you going to end up with?" He paused. "What I'm trying to say is that your relationship is built on shaky ground. You two are very different on so many levels. On top of that, you have your issues with your health. What kind of future do you have together?"

"Well, sir—" he cleared his throat—"I know you have some concerns about my health, but I assure you—"

"What can you assure me? It's not your health I'm worried about. My fear is that my daughter will be tied to you." He pointed at him. "What will happen if you get severely sick? How will you support yourselves financially? Olivia is used to a particular lifestyle. What kind of life would that be for her?"

Nick didn't need James Montgomery to remind him. The fear

of a relapse always overshadowed his future, and he loved her too much to put her through something like that.

"I'm running out of time, son. I need to know she will be taken care of. I'm not sure you're the right person."

"And you think Dario is?" Nick snapped his eyes up.

"No. I have come to realize that Dario might not be the person I thought him to be."

James calmly played with his glasses between his fingers. "At some point you have to understand where I'm coming from. I've loved Olivia since the day she was born. I'll love her every minute, up to the very last breath I will take. I can tell you you'll never experience that kind of love until you have children. And I can only hope she meets a man who is worthy of her. Someone who will love her and respect her and will take care of her like I do. And you must know, I leave great shoes to fill." He narrowed his eyes at him. "Do you think you are capable of filling my shoes, Mr. Montgomery?" he asked.

"No, sir ... I mean, I don't believe that any man is capable. But I love your daughter, sir."

His eyes softened. "Maybe so, or maybe it's just an infatuation," he murmured. "Love is more than something you feel, son. Loving someone means putting someone above your needs, and it also means letting go when needed." James leaned in closer.

Nick got that James Montiano might never accept him, but in the long run, did it even matter? He felt ashamed that the thought came to mind. But he wasn't a bad person. He did deserve Olivia. He wasn't going to walk away from the woman he loved, and James Montiano needed to accept that. Nick got up slowly from his chair.

"I feel there is something else I should tell you, but I'm not sure it's my place to do so."

"Is it something that has to do with Olivia?" Nick frowned.

"Yes, it always has something to do with Olivia."

Dear girl with the red scarf,

Sometimes our worst enemy is
ourselves, and it's our self we
either put up with or have to
face.

Trust me, after all,
I am Mr.universe ☺

31

AFTER DARK

THE MOOD OF THE PARTY TRANSFORMED INTO SOMETHING ELSE once the sun went down. It was a festival of lights. The candles inside the mason jars lit up the walkway from the house to the gazebo and all along the perimeters of the dance floor. Olivia was sitting underneath the gazebo when Nick finally joined their little group. She studied him for a moment. Something didn't seem right. She could tell from the depths of his eyes that he wanted to talk, but then his eyes shifted to Paul.

"Hey, Nick," Paul said. "Can I get you a beer or something?"

"Water would be good, thanks,"

"I assume you can't drink alcohol?" Paul opened the cooler beside him and pitched a bottle to Nick.

"Let's just say it's better that I don't."

Paul's eyebrows knitted together. "Olivia tells me you take a shitload of pills."

Nick shrugged. "Well, it's a small penance. At least I'm alive."

"No kidding."

Nick looked over at Elise and smiled. "When are you due?"

"Three more months." She rubbed her hand on the length of

280

her stomach. "But I'm ready to have my baby boy right now." Elise laughed.

"No, it's okay. I can wait." The perspiration forming at the edge of Paul's hairline made Olivia wonder if Paul was more stressed out than he claimed.

Nick frowned. "Are you all right, bro?"

"Not really. Since the day we found out that we were expecting, I've been waking up at night in a cold sweat." Paul smiled nervously as Elise settled a gentle hand on his arm.

"He's worried that he won't be good at it ... at being a father."

Olivia knew that Paul had been a little apprehensive, probably because the pregnancy was not planned and Paul had to grow up and be responsible for the first time in his life. Now he had a family to take care of.

"Well, if you ask me, you're doing all right. I know nothing about being a father, but your anxiety only proves you've taken the first step in becoming a father." Nick tapped Paul's shoulder. "I would be more concerned if you weren't worried."

Seeing Nick interact with her brother made Olivia feel warm, an overwhelming feeling that this might work out for them and everyone would see how kind and lovable Nick was.

"Somebody hide me," Nina said as she climbed the steps of the gazebo.

"Is Mrs. Simon talking your ear off again?" Paul smiled.

"I swear that lady has a tracker. I can't seem to get away." Nina laughed.

Nick got up and offered his chair to Nina and then came over to stand next to Olivia.

"Where's Peter?" Olivia asked.

"He's upstairs putting Anthony to bed."

"Wow, look at Uncle Dominic go. He's really burning up the dance floor." Paul laughed.

They looked back at the sixty-year-old man busting awkward

moves on the dance floor, so much so that people around him began to move away.

Olivia glanced up, but Nick carefully avoided her eyes until she tugged on his hand, forcing him to look down at her. She stood up to allow Nick to sit in her chair so she could rest on his lap, placing her arms around his neck. He was careful where he placed his hands.

"Are you okay?" Olivia searched his face, but she couldn't read him.

"Yeah, sure."

"Oh ... oh ... don't look now," Nina said in a half whisper, which made them all turn.

Olivia was sure she went whiter than her outfit.

Dario, who was overly dressed for a hot and humid garden party, walked toward them, so self-assured in every step he took.

Paul looked back at his sister. "Don't look at me. I didn't invite him. I don't know how much more of him I can deal with. It's bad enough I've got to work with the asshole all week."

Before Olivia could comment, Dario was in front of them. She felt Nick's body tense underneath her, and she wondered if this was the reason he seemed so distant and cold toward her. She was afraid that Dario had gotten to him at some point in the evening and told him about the kiss they had shared in his condo. She should have told Nick, but what was the use of him getting upset? What was the use of Nick judging her, because she had had no business being there in the first place?

"Good evening, folks," Dario said. Olivia could feel his eyes burning, but she didn't look in Dario's direction. Instead, she kept her eyes on Nick. The group's low mumbles indicated it was just as awkward for them as it was for her. Nick finally looked at her with a weak smile, evidence he was not pleased with the turn of events.

Paul handed Dario a Corona, and Olivia's ex found a spot leaning on the wooden railing across from her.

"Hey, Nick, I didn't think you were going to be here tonight," Dario said, like he had just seen him for the first time.

"Likewise," Nick replied.

Olivia didn't like where this was going. Everyone remained silent, shifting uncomfortably in their chairs.

"Nick, I love your tattoo. Is it a compass?" Nina asked, in some attempt to change the air.

"Oh, cool." Dario raised the bottle to his lips as Nick watched.

Olivia knew it was sarcasm, because Dario hated tattoos. He thought the people who had them were beneath him. Olivia thought it was sexy, especially since it had some personal meaning. Nick had once told her he had gotten the tattoo on the inside of his forearm long ago. He had chosen a simple style of a compass: thin lines, three circles overlapping each other, and the axis in the middle. He told her every time he looked down at it, it was a reminder of where he had been and where he needed to be, almost like a spiritual compass.

"Do you have one, Olivia?" Elise asked.

Before Olivia could get a chance to answer, Dario took the opportunity to speak. "Oh, are you kidding me? Olivia would never get one."

Olivia pretended not to hear. "No, I don't have one, but I love the white tattoos. Something small behind my neck."

"What kind of tattoo would you get?"

"Olivia's too afraid of needles," Dario interrupted.

"Why don't you let her speak for herself?" Nick said in a protective tone that made everyone in the gazebo look up.

Dario gave a cocky shrug. "No offense, Nick, but I seem to know Olivia a hell of a lot better than you do, seeing how I've been with her the longest."

"You must like it, don't you? You think you still have some pull on her." Nick gently removed Olivia's legs from his lap and stood up. "That's why you're here. That's why you won't sell the apartment."

"I'm here because I was invited. Like it or not, I'm still a part of the family and a part of Olivia's life."

"Nick, please, let's just go." Olivia, not able to get Nick's attention, turned back to Paul, who was now standing. She was so afraid this situation was getting out of hand.

"Nick, I need your help." Nina tried to defuse the situation. "Come with me to the garage. I need more chairs for the guests. He's not worth it, Nick," Nina whispered to him, as he finally realized she was right and followed her.

When Nick and Nina were out of sight, Paul said, "Dario, I think it'd be best if you left."

Olivia glanced at him and walked out of the gazebo.

*

JUST WHAT OLIVIA had imagined would happen happened. She left Nick for a moment to help her mother bring out the birthday cake. There was the sound of a woman's voice screeching, coming from the garage. When she got there, she found Dario in the garage with a bloody nose, and Nick was nowhere to be found. Nina told her that not long after they'd walked in the garage, Dario had followed them in. He'd continued to provoke Nick, and that was when he said Olivia had kissed him.

"You!" She pointed her finger at Dario and walked closer. "You know that's a total lie! You're the one who kissed me."

"I told you the guy is fuckin' crazy, Olivia," Dario said. "Ouch!" Dario yelped when Nina roughly placed the ice pack to his face. He scowled at her, and Nina just shrugged.

"Dario, you manage to ruin everything for me ... my life and my self-esteem. You manipulated, kept me from things I love. You twisted everything for your own gain."

She looked at him with all the rage she had inside. Olivia realized it wasn't worth it. After all these months, she was finally able to move on. She was ready to say the words.

"I forgive you for the shitty things you've ever said or done. I forgive you for cheating on me. I'm granting you my forgiveness, but it's not for you. It's for me, because if I don't, you'll always exist in this space in my life, and I need the room for better things."

Dario's eyes landed on his shoes. Olivia was so caught up in her emotions that she didn't hear anyone coming in.

"Dario, you need to leave." A deep voice came from behind her. Olivia turned to see her father. "You're not welcome here anymore."

Dear girl with the red scarf,

I'm going to share with you what I recently
got some perspective on, so listen carefully.
For one, you can't prophesize the future. But
I do believe the universe gives us clues along
the way. It's up to us to be brave enough to
open our eyes. you got to explore every
opportunity, and if you're lucky enough, one
might lead you where you want to be. Seriously,
what are you waiting for? you've got the world
at your fingertips. I know you have this
constant sense of determination and fire in you.
you have so much talent. Show the world what
you can do. Shake it up, turn it upside down.
Run the risk it will be worthwhile, i promise.
                Trust me, after all,
                I am Mr.universe ☺

32

AFTER IT ALL

OLIVIA WENT TO NICK'S APARTMENT, BUT WHEN THERE WAS NO answer, she decided to go down to his studio. Dan, who was coming out the door, met her in the hallway. He closed the door behind him, muffling the ear-splitting music.

He gave her a grim smile. "Trust me, you don't want to go in."

"He's upset?"

"That's putting it mildly." He paused. "Look, he didn't tell me what happened between you two, but I know my brother well enough to tell you to just give him room to cool off, okay?"

Olivia waited until he was out of her sight before going in. She couldn't wait any longer without talking to Nick.

After the party ended and everyone had gone home, she had found herself alone in her parents' backyard, looking at her phone and hoping he would call her and allow her to explain.

He never did.

By the next morning she had gone from disappointment to anger over the way he had acted. After all, she hadn't done anything wrong. Nick, of all people, should have known that.

Olivia opened the door, walking into the blaring music. Nick had his back to her, mixing his paint colors. Without even seeing his face she could tell by his stiff, rigid posture that he wasn't happy. She reached over to the radio to press the off button.

"Dan, I thought I told you to leave me the fuck alone." Nick turned. His icy eyes softened. "What are you doing here?" Nick said in a melancholic voice.

"I wanted to talk."

He shook his head, focusing his eyes on his hands as he cleaned them with a rag. "Sorry, Olivia, but I don't feel like talking right now."

"But I do. I want to talk about what happened last night."

"Please, Olivia, just go home,"

"No, just listen to me for a minute."

She got startled when Nick swiped everything off his work-table, causing each item to crash on the floor. The paint he was mixing just moments before was now splattered all over the concrete floor, adding to the mess of empty paint bottles and dirty rags.

This was the first time she'd witnessed Nick's aggressive behavior. He didn't scare her, because she knew he would never hurt her, but she knew way too well that this kind of aggression always led to violence. But Nick wasn't Dario, which she had to keep telling herself. Nick was acting out from being hurt. Dario would act out because he wanted control. She could imagine how Dario must have woven the story to him, making it more than it was.

If only he would allow her to explain, then everything would make sense.

"Is it true? Did you kiss him?" he asked in a hurtful tone, walking closer but not close enough to touch her.

"He kissed me."

He walked away and kicked the trash can to the other far side of the room.

"Last week I was supposed to have lunch with my dad. He

never showed up, and I got worried, so Dario helped me track him down."

"Of course he did," he said drily.

"I don't know what Dario told you, but the kiss was unexpected, and it meant nothing to me. I made it clear to him I never want it to happen again," she said.

He studied her for a moment. "Did he try to do anything else?"

"No."

"Did he do anything to hurt you in any way? Because if he did..."

"No, no, of course not."

"I just don't understand why you didn't fuckin' call me instead."

"You're right, I should have. I had no business being with Dario that day. The only reason I called him was because I thought they were together." She paused. "I didn't tell you because I thought it wasn't worth getting upset over. It's the only reason I kept it a secret from you."

"Well, I'm upset just the same. You know you can come to me for anything?"

Olivia felt something else in that question. "Yes, I know."

"Shit, I ruined your father's birthday party. I feel like such an asshole." He placed his hand on his face. "It was exactly what Dario wanted, and I played right into it. I let him get under my skin. I should have just walked away...I just couldn't let him talk about you like that."

"What did he say to you?"

"It's not important now. The guy is a creep. I'm sorry for the way I behaved, but I'm not sorry for breaking his nose." He gave her a half smile. He slowly turned away and walked back to his worktable. "So, when were you going to tell me about the job offer you got in Milan?" Nick said as he began to throw everything into a black garbage bag.

Olivia knew that the only people who knew were her sister and her father. And out of the two, it could have only been her father who had told him.

"I want you to be honest with me. Why didn't you tell me you got that position for a magazine in Milan?"

"I didn't think I needed to tell you, because I'm not accepting the offer." She shook her head.

He frowned. "Then why would you apply for the job?"

She threw her hands in the air and blew out a long breath. "I don't know, I guess because it was W. Moda Italia! I wanted to see if I was capable of getting the job. It was a long shot. I didn't think they were going to call me back for an interview on Skype." She frowned at him. "I don't know why you're making a big deal about it. Look, I applied to get my cousin off my back. Never in a million years did I think I would get the position. Anyways, I turned it down."

Olivia placed her hands in her pockets, feeling the cold metal of her keys between her fingers. She just wished he'd walked over and taken her in his arms like he usually did, but there was something different about him, something somber, like he was afraid to come close to her. He remained silent as he cleaned up around him.

"You should take it."

"What?"

"Yeah, it's too good of an opportunity for you to pass up," he said, without meeting her eyes.

"I'm not going anywhere ... I'm staying here with you."

He searched her face. "Like you said, opportunities like that don't happen every day. You have to take it."

She shook her head. "No, I don't. I've already made up my mind, Nick. You know why my father told you ... He just wants us to break up."

He allowed the trash bag to slide out of his hand. "For once I agree with your father."

Olivia laughed. "My father doesn't want me to go. He expressed that already."

"That's not what he told me yesterday."

Olivia shook her head. "No, I don't believe you. He was always against the idea."

"People are allowed to change their minds, Olivia. Maybe your father realized this might be good for you, to get away from all the bullshit that's happening in your life. It would mean a clean slate."

"Oh my God, you're serious." She frowned.

"I couldn't be more serious. It means you can get away from Dario. You know if you stay, he will only find ways of making your life harder. I'd rather you be miles away from him, safe from that asshole, even if it means you'll be away from me, too. Take the job," he said softly.

"No. You know I can't leave my dad, not now."

"You're not a fuckin' lifeboat, Olivia. Stop trying to save everyone. This time, you need to focus on yourself. Your dad has other people in his life. He'll be okay."

"I don't get it. Don't you want me to stay?"

"If it were up to me, I'd want you to leave, and that's the honest fuckin' truth. I know this is your dream, and I don't want to be the one who stands in your way. I could never live with myself if you resented me for it."

She searched his face. "I could never resent you."

"You say that now. We can't be everything to each other, Olivia. You're going to have to start fighting your own battles."

"Then what about us?" Olivia asked. "How is this going to work out?"

"I love you, Olivia."

Olivia could see the sadness in his eyes. "Why does that sound more like a good-bye?"

He walked up to her and placed his hands on her face. "Make me miss you like hell. I want you to go out there and show them what you're made of." He searched her face. "You're so talented, Olivia, and you'll be wasting it all away if you stay here."

Olivia frowned. "You're breaking up with me?"

His shoulders fell, and there was a glaze over his eyes. "I don't see a point in staying together, not when we're living in different time zones." He paused. "I can't do long-distance relationships, Monti. I'm sorry."

"It doesn't have to be a long-distance relationship, Nick. You could come with me. You could finally check off living abroad on your bucket list." She put her arms around him.

His eyes finally met hers, and he gave her a weak smile. "You know there is nothing I would want more, but I can't. My doctors are here, and I can't just leave Dan. I'm the only thing he has left." He looked down at the floor for a moment, then found her eyes. "I ... I think it's best we both go our separate ways."

"So that's all you have to say?" She shook her head, pulling his hands off her face and taking a step back. "How can you tell me you love me one minute and the next push me out of your life?"

"I'm not pushing you out. I'm letting go."

"Maybe my dad has been right all along about you."

"Maybe he was," he said softly. "I never meant to hurt you."

"Go to hell, Montgomery!" She couldn't look at him any longer.

She turned and walked out. When she reached the street, her eyes began to water. Now she knew what it felt like to crash and burn.

Dear girl with the red scar,

People will come and go in our lives.
Most of them we won't give a second
thought to as soon as the door closes
behind them. But I had always
imagined that you would leave the
deepest, everlasting mark.

Mr. universe

33

THE ART OF LETTING GO

OLIVIA SLAMMED THE DOOR. IT MIGHT AS WELL HAVE BEEN A DOOR to his heart. The noise was deafening, swift and quick. Just like that, it was all over.

He wondered how long it would take for it all to sink in, what he had done to the both of them. It was the most difficult thing he had ever had to do. Nick had to muster all the strength not to go after her, because he knew he was doing the right thing. When you love someone, you shouldn't hold them back. You have to set them free.

So, Nick let her go. In the words of a poem he had once read: *how can I live without her? Kills me.* And Nick let it kill him.

Dear girl with the red scarf,

I miss you (I miss you).

Mr.universe ☹

34

INTERESTING GIRL ON
THE INTERNET

PRESS PRINT
Interview Vivre magazine/ May 2016
By Giovanna Oddi, translated by Bianca Jones

WHY SHOULD YOU KNOW HER?

OLIVIA MONTIANO IS a twenty-four-year-old beauty from Montreal, who works behind the scenes as a stylist for magazines such as W. Moda Italia and L Magazine. She has become an overnight sensation thanks to street style and social media, which has made her the go-to girl for fashion. Whatever this girl shows up wearing, it automatically flies off the shelves. Her style is photographed and copied all over the world. She is an asset and in demand, a hot commodity for designers and fashion magazines. After playing phone tag for weeks, she finally agreed to meet me for an interview at a café near where she worked for W. Moda Italia. I have seen the pictures online, and now, seeing her in person I can see what the buzz is all about. She said she never modeled, but she is stunning to look at. She reminds me of Sophia Loren with a modern edge. Miss Montiano is wearing a gray, fitted sweatshirt printed with a cowboy, with the text: *Billy the Kid*. Underneath that she wears a crisp white shirt and a pair of light, faded blue jeans, coupled with Manalo black pumps. I'm sure as soon as this article is published, all these items will be hot sellers.

WHAT DO you think when people dub you a style icon?

"IT'S SURREAL." She laughs. "I've been an assistant designer in Montreal, and now to get so much attention on what I wear...it's just funny, the irony of how things happen in life. But no, I don't consider myself a style icon. I'm just passionate about clothing and love to create looks. I guess, to me, it comes naturally. I want to create a beautiful image, and if I get people to react to it, then I think that's great. Then I've done my job."

HOW WOULD you describe your style?

"MY STYLE IS much different from when I first arrived in Milan nearly a year ago. I do adore the Milanese style, so sophisticated, more than you'd normally see back home. I am not a fan of minimalism; more color, more jewelry the better. I believe great accessories complete an outfit. I love to mix pieces that you wouldn't normally think to put together, but somehow it works."

WHAT DOES fashion mean to you?

"FASHION IS A FORM OF ART, a way to express yourself through clothing. It should be fun, and you should never take yourself too seriously. Fashion is a way you can always reinvent yourself. In some way, fashion determines who we are ... doesn't it?

WHO INFLUENCES YOUR STYLE?

"OH, I have so many designers I love dearly that inspire. Even those who are not in the fashion industry ... like my dear friend, who's an artist back at home in Montreal. He wears these lame graphic T-shirts, but he remains true to his style, and I guess, in retrospect, he influenced me. Dress the way that makes you feel comfortable, and dress to please yourself. You shouldn't have to change for anyone. So yeah, he's been a great influence on my style. Now I put on one of those lame graphic tees and pair it with an overly beaded pencil skirt and some heels, step out, and it will be all over the Internet by tomorrow morning. He would be so proud." She laughs.

WHAT DOES your boyfriend think of your newfound fame?

"No. No boyfriend. Who has time for a boyfriend? During fashion week, I sometimes work twenty hours a day. Believe me, I do not stop. My job is my life, and it doesn't leave room for anything else."

WHEN ARE you going to design your line?

"Ah, it's funny, people keep asking me that. Like I said, I had worked as an assistant designer, so I don't know, maybe I will get back into it. It's something I've been thinking about somewhere down the line. Right now I am so busy, but yeah, it's never too far from my mind."

Where do you see yourself in a year from now?

"Who knows? I might stay here in Milan or go back home to Montreal. But one thing is for sure: working for W. Moda has been a dream come true. I will be forever grateful for Celina Toridini for giving me the opportunity to work for her magazine. It certainly has opened some doors for me and taken my career on a new path. My phone is ringing nonstop. I'm humbled by the attention that I've been getting. I'm finally living out my dream."

ONE YEAR LATER

35

COMING HOME

Olivia arrived at Trudeau Airport with a carry-on bag and a small suitcase. She had flown in from Milan to visit her family for a few weeks.

Her job was very demanding. When fashion season began, it was nonstop, running from one show to another. And when the season was over, she was busy planning the next photo shoot for the magazine. Working for the W. Moda Italia had opened many doors for her. The exposure to Italian fashion had given her a better outlook on style, better than the garment industry in Montreal ever could. Her contract was coming up for renewal, and Celina wanted her to stay, but this newfound fame had opened up all kinds of opportunities. She wasn't sure what she wanted to do next. She needed time to think, so it was a vacation well deserved.

It had been a while since she'd seen her family, and she missed them dearly. Olivia had Skype time with her sister and mother often enough, but it wasn't the same. Olivia had enough distractions, pouring herself into her work to make her forget how homesick she was.

And then there was Nick. A small part of her was afraid to

come back, because Nick was never far from her mind. After they went their separate ways, she had never attempted to reach out to him. Olivia didn't see the point in chasing someone who didn't want her in his life. She had begun to wonder if he'd even loved her at all.

Once she'd gotten to Milan, things had gotten better. She was finally living her dream, but her heart had never recovered, maybe never would. After her apartment was sold, Paul and Peter managed to place the rest of her belongings in her parents' basement. She came back to Montreal for a couple of days for the signing of the sale, which was the last time she saw or heard from Dario.

After her father's sixty-sixth birthday party, things had gone downhill for Dario. It was finally revealed that he was doing illegal things through her father's company, so he was immediately canned. Once her father officially retired, Paul was made chairman of the board. And now baby Christina was almost a year, and with his wife, Elise, Paul's life was finally falling into place.

The charges against her father were dropped. The media's coverage of her father's case ceased to exist, but James Montiano's condition just worsened with time. According to her mom, these days he liked to sit in front of the TV and not interact much with anyone around him. It had been hard for her mother to watch him transform, and a big part of Olivia felt sorry for leaving.

One of the very last things her father told her before going was, "It seems I've made the wrong choice for the right reasons, you understand? If only I had opened my eyes, I would have known what Dario was really like. I would have never allowed him to hurt you."

"I know, Daddy. It's not your fault. How could you have known? I kept it from you because I didn't want to disappoint you. I wanted you to be proud of me." Olivia's eyes had teared up.

"You could never disappoint me. I just want to see you happy."

He smiled, his eyes glazed. "There is nothing in the world that I love more than you. I am so proud of you." He removed his glasses to wipe his eyes. "My darling, what am I going to do without you?"

She'd wondered the same thing.

Peter was the one to pick her up at the airport, driving her to her parents' home, where she received a warm welcome, feeling like a superstar. Being back home seemed so foreign to her.

"What?" Olivia looked up at her sister, Nina, sitting in a chair beside her. Olivia had her legs pulled to her chest. They were under the gazebo in their parents' backyard.

"You look so grown up, your hair ... your clothing ... You seem like a different person," Nina said as she ran her hand through Olivia's new, much shorter hairstyle.

"You like what I'm wearing? Wait until you see what I brought back for you." She smiled.

Nina hugged her again. "I'm just so happy you're finally home."

"You missed me that much, hey?"

"You have no idea, little sis."

"How's Mom doing?" Olivia gave her a sideways glance.

"You know Mom. She's built like a tank, but soon she's going to need someone to help her with Dad."

Olivia knew her mother had refused the idea of sending their father off to a home. "Maybe I could help you find someone before I go back."

Nina nodded. "Hey ... uh ... I know you told me you didn't want to talk about Nick, but since you've been gone, he's been coming around quite often."

Olivia shook her head, perplexed. "What for?"

"I don't know. Maybe he missed you as much as we did." Nina shrugged. "He's been good with Dad, helping Mom out. We don't mind having him around."

"Mommy?" Olivia's nephew called out from the patio door.

"Yes, Anthony, I'm coming." Nina got up from her chair. "I just thought you should know."

"Mommy..."

"Go, I'll be in soon," Olivia said, looking up at Nina, who was smiling like she was trying to hide something. Before Olivia could say anything, Nina had turned and walked across the grass, going inside the house.

As Olivia leaned back farther in her patio chair, her eyes settled on a red card sitting on the coffee table across from her with her name written on it.

Dear girl with the red scarf,

What do you say we finally meet?
Come and find me tomorrow at 7:00
pm at 556 Notre Dame street. I'll be
wearing something red.
Always yours,
Mr. universe ☺

OLIVIA LOOKED AROUND, but she was alone in the yard. She glanced back at the address and realized why it was familiar.

It was located in Griffin Town.

36

LOVE RETURNS

Olivia stepped out of her father's black Mercedes onto Notre Dame Street. She took a second glance at the address and realized it was close by. She tucked her black clutch under her arm and began to cross the street. She followed the addresses up until she found it. It was an art gallery with a sign in red block letters: The Proverbial Mr. Universe Atelier.

Olivia smiled. She knew where she was. This spot was the space where Nick had once told her he would open his gallery one day.

A crowd of people flowed in and out of the front entrance. Gray stone framed the entrance, and the big windows were tinted, not allowing her to see the inside.

"Olivia?"

"Jessica, what are you doing here?"

"I was just leaving. I didn't know you were going to be here." Jessica turned back as though she was looking for someone.

"To be honest, neither did I. What's going on in there?"

"It's the gallery's grand opening," Jessica said, but before she could say anything more, a tall guy came right up behind her, wrapping his arm around Jessica's waist.

"Hey, I know you. Luke, right?" Olivia smiled. "I didn't know you two were together."

Jessica raised her left hand.

"What? Are you engaged? Oh my God ... Congratulations, guys!"

"I was going to surprise you tomorrow at lunch. We're still on for tomorrow?"

"Yes, of course."

"You should go in. He's waiting for you," Luke said.

"We'll talk more tomorrow." Jessica blew kisses at her as she and Luke walked down the street.

THE GALLERY WAS OPEN-CONCEPT, modern, with high ceilings that exposed the plumbing and heating system. She only took a few steps before being greeted by uniformed women holding trays of champagne. Olivia took one and continued to scan the room. Though she felt she was being watched, there was no one she recognized. No one wearing red.

She walked into the next room. The walls were white and filled with art, and a sculpture stood in the center of the long room. As she got closer to the far back of the space, there it was.

The canvas hanging on the wall. Of course it was familiar to her, it was her face. Written at the bottom of the plaque was the title and artist: *Mavourneen, My Love,* by Nick Montgomery. It was the painting Nick had started long ago that she had never gotten to see finished.

"So, what do you think?" a familiar voice said.

A tall man stepped right beside her. Her heart began to race faster. It seemed her heart had recognized him before her eyes did.

A version of Nick Montgomery she had never seen before. His

hair was much shorter, and he was clean-shaven, smartly dressed. He looked handsome. Their eyes locked, and he smiled at her. It felt as if no time had passed.

"I was hoping to see you." He paused. "I'm glad you came," he said, with his hands in his pockets, as though he didn't know what to do with them. It was funny to Olivia that so much time had passed, but things felt the same between them. His hands in his pocket and her hands on her clutch ... They didn't know what to do with themselves.

"So this place is yours?"

"Half mine. George is my business partner."

"I'm so proud of you," she said. "Really happy for you that you are finally living your dream."

"And you look ... wow ..." He paused. "Beautiful."

"My hair is really short," she said, passing her hand through it.

"I like it."

"You do?" He nodded his head in confirmation. "And look at you! You don't look too shabby yourself." She smiled.

"You like the change?" He ran his hand down his vest.

"I do, but to be honest with you, I kind of miss the old Nick," she said as he placed his hand on his jaw.

"Well, one word from you and he can come back, lame shirt and all." He gave her one of the goofy smiles that she had missed.

Her eyes softened, and she looked back at the painting, wondering if things could ever go back to the way they were.

"I thought you said would never shave."

He shrugged. "People change for the ones they love."

She didn't know what that meant. Did he have a new girlfriend? He was willing to change his appearance for someone else, but not for her? Now she thought she was going to be sick.

"Where are Dan and Amanda? Are they here?" Olivia's eyes looked around.

"No, they're on their honeymoon," he said.

"Right, they got married last weekend. Did they receive my gift?"

"Yes, they wanted me to thank you." He looked at her, and she shyly looked away.

"I'm sorry I missed it. I got the invitation, but I—"

"Olivia, you don't need to explain."

She nodded.

"Guess what!"

"What?"

"I'm trying to work on my relationship with my dad."

Olivia's eyes snapped up. "Really?"

"Yeah, well, at the wedding we started talking. In a couple of weeks, I'm supposed to fly to Calgary and stay with him and his family."

"That's great, Nick. I'm happy things are finally coming together."

"You think they are?"

"Of course." She smiled. "You're painting again. You have this place, and now you're talking to your dad..."

"I promised myself that the next time I saw you I wouldn't let it show how much I've missed you, but now that you're here, that's all I want to tell you."

Olivia saw a shadow cross his face, like he was hoping she might have felt the same way, and she did.

"You know what I miss the most about you?" He looked around the room before his eyes met hers again.

"What's that? My smart mouth?" Olivia smiled.

He laughed. "Yeah, that too, but no ... it's your brilliant eyes, the way they can find mine in a crowded room. How they can make me feel like I am the most important person in it," he explained, as her smile faded. She never thought it would still be difficult to be around him.

"Want to get out of here?" he whispered.

"Shouldn't you stay? I mean..." She looked up at him with hopeful eyes.

"Yes, I should—" his eyes scanned the crowd—"but that's what partners are for."

Nick took the champagne glass out of her hand and placed it on the table behind him, picking up his suit jacket from the chair beside it. Olivia didn't flinch when his hand slid into hers—a perfect fit. It was natural, like it had always been between them.

37

LOVE STILL EXISTS

Nᴉᴄᴋ ʜᴀᴅ ʙᴇᴇɴ ᴡᴀɪᴛɪɴɢ ꜰᴏʀ ᴛʜɪꜱ ᴠᴇʀʏ ᴍᴏᴍᴇɴᴛ ᴡʜᴇɴ ʜᴇ ꜱᴀᴡ ʜᴇʀ again, a moment he had been sure he would never get. When she first walked in his gallery, it was as though his eyes were starving. He wanted to take in every inch of her. She wore a knee-length black dress, her hair straight down to her chin and much lighter than he remembered it to be. A year apart might have changed her, but she was still his Olivia.

He had taken her up on the roof of the gallery, and there they were under a clear night sky. A gentle summer breeze lightly danced on Nick's freshly shaven face. He couldn't remember the last time his face had been bare. They stood side by side, neither of them wanting to break the silence, neither of them knowing what to say next. He gazed up at the sky and felt some premonition, like something extraordinary was about to happen.

"Look at the stars." Olivia wrapped her arms around herself. Nick thought she might be cold, so he brought his suit jacket and draped it around her shoulders. Her eyes focused on the red pocket square. She brightly beamed up at him. "It's nice to finally meet you, Mr. Universe. I was secretly hoping it was you."

His smile widened.

"But there's something I need to know. Why would you go through the trouble?" she asked.

"I guess it was a way to reach out to you. At the time, I didn't think anything of it other than doing something nice for someone else."

She smiled and bobbed her head in disbelief. "How did you manage to pull it off?"

"Ah ... well, I had a little help from everyone."

"Was my sister in on it? Jessica?"

Nick nodded, sliding his hands into his front pocket.

"I can't believe they kept it from me."

Nick gave her a sideways smile. "It wasn't easy, but we managed to pull it off."

"Okay, I guess my next question is, why Mr. Universe?" She brushed the strands of her hair away from her face, the moon's glow softly highlighting her features.

"Well, I suppose I got the idea from you."

"Me?"

"Yeah. I guess I wanted you to believe in something."

She frowned. "What do you mean?"

"Long ago, before we knew each other, you walked in the café looking so sad. I didn't understand what was going on in your life at that point, but I felt you were in some trouble. I kind of overheard your friend say to you that it was the universe sending you a message. You responded that you didn't believe the universe could provide you with any guidance in life."

"I said that?" She smiled. "Okay, so why didn't you admit it was you when I suspected it was?"

He shrugged his shoulders and smiled. "If I told you it was me, it might not have meant the same to you. Being anonymous gave me the freedom to continue writing those notes, especially after I had a better insight into your life."

"I guess."

"So. Monti, the question is, do you still think the universe can't provide you with any guidance in life?"

She gave him a sideways glance. "Hmmm ... all right, I admit our lives kept crossing under the strangest circumstances. I don't know if that makes me believe in the universe or some fate, but I must divulge I believe in something." She paused. "Whatever it is that brought you into my life, I'm grateful for it. You made me realize I have been ignoring myself, trying to please everyone, when in the end I was the one who was suffering the most. You're the only one who accepted me for who I am. You took the time to figure me out, even before I ever did. Now I get it. I get what you'd been trying to do all along. With all those handwritten notes, you were attempting to help me figure myself out. You opened my eyes, and I never thanked you for it."

"You did it all on your own, Monti. I was just there to shake you up a little." He smiled. "But you know I didn't get the short end of the stick. You brought so much to my life as well."

"I didn't bring anything into your life, Montgomery." The serious expression on her face made him think she wasn't kidding.

Nick frowned. "What? You have done more for me than I can ever imagine. You inspired me like no one else had. Do you know how much I adore you, how special you are to me? You filled me with peace and reassurance. Most importantly, you loved me." He paused. "Do you know the moment I knew I loved you? It was the first time you looked at me. I showed you my deepest secrets, and instead of walking away, you clung to me like a last breath. I had never imagined a person like that could ever exist for me."

Olivia's eyes became glossy, and she looked away.

He knew a year ago he had made the painful decision to let her go. And he had tried to be strong, but now, having her so close, everything came rushing back again. All the feelings, all that love and emotion had caught up with him at the moment. He had made himself believe that living with her ghost would be enough for him, but he couldn't have been more wrong.

"Why is this so hard?" She looked down at her hands.

"I know what you mean." Nick let out a frustrated sigh.

"I hope you've been seeing other people. I know it sounds strange coming from me, but I do care about you, and I do worry about you, Nick. I want you to be happy," she said as he pushed off the wall and slowly paced around.

"Well, since you've been gone, I have been keeping myself busy with my art and then this place. There wasn't any time for anything or anyone else. Don't think I have forgotten what you mean to me, Olivia." He faced her with his hands in his pockets.

"So there hasn't been anyone else?" she asked in a small voice.

"How could there be?"

She turned back to look at the view of the city before them. He knew she was trying to avoid his eyes.

"Do you know why I chose to be alone? It's quite simple. You see, I've come to realize that there are some people you love for a moment and the ones you love for a lifetime. And, Olivia Montiano, you are a love of a lifetime. If I can't have you in my life, then I don't want to be with anyone else. You've occupied my mind, and you're still in my heart, Olivia. It doesn't leave room for anyone else."

Her mouth hung open slightly. "I don't see where we can go from here. So much has changed, and we can't live in the past, Montgomery." By the tone of her voice, it was evident he'd upset her.

"You're right, but I've got nothing else but the past. It's the last place where we seem to exist," he said.

She shook her head and started walking away from him.

"It feels impossible to let you go. I know I should, but I can't."

"That's not fair, Montgomery. All this time, it's been hard enough to get through without you, and now you're not being reasonable. What I think you're asking of me...It's best we both forget, especially when I recall you were the one to push me away." She paused.

"I didn't push you away. I wanted you to spread your wings and fly. I told you once that if I followed that thread it would always lead me back to you—well, it works both ways."

He walked closer to her, but she continued to walk farther away from him.

She began talking rapidly. "I am not one of your projects that you can mold and create. It doesn't excuse you from the fact you left me with a broken heart. I don't think I can ever trust you again."

"Don't forget, Olivia, you're not the only one who's been hurting through all this."

"I don't get it, Montgomery. Why now? What's changed?" Her arms made a smacking sound when she placed them at her sides.

"Nothing changed. That's the thing. I still love you, Olivia."

She looked off in the distance, trying to process.

"Do you ever think of me at all?" he asked.

"I think of you much more than I should." She gave him a weak smile. "But it doesn't change the fact that I'm going back to Milan in two weeks. Where does that leave us?" She paused and looked up at the night sky.

"I want to see you again," he asked.

"Then what? Let's make it the last time? Then never again? And besides, your place is here and mine is in Milan. How could this ever work out?"

"No, you're right. It could never be the same. That's true. Maybe I should let you go, but I don't want to," he said as he came closer, and she turned and looked up at him.

"Montgomery, what if everything that was meant to happen has happened for us? What if that is it for our story?" she asked.

"See, I'm a shameless optimistic. I can't tell you what will happen tomorrow or the day after that. But if you should ask me, if I believe there is still hope for us. Yes, I do. What I see here is the possibility of you and me, and I don't want to run the risk of losing you, not the second time around. If you take a leap of faith with me here, then maybe there is still a chance for us. As long as there is still hope and love, we'll find a way to make it work ... Trust me, after all, I am Mr. Universe."

"You're incorrigible, Montgomery," she said, her face softening. "It's all your fault, you know. You made me care too much and ... love you too much."

"I'm sorry. I just wanted to do the right thing, Olivia. I guess I messed up. Maybe I should have done things differently. Please give me a chance to set things right."

"I don't see the point. I'm sorry ... it's just too late."

Nick watched her walk away from him, heading toward the door to go back inside.

"Olivia," he called out to her, and she halted in her steps. "Let the universe decide. Roshambo me for it."

She turned to face him, but didn't walk back.

"Roshambo. If I win, you give me one day. If you win, then you can walk away and never see my face again."

She placed her hand on her forehead and shook her head. "You can't base the future of our relationship on a kid's game."

"You don't get it, do you? We belong to each other, and no matter what, our lives will always revolve around each other. And I have a feeling that tonight is our night. You know how I know? Because the universe has been presenting countless opportunities for us to be together. All those times we crossed paths ... when they did, our direction changed for the better. No, I believe we were meant to be together." He smiled. "Look, love is more complicated than we think, Olivia. Love is messy. Love is hard work. But when you know we are good together, then you have to make it count, and I desperately want to make it count. I want you to know I never wanted you to go. The truth is, if we walk away from each other, we will never find what we have with anyone else."

He pressed his forehead to hers.

"Roshambo," he whispered.

"All right ... okay." She took a step back.

"Ro. Sham. Bo," they said in unison.

She smiled.

"Okay, you win, Montgomery. So what now?" she whispered as he gently pulled her into his arms.

"Everything." He searched her eyes. "And I wouldn't have it any other way."

He placed his hand on her face and leaned in closer, claiming her mouth, subduing her into silence. On that very rooftop, on an evening which had begun with no promise that anything magical could materialize, they both realized that anything could happen, and everything was all they ever needed.

THE END

OTHER BOOKS BY MARIA LA SERRA
LYRICAL LIGHTS

He was the oxidizer to my metal.
But sparkles give a brief burst of light;
then you're only left in the abyss.
He went right, and I went left...
In a world that's a stage, can their love thrive under the lights?

ABOUT THE AUTHOR

Maria La Serra lives in Montreal with her husband and two daughters. Before becoming a writer, she worked as a fashion designer. She will try everything at least once except for skiing or hiking or camping—okay, anything relating to activities done in the great outdoors.

When she's not working on her next book, you can find her spending time with her family.

The Proverbial Mr. Universe is her first book.

Email Maria at: authormarialaserra@gmail.com
Newsletter Signup: http://eepurl.com/bVUV19
Facebook: www.facebook.com/authormarialaserra
Instagram: www.instagram.com/maria.laserra
Twitter: http:// twitter.com/authormlaserra.
Website: maria-laserra.com.